Praise for Annmarie McKenna's
Seeing Eye Mate

Blue Ribbon Rating 4.5 "SEEING EYE MATE is a book that is jam-packed full of mystery and suspense that will keep the reader on edge through the entire book... The reader will be drawn into the hunt for the evil werewolf and become apart of this exciting adventure. AnnMarie Mckenna is a talented author and has a very promising career in the ebook industry."

~ *Angel Brewer, Romance Junkies*

"*Seeing Eye Mate* kept me turning the pages and I couldn't put it down until I read the final word. Just when I thought I had the storyline figured out, I realized I was wrong. I love when an author can keep me from guessing the plot and Annmarie McKenna did just that very thing... I have happily placed *Seeing Eye Mate* on my keeper shelf and have decided that Annmarie McKenna is one author I want to keep reading!"

~ *Talia Ricci, Joyfully Reviewed*

Seeing Eye Mate

Annmarie McKenna

A SAMHAIN PUBLISHING, LTD. publication.

Samhain Publishing, Ltd.
2932 Ross Clark Circle, #384
Dothan, AL 36301
www.samhainpublishing.com

Seeing Eye Mate
Copyright © 2006 by Annmarie McKenna
Print ISBN: 1-59998-356-7
Digital ISBN: 1-59998-156-4

Editing by Sasha Knight
Cover by Scott Carpenter

First Samhain Publishing, Ltd. electronic publication: October 2006
First Samhain Publishing, Ltd. print publication: January 2007

Dedication

To my editor, Sasha.

To Maria, Regan, Judy. Thanks for your endless critiques.

To Christine for the final boost of encouragement.

And to my sister, Sharis, who has to go through long dry spells while waiting for the next installment.

Chapter One

"Eight ball, corner pocket."

Caelan Graham tipped the bottle of Bud Light to his lips and took a long drag as he pointed his cue stick toward his chosen spot. He tried to alleviate some of the tension strumming through his charged body by rolling his head on his shoulders. Tonight was a full moon and he was restless. He needed a good, long fuck and a run through the woods, preferably in that order. Since he'd come here tonight to fill Eli in on the latest pack developments, it didn't look like either the fuck or the run was going to happen in the immediate future. Instead, he'd settle for winning another round of pool.

He set the bottle on the edge of the table and lined up his shot, rocking the stick three times before striking the cue ball. With a satisfying clack, it careened into the eight ball, knocking it into the pocket.

"I win. Again," he said flatly. This was getting way too easy.

"Goddamn it!"

Caelan ignored the pissed off shout of his younger-by-two-minutes brother, Eli. Maybe tomorrow night he'd go for a run. The woods around his and Eli's ranch had been calling to him for days now. Their land sat about an hour outside of St. Louis.

It was close enough to the city for practical purposes, yet far enough away from urban sprawl to provide hundreds of acres of wooded area for his kind to roam freely.

The steady flow of jobs at Graham Securities had kept Caelan too busy to even think about shifting lately. Not to mention the ongoing duties as his pack's Prime.

He held his palm up just in time for Eli to slap a dollar bill into it. They'd long since given up playing for bigger money, or Eli had rather, for the simple fact he lost all the time. Shaking off his longing to slip into wolf form for the moment, Caelan chuckled and scooped up his beer. He headed to one of the few empty tables in the typical-for-a-Friday-night packed bar.

"How'd it go last night?" Eli asked, yanking a chair around. He straddled it and placed his arms along the top of the backrest.

So much for the happy moment. Caelan didn't even want to think about how the pack meeting went last night. Or how it had ended with a knockdown, drag-out fight. But since Eli had been on another assignment and hadn't made it to the meeting, Caelan had to inform him of the situation. He cocked his head and leaned closer so they could talk without being overheard. No one seemed to be listening. They were too busy drinking, dancing and having a good time. "Jared Ramsey's mate was killed two nights ago. She's the third one in two weeks."

The Ramsey pack was settled in Junction City, about a hundred miles from the Graham pack. It hadn't taken long for word to spread about what had befallen the young woman, especially not with Jared being the Prime's son.

As the Graham Prime, it was Caelan's duty to protect every member beneath him. So far his pack hadn't been touched by the brutality of the three attacks.

"What kind of fucking sicko would do that to an innocent woman? Hell, three women." Eli smacked his hand on the table, making it wobble precariously. Their beers skittered across the top, nearly taking a fatal nosedive off the edge.

Caelan grabbed both sides of the small, round table before it collapsed and made him lose his one drink for the night.

"Shut up, Bro. You want the whole damn place to hear you?" he growled.

"He killed another one of our mates, Cael," Eli hissed.

Caelan nodded in agreement, understanding the implied "our" encompassed all mates in the shifter community. "I know what he did, E." Every pack for three states knew what the asshole had done. It was finding out *who* he was that had them all chasing their tails. Literally. "The elders have asked all the packs to unite so we can pass information and better protect our mates."

Talking about mates made Caelan suddenly glad he hadn't found his yet. *Yet* being the operative word. The pack elders were pressing hard for him to do so and ensure the next generation of Prime. Hell even Eli was nudging him in the same direction. Of course Eli didn't want the responsibility of Prime, which would be his should anything happen to Caelan.

This situation gave Caelan the ultimate enticement to stay away from women right now. He didn't need the added responsibility of protecting a mate from the same person he was hunting. His brain knew that; his cock argued every step of the way. The insane growing compulsion to fuck was making Caelan growl and snap at everyone he came across. Especially when one of the elders had suggested to him that his need meant he was getting closer to finding his mate.

Thus the fight outside the pack meeting last night. Everyone's tempers were already hot with the news of yet another attack. It had only taken a not-so-private conversation he'd picked up on for Caelan's overloaded nerves to explode.

"Methinks our Prime needs to get laid," Caelan had overheard.

He ground his fist into his thigh. Damn Michael Hayward to hell and back for being the one shifter in their pack able to pick up on Caelan's need to get laid. No, that wasn't entirely true, the elders thought so also, but their flat-out innuendos didn't piss him off near as much as the bastard Hayward's did. And leaving a bruise the size of Texas on Hayward's jaw hadn't eased the pounding need to fuck a woman either.

"*Ooowee.* Now that is one fine-looking specimen."

Caelan snapped his attention back to Eli. God, but the man could change a subject quick. Of course, since Caelan's mind had been on getting himself a woman too, he couldn't fault his brother much. Caelan grinned. Having a woman, not keeping her, just having her. For the night. Or two, maybe. Not forever. Not now, anyway. Later.

Eli slapped his hand down on the table again. Caelan snatched his beer and balanced it on his knee while his fool brother stared and slobbered at someone over his shoulder. Caelan didn't even bother to turn around.

"Cael, brother, I think you're going to have to find someone else for that job tomorrow morning. I'm gonna be busy with that little filly over there."

Caelan snorted. Born identical, neither of them ever had trouble attracting the opposite sex. More so for Caelan, being Prime. Females, both human and shifter, were always vying for his attention, but then, the humans didn't know what he was.

"She's close to her heat. Hot damn is she gonna be sweet." Eli rubbed his hands together like a kid at Christmas.

Caelan had to admit a female in heat or even within a few days of it, was nearly irresistible, wolf *or* human. Any babies born to a human woman, like he and Eli, were considered special, as they could control their shift and change to their wolf form whenever they chose. A pureblood shifter was forced to deal with their transformation once a month, on the night of the full moon.

Unfortunately, or fortunately depending on how you looked at it, the only way to impregnate a human was for her to be your mate. That in itself virtually ensured an offspring.

Despite his desire to avoid women for the foreseeable future, Caelan found himself sniffing the air. The fruity scent of a very alluring woman wafted across his nose, and Caelan froze. The hair on the back of his neck rose and every muscle in his body tightened in response. Including his cock, which stood at attention like every good soldier ought to, demanding to be buried as deep as it could get in the woman's pussy.

"Son of a bitch," he said succinctly. He dropped his chin to his chest, closed his eyes and counted to ten. Then he begged whatever god was listening to make this situation a dream instead of the reality he feared it to be.

He didn't need to open his eyes to know that it wasn't.

Eli droned on beside him. "*Mmm-mmm.* It's gonna be a long night..."

Caelan couldn't contain the canines that lengthened and sharpened inside his mouth. A low growl emanated from his throat as he listened to his brother continue to talk about the woman Cael had yet to look at. He instinctively knew the woman he smelled and the object of Eli's current wet dream were one and the same.

"I thought you wanted Nikki," he snarled.

11

Caelan glanced up to see a different kind of heated desire cross Eli's face. A look that changed from I'm-gonna-roll-in-the-sheets-for-fun-tonight to she's-mine-forever. Caelan wondered if there was more to the story with Nikki than Eli was letting on.

Eli stood, clearly shaking off whatever had been in his head a second ago, ready to swoop in on his prey, a stupid grin splitting his face.

Caelan reached out and grabbed his twin's arm. "No."

Eli tried to shake him loose, his smile slipping. "What the hell, Bro?"

"She's mine." His voice rumbled out of his chest, and he grimaced. He looked up at Eli, begging with his eyes for his brother to understand.

He did.

"Damn it." Eli slung himself back into his chair, pouting and jostling the table again. "Ain't this just the perfect fuckin' time!"

Caelan had to disagree with him. This was the *worst* time to finally find his mate.

🐐 🐐 🐐

Tieran Jones stood just inside the doorway of the packed Cahoots and Boots Country Bar. Line dancers strutted their stuff to the rhythm of the twangy music filling the air, their boots stomping and slapping in perfect timing. There was a full bar to her right, a small pool table area to her left.

She shivered despite the stuffy buildup of heat generated by the multitude of bodies, and cursed herself for having entered the bar in the first place.

Damn her car to hell, too. Stupid thing decided to break down right out front. She'd never had a problem with it before. After sitting most of the day because of her job as a research librarian, Tieran was more than ready to be home. She sighed. So close, yet so far away. She did have to pee pretty badly, might as well go while she was here. At least there hadn't been a cover charge to get in. Nothing like paying five bucks to use the toilet.

Tieran picked her way through the crowd, carefully dodging the undulating bodies. There were way too many chances for an accidental vision here, something she wasn't prepared for tonight.

How in the hell did it just so happen to be this place where her car decided to take a last hacking breath?

"It is fate, my dear."

"Yeah, screw fate, Gramama," she mumbled under her breath to the woman who'd been dead for going on ten years now. Well, dead to everyone except Tieran, who, as a medium, still conversed with her regularly.

"Do not sass me, young lady."

Tieran resigned herself to her *fate* and searched for any sign indicating a bathroom. She really did have to go bad enough her walk might be construed as a waddle.

The bathroom wasn't any less crowded or less noisy than the main bar. Women were lined up in front of the mirror primping themselves and she wondered what for. In her opinion, men were the scourges of the earth. So what if her world was colored by her one terrible attempt at a serious relationship. It had ended in disaster, thanks to her "gifts". She was definitely better off without a man.

Tieran stared at the women, itching to blurt out, "They're not worth it, girls."

"Some are, my dear." Her grandmother's semi-scold came through loud and clear.

Maybe, just maybe, there really was some man out there for her, but Tieran wasn't inclined to test the theory ever again. Once burned and all that.

By the time she'd done her business, the area had cleared enough so she could safely wash her hands without rubbing shoulders with anyone. She could see it now—bumping into a woman who was wearing a too-short skirt and a barely there top. She'd probably envision said woman getting it on with some gross man she'd just met out at the bar.

Of course, the vision wouldn't be the worst part. It would be the massive headache and nausea that followed. Occasionally a vision was so powerful she blacked out completely and woke up disoriented some time later.

She looked at her watch. A whopping five minutes had gone by. The towing company had said it would take them about thirty minutes to get to her. She snorted. If she was lucky, they might get here in an hour.

Maybe she'd get a drink since she'd worked through dinner. This place had to be better than sitting outside and waiting in her car. Alone. In the dark.

Along one wall was a row of seats, several of them unoccupied. She chose one, the middle of a group of five, hoping that anybody else who wanted to sit would wisely choose one that wasn't on top of her. Kind of like those people who park their car way out in the parking lot so it doesn't get touched. She smiled. She'd always been tempted to kick a tire to see what would happen.

The nape of her neck prickled. Someone was watching her. She gritted her teeth and pursed her lips when the feeling didn't go away. Years of being laughed at and teased hadn't developed the thick skin she needed to shield the pain the ridicule had caused. She felt like she was being mentally undressed. The man must have x-ray eyes or something, and was using them to strip her bare, skin and all. She would just take a quick peek. No, a glare. Yeah that's it, a glare. She'd ensure that he'd never look in her direction again.

And pigs might fly. The way her senses were screaming, she doubted much of anything would make him stop looking at her.

"Be nice, Tullabelle."

Tieran relaxed at her gramama's use of her childhood nickname. It was the one thing that could make her smile in an instant, but if she let the woman get the upper hand...

"You be nice! I'm practically chafing here with all these bodies, as if you hadn't noticed," she grouched.

"Temper, temper."

Ooh, that ornery old woman. Even from her grave she still gave Tieran what for. Thank God she was the only dead person Tieran could speak with. Having visions was one thing, but she'd heard about mediums whose brains were constantly filled with buzz from the dead. Worse, she thought, would be the empaths whose entire lives were bombarded with other people's emotions.

Tieran peeked toward the pool tables, where the stare originated. The only thing she picked up was eyestrain from peering out of the corners of her eyes. Darn it, she'd have to turn her head. On the pretense of popping her neck, she twisted sharply to the left, then back to the right.

Bingo! There he was.

Boy was he ever there. Dark hair, dark eyes, though she couldn't tell what color in the dim light of the bar. He was sexy as sin and smirking like the devil. Except that she'd already

15

been with the devil and he'd used her and left her with a broken heart. Asshole.

She glowered at the man, drawing her eyebrows together in hopes it added to her intensity.

Apparently he didn't take the hint. Some guys really were as dumb as a box of rocks. Her skin tingled in exasperation and...something else. Heat pooled low in her belly. No. No way. Uh-uh. She would not let him make her feel this way.

It was hard to keep up the look when the man had such a scrumptious, I-could-lick-you-all-over body. She tried another tactic, turning on her scowl. This time she raised her eyebrows and sucked her cheeks in, making it clear she wanted no part of what he was offering.

Two sets of matching eyes peered back at her. One pair, the original ones, perused her body, while the other turned her scowl back at her.

Holy shit! Stunning, identical twins.

"Watch your language, Tieran."

"Shh. Go away, I've got a situation. And stop laughing."

Tieran bolted upright in her chair. Oh my God. Her car hadn't simply broken down, her grandmother had played a hand. She didn't know how and she didn't care. Tieran just wanted to know why her gramama had manipulated things to put her here. *"Fate schmate. You did this. You set me up! Why you rotten...of all the low things to do."*

"Ah, ah, ah. That's no way to talk to your grandmother. Listen to me, Tullabelle. They need your help. Let them come to you. I promise they won't hurt you, not like that little maggot Peter did."

Tieran snorted. *"Now who needs to watch their language?"*

"Tieran, I sense evil here tonight. Be careful, please."

"First you tell me to let two strangers come to me and then you tell me you sense evil? From who?"

"I don't know, dear. I only see that you can help."

"Yeah, yeah, yeah. Help."

With what? she wondered.

🐾 🐾 🐾

Caelan turned back from getting his first look at the woman predestined to be his mate. What he'd seen hadn't been too encouraging. Her dark eyes had practically glittered in the dim light, shooting daggers at him. Then they'd widened as her gaze darted back and forth between him and Eli. He smiled at her obvious shock upon seeing the two of them side by side.

Her expression had turned obstinate as hell, making his already hard cock grow further with painful anticipation. Any more pressure against his zipper and he'd come in his pants. Either that or split the seams.

Caelan chuckled. Once he got a hold of her, it would be an absolute pleasure to tame his little spitfire mate. He wanted to take another look at her but forced himself not to. Having smelled her, he'd know if she moved by the direction of her scent. After they mated for the first time, their connection would be unbreakable.

His smile fell. What the hell was he thinking? There couldn't be a more deplorable time to discover her. The thought grated. He'd have to be on her like white on rice to ensure her safety, yet somehow not come off like a stalker while he pursued her. Not to mention the fact he had to do this while still actively searching for the Mate Killer. Oh, then there was the small matter of his getting her to understand his ability to change forms.

"So you gonna get over there and claim her, or what?"

Caelan cleared his throat. "Somehow I don't think it'll be that simple."

"She *is* giving you the evil eye."

"Me? I believe she included both of us in that look."

Eli shrugged. "Yeah, but she's your mate." He stood and smacked Caelan on the back. "Since it looks like my plans have changed and now I have to go in to work in the morning after all, I'm gonna hit the john and get going. Good luck."

"Asshole."

"Hey, just supporting my Prime."

Caelan jabbed a quick left hook at his twin.

Eli laughed and ducked out of the way, then sobered. "She's gorgeous, Cael, I'm envious."

"Thanks, E, that means a lot."

"Now, go get your bitch and try not to think of me while you're fucking her tonight," Eli mocked, batting his eyelashes at Caelan.

Caelan growled at the sharp teeth glinting behind his brother's smiling lips. Eli left, chuckling loud enough that people turned to see what they were missing.

Caelan inhaled her scent again, instinctively picking hers out with ease over the entire crowd. Spicy-sweet and laced with a twinge of anxiety.

Anxiety? What was that all about? His fingers tightened around his beer. He hoped she was here alone. Too bad if she wasn't because she would be leaving here with him.

Enough. He'd just go over and introduce himself. And then what? "Oh, and by the way, I can shape-shift into a wolf?" Yep, that'd go over really well. Damn. He'd always imagined his mate would be a shifter like him. Not a human. Things would be so much easier...

🐺 🐺 🐺

Motherfucker. He punched the stall door, ignoring the searing pain shooting up from his knuckles to his shoulder. They were supposed to come here tonight to relax. He expected they might find a nice piece of ass, but not this. How could that son of a bitch possibly have come across his mate tonight, of all nights?

To top it all off, the bitch would soon be ripe for conception. Caelan would have her full of his seed before mid-week.

His canine teeth exploded in his mouth, sharpening into points that pricked at his still-human mouth. The bones in his fingers popped and contorted, shortening to create a paw, the nails elongating into razor-sharp claws.

Closing his eyes, he inhaled deeply and fought the shift, resisting the urge to transform and tear through the crowd outside the bathroom door. Common sense prevailed over his inner wolf. Detection at this stage of the game would be detrimental to his cause, to the entire pack.

His human DNA took over, reshaping what had already slipped into wolf form. The pain was negligible compared to the thumping anger in his head.

He thought again of the girl, memorizing her face for future reference. She'd have to go. Or maybe he'd keep her, if Caelan didn't get the chance to claim her before he made his move.

19

He'd have to act quickly, up his timetable now that the cunt had entered the picture. And he'd have to keep a close eye on her, to make sure she didn't see something she wasn't supposed to.

He curled his lip and snarled. He'd come here tonight to get a feel for how his plans were working and hadn't been disappointed by what Caelan had revealed.

Every day he was one step nearer to the position that should have been his since birth.

🐈 🐈 🐈

Caelan turned in his chair and rested his arm along the back.

"What the hell?" he yelled, and winced when several people looked his way.

Two different people now occupied the set of seats where she'd been, but her scent still lingered as if she hadn't left. He was losing it. He'd gotten so caught up in thinking about her he hadn't even noticed her moving. Caelan scanned the bar, looking for the pale brown hair that had hung in a simple bob around her shoulders. He stood, his heart pounding now, the anxiety he'd smelled on her transferring to him.

He searched the crowd, his gaze flicking over everyone until he reached the door.

"Son of a bitch," he snarled. She was following a behemoth of a man in a grubby jumpsuit. Caelan pushed his way through the gyrating mass of people, knocking into a couple two-stepping their way around the dance floor. It took precious seconds to untangle himself.

"Sorry." He helped balance the woman and man, then sprinted for the door.

He slammed it open causing the heavy metal to bang against the wall outside. Cars jammed the parking lot, but he saw no sign of his mate amongst them.

"Damn it." He dug a hand in his pocket and tore his keys out. While he stomped towards his truck, he cursed himself for letting her get away.

He was supposed to be able to sense his mate at all times, so how had she done this exactly? Why did his intended have to be as slippery as a wet bar of soap? He groaned as the imagery of wet soap and lust-filled longing took over common sense. What he wouldn't give to be at home in the shower right now, using that soap on her slick, heated skin, instead of chasing after her.

His cock demanded to be let loose. He adjusted himself to relieve a minuscule amount of pressure.

He swung open the door to his F-150 and stepped up on the running board. Flashing lights to his left drew his attention. Yellow beams slashed the night from the panel atop a tow truck. In front of it sat a small, white four-door. The dim streetlight above them wasn't much but it did allow Caelan to see a figure.

The same man he'd seen inside the bar now stood near the rear of the car and spoke through the open driver's door to someone in the front seat.

Another car's headlights lit up the scene and Caelan caught a quick glimpse of a cap of light brown hair.

"Un-fucking-believable." He stepped back down to the ground and shoved the door shut.

At least now he knew what the anxiety had been about.

He shook his head. "You won't get away from me this time, sweetheart."

🐈 🐈 🐈

If this jerk hit on her one more time... And to think she'd been ecstatic that he'd gotten here early.

"Patience, Tullabelle, he's coming."

"Who's coming?" Tieran scanned the parking lot but didn't see anyone.

"Hey, honey, I'm gonna have to give you a tow. Why don't you hop on into my cab, I'll give you a lift."

Eew.

The slob tried to smile around a glob of tobacco, revealing more than one missing tooth. What kind of woman did he think she was?

"I don't think so. I'll call a friend to pick me up." She tried to speak as sweetly as possible, but must have sounded a tad bit repulsed. The man's eyes narrowed and he spat a big wad of gross, black tar at the ground near her shoe.

"S'no problem, lady. Jump on in."

"The *lady* said no thank you."

The tow-truck driver jerked at the sound of the deep, gravelly voice. Tieran's heart pounded. It was them, or rather, one of them. Whether it was the playboy who'd smiled at her or the one who glared back, she couldn't be sure. Hell, she hadn't seen anything past their gorgeous faces to tell them apart.

His dark brown hair reflected the dull light above him. He had his hands tucked into the pockets of his black jeans, lending to his air of casualness.

His expression, however, was anything but casual. His feral eyes pulsed and flashed an eerie, yellowish-brown beneath deceptively long lashes. Tieran expected that at any second he would pounce. God help the poor soul he landed on.

"I told you."

She ignored her gramama's words just as she tried to ignore the quickening of her heartbeat and the hardening of her nipples beneath her shirt. *No more men. None. Stop looking at him.*

She couldn't and had to swallow to keep her tongue from coming out and licking her lips the way she wanted to lick his body.

He was all male and she wanted him. Bad. Wanted to feel him between her thighs. Wanted his mouth and hands on her, caressing until she screamed out with her climax. Why? She'd never wanted Peter this way. Not even in the throes, or lack thereof, of passion. What was a throe anyway?

"Focus, Tieran."

Her cheeks caught fire at her gramama's command, jerking her completely out of her fantasies.

"I reckon it ain't none a your business." The tow-truck driver's voice made her skin crawl and she barely refrained from rubbing her arms to ward off his ickiness.

A low growl—that's the only way she could describe it—issued from her savior's mouth and he cocked his head. Her savior?

"She's here with me. I'd say that makes it my business." His low voice rang with menace.

Take that! She was suddenly sorry she'd glared at him earlier.

The disgusting man straightened to his full height and was still about a head shorter than Mr. Yummy. Tow-truck man spit again, some of the loogie landing on the interior panel of her door.

Sick. "That's a really disgusting habit," she blurted.

"You just can't keep your mouth shut, can you, Tulla?"

Tieran mentally shrugged. The towing man continued to stare at the other man, whose lips had curved at the edges for some reason.

"I think he likes your attitude, Tulla. Wonders never cease."

For long seconds no one moved or spoke, until finally, the towing man turned his head away from the car and spit for the third time.

Tieran could take no more. She gagged and her eyes watered.

"You're on your own, lady." He turned and stomped back to his truck. The engine roared to life. Gravel spewed out behind the tires as he reversed and took off down the street.

She sighed in relief. Thanking God was a bit much considering she still had a broken-down car to deal with, but then she remembered her savior. "Thank you."

He stepped forward and planted a big hand on the top of her door, preventing her from closing it. "My name's Caelan Graham."

Please don't tell me that. I don't want to know and I don't want to get involved again.

"He's different, Tullabelle."

"So? Butt out."

"And yours is?" He crossed his arms over the edge of the door and rested his chin on his muscled forearm. His posture clearly said, "I have all night."

Fine. *Damn it,* but fine.

"Tieran."

He seemed to ponder that for a moment. "What kind of name is that?"

"One step above Nareit." Why did everyone in the world have to question her name?

"Be nice to him, Tulla."

Caelan—could you have a sexier name?—smiled, letting her attempt at an insult roll off him, melting the icy demeanor she was trying to portray.

Aargh!

"Nice to meet you. Now, I have to go." She yanked the door away from him, causing him to stumble, a surprised look on his face.

"And just how do you plan on doing that if your car doesn't work?"

He had her there. She jammed the key in the ignition, praying it might start now that it had rested for a while. Right. Nothing would ever be that easy for her. She held her breath and turned her wrist. The engine purred to life. Feeling like a snot, she turned to Caelan and graced him with a bratty smile.

"See? It's fine. Just needed a minute to cool down I guess." Even she didn't believe that.

As she pulled away, she glanced in the rearview mirror at Caelan who stood with his arms across his chest, grinning.

She found herself smiling back and shook her head. Fool.

Was she referring to him or to herself? Crap. What did it matter now? He was gone.

And her grandmother had said she was supposed to help him with something. Double crap. She'd gotten so flustered by the tow-truck driver and Caelan's heated gaze that she'd forgotten the reason her car had conveniently chosen that moment to break down. As soon as she got some rest, she'd find out exactly how her gramama had made that happen.

"I can explain, Tulla, and don't worry, my dear. He'll find you."

Tieran wasn't even going to think about why that idea made her panties wet.

🐈 🐈 🐈

Caelan dropped his arms to his side. His slippery little mate had gotten away again. No problem. At least now he knew how to find her. He had her name and license plate number. Owning your own security company sometimes had its privileges.

Tomorrow. He'd go to her tomorrow after he finished the job he had in the morning. Then he'd sit her down and enlighten her with reality. His reality, not hers, since her version would be vastly different. Then he'd take her to bed and have his way with her, making her position in his life concrete.

And that was the only way it could be.

Chapter Two

Caelan slapped the file folder down on the cluttered desk the next day and ran a hand over his face. Damn he was tired. His eyes were gritty from the number of hours he'd worked lately. They had to find this guy before he got to another one of their mates. He ground his teeth together, surprised the shifter community hadn't been outed yet. It would come to that very soon if no one could identify the man responsible. Caelan was no closer to finding the bastard today than he was yesterday. Or two weeks ago for that matter.

He was failing his shifters. All of them, even if none of the mates murdered so far had been from his pack. Caelan still felt responsible. Fat lot of good he'd do them in his current state of mind.

He cursed himself for not being able to concentrate this morning. He'd been too fucking busy thinking about Tieran. When he'd woken up this morning his dick had been so hard he'd had to jack himself off. Something he hadn't had to do since high school.

Imagining Tieran's head bobbing up and down as she sucked him off had done the trick, but it just hadn't been the same as having her do it for real.

He wished now he had been more forward last night. Somehow gotten her to come home with him or something. His body already knew what it was missing even though he hadn't completed the transfer of body fluids.

Yeah, right, Graham. Letting her see the real you would have gone over well. Probably would have sent her racing for the hills.

"You find out anything?" Eli settled his tall frame into the chair across the desk.

Jesus, Caelan was so preoccupied with his mate he hadn't even heard his brother come in. Not good. "You look like hell. Have another late night?" His brother was an eternal rake. Caelan thought maybe Eli was trying to deny his future.

Eli grinned but the smile looked forced.

"You could say that." Eli raked a hand through his hair. "Got a lot on my mind, I guess." He gestured with a jerk of his chin to the papers strewn across Caelan's desk. "What ya got?"

"Anything I can help with?" Caelan asked, ignoring his brother's attempt to change the subject.

"No, not until we get this killer business behind us. My problem can wait."

"If you've got an issue—"

"I don't, Cael. Well, I do, but nothing serious. I'll get to it later. What do you know?" Eli pointed to the papers again.

Caelan sighed and let the issue drop. Sooner or later Eli would get around to telling him. They had no secrets. He hoped.

"I know where she lives, where she works, her debt-to-income ratio, her education and where she shops. Hell, I can probably even tell you her bra size."

Eli's face lit up with a wolfish grin, no pun intended. "What? All that and no name? I was talking about the Mate Killer, anyway."

Caelan fisted his pencil until he heard a crack.

"What size are they?" Eli continued, wiggling his eyebrows.

"Tieran, and no, I didn't find out anything." He would ignore his little brother's comment about Tieran's cup size for now. "You won't get a rise out of me that easily."

"No, I can see you're in no way affected by the very hot human who's got you sporting a permanent woody."

Caelan itched to wipe the smug look off his little brother's face. Eli would get what was coming to him sooner or later. He couldn't escape finding a mate forever. Caelan had a feeling it would be Nikki who brought Eli to heel. "The police have no leads, even after last night," he said, striving to keep his voice normal.

Eli brought his chin up sharply, his eyes narrowed. "What happened last night?"

"Another one," Caelan said solemnly. "They think she was attacked by a pack of wild dogs or coyotes."

Eli snorted. "Coyote are wild dogs, aren't they? Wait a minute. Why did he take one while in wolf form? That's a pretty big leap from his previous attacks. Maybe he fucked up."

Caelan shrugged. "And maybe we're dealing with a full-blood shifter. The moon was full last night, he wouldn't have been able to get out of it. Or it could be he just knows what the hell he's doing. It might be a ploy to throw us off, to make us think he's a full-blood so we'll back off looking at the half-bloods completely. Not to mention he's been very careful not to kill in the same way twice, even in his human form."

Eli leaned over and braced his elbows on his knees. "Okay, so we know all the women targeted so far have been mates. There has to be some way of leading the police in the right direction. Hell"—he threw his hand in the air—"we've got fucking shifters on the force. Can't that asswipe, Hayward, drop a hint or something?"

Caelan shook his head. "Not without giving himself away in the process. But since we haven't been able to trace a scent marker, there aren't a lot of hints to drop. Our police shifters are stuck using conventional methods just like the human crime scene techs. And so far, there's been nothing to pick up."

"Shit. By the time they get all their i's dotted and t's crossed, we won't have any mates left." Eli slapped his thighs and rose from his chair. "You going to see her now? In the flesh I mean?" His smirk said he'd known all along where Caelan's thoughts had been today.

Caelan threw his pencil down. It bounced off the desk and javelined toward Eli who caught it with a lightning-quick reflex, his grin spreading from ear to ear.

"Yes, I am."

Eli nodded once. "Keep her safe." He strode to the doorway. "I have a feeling she's going to do great things for us."

Caelan snorted. "The great eagle in the sky tell you that?"

"No." He laughed. "Just my gut. Later, Bro."

"Yeah, later. Hey, don't you have a meeting tonight? Who is it with?" Caelan asked his brother's retreating figure.

Eli tapped his fingers on the doorframe, a strange look marring his features. "Yeah, with Dane Christian."

"You ever figure out what he wanted?"

This time it was Eli's turn to shake his head. He stared out the window of their home office, almost distracted by whatever he saw. "He said a friend recommended me. Mentioned something about needing me to do something for him. I'll see what he wants and get back to you after." He gave a two-finger salute and walked out.

Caelan sifted through his papers until he found the file with the bright pink tab. Not that he needed to look at it again, he'd memorized the contents.

Twenty-one sixty, West Springdale. His mate had been living in the same city as him all along.

It was time.

🐐 🐐 🐐

Tieran stared at her front door with pure contempt. She'd woken up later than usual this morning, courtesy of the erotic dreams she'd had of Caelan—all night long, thank you very much—and now she was grouchy. Lack of sleep was not the only reason for her current mood, though.

She'd worked an extra long day yesterday trying to finish her current project then had to deal with the situation last night, only to get up extra early this morning to go back into work.

"My hands are full, my head is splitting and now I've dropped my keys. Do you think you could just open sesame?"

She glared at the door, willing it to open, and sighed when it didn't. She blinked hard and nodded. Nothing. Were you supposed to cross your arms also?

"What happened to the psychokinesis, Gramama?"

"Aw, sweetheart, it didn't pass to you."

"Damn. Oh all right." Tieran bent down to retrieve her keys and rapped her forehead on the wooden frame. She had to bite

31

her lip to ease the pain in her head and hold the tears at bay. With a sniff, she rotated her neck, popping the kinks out.

With her bags teetering, Tieran unlocked and turned the knob, only to discover that because of the rising temperature, or whatever other reason the door chose today, it was stuck again. It would take more than a twist of the wrist to get through this stubborn piece of wood. Preparing herself for the battering, she shouldered the door open. It flew inward with little resistance, causing her to stumble forward and step on one of her plastic grocery sacks.

When she tried to straighten, she nearly ripped her arm out of its socket. The corner of a box inside the taut bag gouged a hole, then used its scalpel edge to slice its way out of the confining plastic. It leapt to the ground, urging all its fellow inmates to follow.

Before she knew it she was on the ground on her hands and knees, just inside the foyer, the door standing open, her butt in the air, her keys stabbing her palm, and approximately thirty bucks worth of groceries strewn about the hardwood. Her dinner, the offending box of frozen grilled chicken fettuccine, was smashed beneath her knee, where it had gotten caught in its misguided attempt to keep from being eaten. Ironic, the damn thing had accomplished exactly what it had set out to do.

"Tullabelle, you really should be more careful."

"Thank you, I appreciate the help."

Groaning, Tieran hung her head and slapped the floor with a hand still entwined in the handles of her now-shredded bag. She stood, with as much grace as possible, and turned to the door.

"Someday, I'm gonna shred your ass, then we'll see who's laughing." With the toe of her shoe, she kicked the door with all her strength and smiled in satisfaction as it slammed against the frame. The moment was lost, however, when it flew back open and smacked against the wall, leaving a small dent where the knob hit. As always, she did not get the last word.

Her smile faded into a snarl. In order for the door to shut, you had to turn the knob to loosen the locking mechanism, which she did now. It was just one of the quirks "possessed"— and she meant that in every sense of the word—by the house her gramama had lived in until the day she died. Tieran loved the house because it was where she felt the safest, but it was the most ornery dwelling on the planet.

Pushing her disarrayed hair out of her face, she stalked toward the kitchen, ignoring the mess surrounding her. Her shoulders drooped when she squashed a loaf of bread and kicked a can of green beans under the desk.

"So much for walking away from a conflict," she muttered.

Ten minutes later, Tieran sat in her breakfast nook with a cold Mountain Dew and a bag of Doritos. Lunch. The paper lay open in front of her and she skimmed its contents while she crunched the spicy, cheesy chips.

Blah, blah, blah. She turned the page and wondered why she'd even opened the stupid thing.

Then she saw why. Staring back at her from the bottom of page four was a woman with long, loose, blonde hair that hung like a curtain around a heart-shaped face. Tieran's eye twitched.

"No," she groaned. "Not today, please." She rubbed at her eyelid and prayed it was a simple twitch and not a precursor to a vision. Who was she kidding? She'd never had a normal *twitch* in her entire life. The stupid twinge was the only warning she got before a full-blown vision. The precursor might happen an hour before, or a day. There was no telling. Good thing she was off rotation the next three days.

Her visions were a curse and a blessing. Most of the time they were simple scenes from someone's life. She could put those out of her mind. Others, the ones that followed the twitch in her eye, usually depicted something bad that had happened, or was going to happen. Those types stuck in her head for days, causing her to replay them over and over.

"Do not resist him when he comes, Tullabelle."

"He who?" she asked, knowing full well who her gramama was referring to. Tieran hadn't been able to put the plea to help Caelan Graham out of her mind since she'd left him standing in her dust.

"He needs your help."

"Yes, you've said that before. If you know he needs my help, why can't you just tell me the reason?"

"You know I can't, Tulla." Her grandmother's words were filled with remorse.

Tieran did know that, it just confused the hell out of her. Her grandmother sometimes knew what would happen after one of the visions, but not what the vision was about. Tieran sighed, it looked like she was in for another long night.

Stretching her arms above her head, she worked the kinks along the length of her spine. It was only early afternoon but she was exhausted. The sheer magnitude of an upcoming vision was daunting enough without being tired.

Stumbling toward her bedroom, she unsnapped and unzipped her jeans, prepared to strip down to just her panties and T-shirt and take a nap. She'd be asleep as soon as her head hit the pillow. Cleaning up the foyer could wait.

The instant she sat on the bed to kick her shoes off, someone knocked at her door. For a second, she thought about answering it but then shook her head. Whoever it was could come back later. She flopped down onto the quilt her gramama had made years ago, the material soft and inviting with its age and memories.

The knock sounded again. "No," she groaned and covered her head with her pillow. "Go away."

"Answer the door, Tulla. Now."

No one who had a little voice in their head had one as commanding as her grandmother's.

She dragged herself off the bed and back down the hall to the front door. At least she was still dressed. The frame shook as her visitor pounded again. Only people peddling the Word came to her door, and she didn't have the energy for God right now. She closed one eye and looked through the peephole with the other.

God was not standing on her porch. Instead it was the incredibly yummy man she'd left standing in her car's dust last night. Caelan.

"This is who you thought I needed to get out of bed for?" Her heart skipped a beat. My Lord, the man was more gorgeous than any man had the right to be. He was even more devastating in the light of day and had an animal magnetism about him that drew her in. Love at first sight? No. Not possible. She hated men. Didn't she?

"Tieran!" her grandmother yelled, yanking her back into focus.

"I'll take that as a yes."

She grasped the knob with both hands and yanked on the door she'd never locked. It burst open with an unwilling protest. Being partial about her privacy, she quickly placed her body in the foot-wide opening.

"Oh, it's you." Did she sound uncaring enough? She wasn't grinning like a lovesick puppy, was she? She gripped the door, too tired to stand here and discuss life with the man who'd so rudely stared at her before.

"He also saved your butt."

"Well, there is that." Not to mention the fact the man was gorgeous.

"It's nice to see you too," he said, grinning.

"Is there something I can help you with?" She tried to ignore his devastating smile and the fact that her insides were melting because of it. Then it occurred to her. "Hey, how did you find me?"

A dimple creased his cheek, making her tummy do a weird little flip-flop, and he shrugged. "I own a security company. Finding people is part of what I do."

"Huh. What about people who don't want to be found?" she asked, lying through her teeth. If her panties got any wetter, her cream would be dripping down her legs. Who wouldn't want to be found by this man?

Me, she inwardly shouted. *Remember Peter and never wanting anything to do with a man again?*

Caelan peered around her head like he had every right in the world to invade her space. "What are you hiding in there?"

Her eyebrows shot up. *"Moi?"*

"Yes, you. You look like you're guarding state secrets in there."

"Oh, that. Well, I was attacked, and there's a mess—" Her breath left on a whoosh. One second she was in her house, the next Caelan had her pinned to the wall outside by a well-muscled arm. A growl vibrated his rib cage. With his other hand he whipped out an ugly black gun faster than she could blink.

"What are you doing?" she shouted, and struggled to disengage herself from his hold. Not that it wasn't nice to be held and protected, but she was clueless as to why he'd suddenly gone security guy on her.

"Is he still in the house?" he whispered, controlling her squirming with what seemed like little effort on his part.

"He?"

"You said you were attacked."

Reality dawned. "By the door, big guy."

"What?"

"The door. It was stuck, and then I tripped over my bags and spilled everything inside. I was too tired to clean it up, so I left it." She leaned in close and whispered in his ear, the urge to lick it strong as hell. "I didn't want you to see it."

He looked adorable standing there with an expression of utter disbelief.

"The door."

"Afraid so."

His eyes closed, his jaw started ticking and he seemed to be counting to himself. She bit her lip to keep from laughing. Then he opened his eyes and leaned even closer to her face. His breath puffed on her nose when he spoke.

"You're gonna be the death of me and I haven't even gotten to know you yet."

He searched her eyes like he meant to find the meaning of life in them and Tieran held her breath. An inch. She'd only have to stretch that far to plant her lips on his. A funny sensation zipped through her body and pooled in her belly. And then he spoke, shattering the illusion.

"What's wrong with your eye?"

She tried to reach for her eye, but the way he had her pinned, she couldn't get her hand past his thick biceps.

"What's wrong with my eye?"

He raised an eyebrow. "Are you a parrot? How do you even know which eye I'm talking about?"

"Because you're looking at this one!" She pointed as best she could.

"Oh. Well, it's just not right." He looked at her with a more critical eye. "The color's not the same as the other one."

"How very PC of you to notice."

He shrugged. Being a big, tough, security man, he probably didn't care if he hurt people's feelings or not.

"Why are you trying to disguise your eye color?"

"Blunt, aren't you? A *lot* of people wear colored contacts, and as you so clearly pointed out, I'm only wearing one. I'm weird enough as it is, I don't need to draw attention to myself through some strange genetic abnormality." Oops, too much. She could tell he'd latched on to her "weird enough" comment. His nostrils flared.

Tieran pushed against his weight in an effort to dislodge him. They'd stood too close for long enough.

"Oh my God!"

"What?" He tightened around her as if preparing for a new attack.

"You're touching me!" Panic set in and then she realized what she'd just said. Oops, again. Her cheeks flamed. It wasn't totally unusual to touch someone and not get some insight about them. It just didn't happen very often. The only truly safe person she'd ever known was Gramama. To this day, even dead, the elderly woman took care of her, shielding her from harm and guiding her down the right path. Caelan, however, was wreaking havoc on her system, pulling her out of her element and her safe zone. She made a fist and before he could realize what she intended to do, punched him in the stomach.

"*Oof.*" The air rushed out of his lips as he doubled over. "What was that for?" he croaked.

"I don't like to be touched."

"And you forgot that little detail until just this second?"

"Yeah, you got a problem with that?"

"No, but my belly does." He rubbed the offended part of his anatomy.

"Sorry."

"No you're not."

Tieran tilted her head and pretended to think about that for a minute. "You're right." She turned to step back inside but was brought up short when his long, slender, lover's fingers wrapped around her forearm. She glared at those fingers like they were burning her.

"We're not done yet." He righted himself, stretching to his full height, which Tieran guessed to be about six-foot-two, a long way off from her own five-six. He was a whole lot of stud-packed man. She found her gaze wandering south to his groin where his package impressively strained his jeans. Apparently the man was big all over.

The dampness between her legs increased tenfold as she wondered what it would be like to fuck him.

Great, now that he'd touched her and she'd gotten zero images from him, she was letting loose with all sorts of dreams. Dreams that included being with a man she couldn't read. Now that would be wonderful.

"*Maybe you were right, Gramama. Maybe I should let him into my life. If for nothing else than...never mind.*"

"*I told you so.*"

She curled her lip at the smugness in her grandmother's words.

Caelan drew a breath and steadied himself after the sucker punch to his gut. His mate could pack a wallop with her diminutive frame. He re-holstered his gun and spared a chuckle for the caveman routine he'd just engaged in. It had to have something to do with his species, and their innate sense to protect their mate.

Of course, he should have picked up on her complete nonchalance when saying she'd been attacked. Instead he'd gone into lockdown mode and prepared to defend her life with his own.

He eyed the door with caution and wondered how she could accuse it of attacking her.

Following her retreating figure into the house, Caelan surveyed the area. It was, in a word, homey. His mouth quirked at the mess she hadn't wanted him to see, and he planted his hands on his hips. Tieran had disappeared. For a split second he thought about the fact that she might run but dismissed the idea just as fast. Why would she have any reason to run?

He flipped the door closed behind him with his heel. It swung back open and slapped him in the rear. Now he could see why she said the door had ambushed her. He pushed firmly on the paneled wood but it still wouldn't close. He frowned at it. Damn thing was possessed.

Caelan turned when an odd breeze wafted across the back of his neck. The hair on the rest of his body stood on end, a testimony to the eerie feeling he was being watched. He traced the room carefully, looking for anything that may have caused the sudden puff of air, and was tempted to start humming the theme from *The X-Files*.

"You have to turn the knob to close the door," Tieran yelled from somewhere deeper in the house.

How had she known he was having trouble with the door? *Because she lives here, you idiot.*

"Where are you?"

"In the kitchen," came her muffled reply.

"The kitchen. I guess I'm on my own to find that. Which shouldn't be too hard for an expert security person like myself." Jesus, she had him twisted in knots and talking to himself.

He froze in the doorway to the kitchen at the sight greeting him. Tieran was bent over, her upper half hidden as she scrounged in the refrigerator. More blood rushed straight to his cock as he stared at her firm butt encased in tight blue jeans. The waistband of her jeans was bowed out, giving him a glimpse of skin at the small of her back.

His fingers itched to touch her and his inner wolf howled, wanting to claim its mate. Cael curled his hands into fists to keep from reaching out and taking what he already knew to be his.

He swallowed, remembering how her eyes glittered and her cheeks grew rosy when she was angry. He'd first seen it last night at the bar, then again a minute ago when he'd stood on her porch an inch away from her face. Would they look the same way when he was buried deep in her wet heat? Would they glaze over when a climax claimed her? He shifted in an attempt to ease himself.

"Since you're being so persistent, I guess I'll offer you a drink."

He had *not* made a sound. In fact, he was well-known for his sneaking ability. She either had supersonic hearing or a strong sixth sense.

Caelan rubbed a hand at the goose bumps suddenly tingling along his neck. "What do you have?" His voice cracked like a preteen in puberty.

"Hmm. Water or, water."

"Wow, great choices. What are you having?" he asked, regaining control before she could see the precarious hold he had on his libido.

"Mountain Dew." She rose and faced him, a green can in one hand.

His attention, however, was drawn to her midriff. Her jeans, he just realized, were unbuttoned and unzipped. A slice of creamy, tanned skin peeked out where her T-shirt had ridden up, looking smooth as silk just like her delectable backside.

"What are you drooling over? You can't have my Mountain Dew."

His attention remained riveted on her belly and he found himself swallowing again. A tiny gem sparkled from where it nestled in her navel. It was the most perfect fucking thing he'd ever seen. He stalked towards her. She seemed to be completely oblivious to the effect she was having on him.

"Water's fine," he choked out. He gestured to the exposed part of her anatomy. "Your pants...umm...XYZ!" he spit out.

Her gaze dropped. "Oh, geez. I find it hard to believe you've never seen a female body before."

He looked to the table and back to her, unable to control his need for her. He could take her right there on the Formica.

Tieran threw her hands up. "Whoa!" Forgetting she was holding the can, she fumbled to fix her jeans. The can fell to the floor at just the right angle and exploded, spraying the sticky yellow soda everywhere.

"*Ugh!*" she yelled. Caelan was rooted to the floor, a silly grin on his face. "You!" she pointed. "Out. Go. Sit on the couch and wait for me."

Now why did her words make him feel like a dog being reprimanded?

"Uh-uh." Shaking his head, he ignored her pointing finger and continued walking towards her. She was soaked from head to toe, and he was going to enjoy licking every inch of her clean.

Her eyes widened and she stepped back, once, twice, and bumped into the counter behind her. Caelan stopped just in front of her, pinning her to the cabinets. He had her between his rock and a hard place.

"What are you doing?" she whispered.

"I'm going to kiss you." He traced a line of soda down her cheek with his forefinger. "And you're going to kiss me back." He framed her face with both his hands, holding her in place, though he didn't need to. She was frozen to the spot.

Her lips were warm and soft as he licked along them, sipping a drop of the soda's sweetness from one corner. He pressed his tongue between her lips, demanding that she open to him, which she did without the slightest bit of hesitation.

He tasted her, dueled with her tongue, bit her bottom lip gently, until she groaned and her body melted into his.

Tieran brought her hands up to his chest and fisted them in his shirt.

He tasted like heaven. His tongue was velvet soft and caressed with the perfect amount of pressure. Their lips melded together, sealing their bond. She flicked at his teeth, surprised at how sharp they were, and how very much she wanted to feel them nipping at her skin. His chest rumbled under her hands.

43

She ripped her mouth away, panting hard. Almost as hard as the erection that was pressed against her belly and not where she really wanted it to be. Inside her.

Caelan's eyes appeared to glow, just like she'd noticed last night. They were mesmerizing and entrancing, pulling her into their depths until she was lost.

"I want you." His head dipped and took control of her mouth again.

Closer. I have to get closer. She lifted her arms and wrapped them around his neck, hugging him to her. His palms were rough when they slipped inside both her panties and jeans. Then he shoved the fabric down and out of the way.

"Step out."

She shivered at his gravelly command, anxious to do whatever he wanted, her need spilling from her pussy.

He helped her out with the toe of his leather work boot in the crotch of her pants, and suddenly her feet were off the ground. The counter was cold beneath her bottom.

"Jesus." She yelped and inadvertently pressed her legs together.

Caelan wrenched them apart. "Uh-uh. Mine." He stared at her drenched pussy, his lungs heaving. His gaze traveled the length of her until he met her eyes with a look drowning in hunger and need.

It fueled her own.

"Now, Caelan."

He grasped the hem of her sticky, wet T-shirt and yanked it over her head. Her nipples stood proudly at attention, begging to be touched, kissed and sucked. Her womb clenched, his jaw ticked, the air around them crackled. She fought to keep herself from covering her breasts, a moment of insanity brought on by memories of Peter's bitter words about her small figure.

There was nothing even remotely resembling disgust on Caelan's face, just pure, carnal lust.

"What do you want, mate of mine."

Okay, that was weird. Who cares? Fuck me, fuck me, fuck me.

God, was she really having sex with a complete stranger? Yes. Yes! The answer was a resounding yes. Nothing had ever felt this good. What was it about this man that had her wanting to scream, "Fuck me, Caelan. Now."

"Gladly."

Oh Lord, she had screamed it. He attacked the button-fly of his jeans, separating the material and allowing his going-commando erection to spring free.

Tieran's breath caught in her throat. His cock was huge, in circumference and length. Her clit pulsed an achy rhythm, despite the fact there was no way he'd fit inside her. Caelan must have seen her distress because he caressed her cheek with one hand, while the other searched between her labia, looking for admittance to her sheath.

He had no trouble finding it and slipped a finger all the way into her core, filling her, but not enough.

Fucking gorgeous. Her head fell back on her shoulders. Caelan shifted her forward until her sweet pussy was lined up with the edge of the counter. His cock was ready to explode and she was more than ready for him, his finger could attest to that.

"This what you want, baby?" He added a second finger to the first, filling her even more, drawing out her juices and coating his palm with it.

"More," she breathed, tilting her head forward and looking at him. Her eyes were glazed over just like he imagined they would be. "Touch me, please." The tendons in her neck corded as she begged.

He placed the pad of his thumb on the swollen nub of her clit and caught her with his other arm when her hips shot off the counter.

"Oh, my God."

One touch and she'd climaxed! Her vagina clinched around his fingers as he continued to pump them into her. He wanted to feel those tiny muscles working on his dick.

He withdrew his hand, grasped his cock, guiding it to her slick folds, and watched the thick purpled head disappear into her tight, wet passage. She groaned, her head thrashing as he took possession of her body. Skin to skin, just as it would always be between them.

She was ovulating. He could smell it on her and he knew what they were about to do would most likely impregnate her, thereby putting her in extreme danger. Damn it. He couldn't stop despite the danger. An uncontrollable need to mate with his mate seized him. If he didn't fuck her, he'd go out of his mind.

Caelan thrust into her, catching her screams with his mouth as she adjusted to his penetration.

"That's it, my own. All of me, inside of you, always."

In about two seconds his little head was going to blow off. He stayed motionless and savored the moment.

"Move," she urged, wiggling against him. "Please."

Aw, shit. "Don't move, baby." He panted and tried to still her to no avail. Fuck it. He withdrew and slammed back home.

"Yes, yes."

His canines sharpened. He lowered his head to the gentle slope where her shoulder met her neck and pressed his open mouth against the tender skin. He rocked into her sopping pussy again and again. Biting her softly, he claimed her with his teeth as well as his cock, marking her as his mate.

With one last thrust, he buried himself inside her to the hilt, and coated her womb with spurt after spurt of his seed.

Chapter Three

"Micah? Is that you?"

The cool breeze lifted Elizabeth's skirt, twisting it around her legs. She shivered at the unusual silence of the woods surrounding their quaint log cabin-style home. Where were the birds tonight, the rustle of the leaves in the trees? Goose bumps formed on her bare arms. From the top of the steps, she searched the darkness.

"Micah?" she yelled louder, wrapping her arms around her waist in a tight hug. A low moan captured her attention. She swung her gaze toward the sound and, slowly descending off the porch, headed in that direction. Her heart pounded. Dried leaves crunched beneath her feet.

"Is that you, honey?"

In the clearing about ten yards from the tree line she stopped and peered into the thick, dark woods. Something moved. Elizabeth squinted to get a better look.

"Stop playing games, Micah, supper's ready." Her voice wobbled.

A shadow split from the surrounding darkness and ventured into the clearing. For a second, Elizabeth tensed then blew out a breath and swallowed. She smiled despite her true feeling. "I was just looking for Micah. Have you seen him?" She fought the urge to shiver. There was something about him she didn't like. Even from the first time she'd met him at the Prime's house. He'd seemed smarmy to her, like he was above the rest of them.

He took a step toward her, his fur lifting with the breeze, and Elizabeth backed up. She twisted her fingers together in front of her. Why was he here and where was Micah? Her belly plummeted. Something was wrong with her mate. Micah would never leave her alone like this. She should have sensed it immediately. Now she smelled the malice on the wind and suddenly she didn't want to be alone with this shifter anymore.

He took an aggressive stance when she started walking backward. His hackles raised, he pinned his ears back and one side of his top lip curled up to reveal his teeth. Elizabeth held her breath. What reason did he have for attacking? She inched closer to the house. If she could get there, she could lock the door and wait for Micah to come home. If he could come home. She whimpered and covered her mouth with her hand to stifle the noise, not wanting to scare the wolf into action.

It lunged at her anyway with a sharp bark. Elizabeth screamed and twisted to run, but it was on her, pinning her to the ground before she could take another breath. He growled and snarled, drowning out her terror-filled screams. His teeth tore into her clothes and her flesh, ripping off strips of both. Searing pain arced through her body and black spots burst in her vision.

With a pitiful volley of fists, she pummeled the creature, still screaming in excruciating horror, but was no match for the much larger animal. After a few minutes of useless fighting, Elizabeth's body grew numb. Her blood-slick fingers fell from the tangle of fur she'd grabbed hold of in an attempt to push him off.

A drop of her blood fell from a pointed tooth and plopped on her cheek. She blinked and took a shallow, wrenching breath. Her lungs were on fire with the effort it took to fill them.

The colors were so beautiful, swirling and dancing in the sky above them.

The eerie silence returned, broken only by a faint whistling in her ears and the harsh breathing of the shifter.

She took another breath, shorter than the last. Cocking his head, the wolf licked its chops and stared at her with glowing yellow eyes. He turned, looking into the woods, and Elizabeth saw the long, fine scar bisecting his left upper shoulder. The hairless strip sharply contrasted with the much darker fur surrounding it. He stood and prowled toward the tree line, never looking back. A howl exploded through the stillness like a shotgun.

Within moments, he was gone, loping off into the night.

Her lungs worked hard to force another breath into her near lifeless body.

Leaves rustled a few feet away. Micah was coming, she felt him. She turned her head to the side and watched as he pulled himself by the strength of his arms into the opening. A gash split his temple, dripping a trail of blood in his slow wake. Halfway to her, he pushed himself to his hands and knees and crawled the rest of the way.

She loved him so much. He would be alone now, without her. "Micah," *she whispered and smiled one last time before ascending into the beautiful lights.*

"Nooo!" The soulful, anguished cry of a grieving shifter followed her.

"Tieran!"

Her teeth snapped together with Caelan's powerful shake of her shoulders. She sucked in a deep breath, revitalizing lungs that felt starved for oxygen. Slowly her senses came back to her.

She was sweaty and dizzy and had to swallow past the lump in her throat while trying to get her bearings. She and Caelan were in her kitchen. Tieran sat on the counter still impaled on Caelan's insistent cock. She had to get away from him. Now, before she passed out. With weak hands, she pushed on his chest.

Jesus, it had been so real. More so than any before. Tieran reached a weak hand up to her cheek and wiped at it. She looked at her fingertips, half-expecting them to come away red.

"Let him help you, Tulla."

She shook her head. No. She didn't want him to know. Didn't want what happened with Peter.

"It won't."

Caelan pulled out, leaving her feeling empty in more ways than one, and captured her hands, placing them on his shoulders. She heard the rustle of his jeans as he drew them over his hips. He lifted her with his hands beneath her thighs, holding her tightly to him, his semi-erection pressed against her throbbing pussy through his still open fly. Tiny pulses of electricity raced through her womb as he carried her, the friction along her sensitized clit making her gasp.

"I've got you, my own. You're safe."

His voice was so tender, laced with concern, not scorn. But then, he didn't know what had just happened, couldn't know. Wouldn't know. She would never hand over control to another man again. Especially not to one she didn't know at all. Regardless of the incredible sex they'd just engaged in.

"You have...to leave." She could barely whisper. The darkness was closing in fast. Soon she'd be unconscious, only to wake incredibly groggy and disoriented with a pounding head.

"Never. I'll never leave you now." He kissed her tenderly on the forehead and lowered her to her bed. She heard herself whimper before the blackness took control.

🐈 🐈 🐈

"What the fuck just happened?" Caelan muttered, unfolding the blue and tan plaid blanket from the foot of the bed and covering her loosely.

In the bathroom he ran a washcloth under warm water, then went back to her too-still form. Tieran never moved as he wiped away both of their come from her thighs and pussy.

The sudden sensation of being watched had the hair on his arms standing on end. He whipped around. Nothing. The room was empty, the house silent. He let out a breath he didn't realize he was holding and shook off the eerie feeling.

Caelan turned back to his mate. She had a beautiful body, slim and slightly tanned. Her nipples stood in stiff peaks atop her small, perfect breasts, and he ached to suck one into his mouth, to mark the sweet skin the way he had her shoulder.

With a fingertip, he traced the bite mark that made her his forever. He'd claimed her by introducing his extraordinary DNA into her bloodstream, not to mention her womb. She was his and he'd never felt more proud. Tieran was feisty and stubborn and all his. Now he just had to convince her they were meant to be together. And somehow reconcile with himself the fact he did all this without her consent.

He idly stroked his quickly hardening cock through his open fly and felt disgusted. His mate was unconscious and he wanted to fuck her again. Before he ended up doing more damage, he jerked his hand off his dick and tucked the blanket around her shoulders, hiding her body from his view.

Caelan painfully buttoned himself up. He'd fucked her on the kitchen counter and hadn't even bothered to take his pants off. *What a charmer, Graham.*

In the corner of the room was an overstuffed armchair. He pulled it over next to the bed and slumped into it. Christ, one minute he'd been coming inside her, the next he'd been shaking her just to get a response out of her.

He'd never had a woman lose consciousness on him before, though he had heard of it happening. At least, he hoped to hell that's all it was, 'cause it wasn't something he wanted to happen again. The look on her face had been downright scary. Almost as if she'd been having a seizure.

And then she'd asked him to leave.

"Yeah right," he scoffed. Like that was going to happen. Leave his mate unprotected? Uh-uh. Not now, not ever. Of course, she wouldn't understand since he hadn't even gotten around to telling her he was a shape-shifting wolf. Hell, they hadn't even gotten past swapping names. The only things he knew about her were from his reports, not from her mouth.

Caelan stretched his legs out. He needed her again and had a feeling he would be in this constant state of arousal forever. With a click, he released his phone from its belt clip and punched in Eli's number.

"Yeah," his brother answered.

"E, I'm at Tieran's."

"You don't sound too happy about that."

"You ever fucked a woman unconscious?"

Eli barked out a laugh. "Once, but then, she was dead drunk. Might have been the alcohol and not my sexual expertise."

"Hmm." Caelan stabbed his fingers through his hair.

"I guess she's good with you?"

"I didn't get a chance to tell her."

The silence on the other end of the line spoke volumes.

"You mated with her, possibly impregnated her, but didn't tell her yet?" Eli's voice was ripe with disbelief.

"Pretty much."

"Damn, Cael. I thought we agreed a long time ago, when we found our mates we'd treat them with more respect. At least give them the chance to understand what we are before going on to more drastic measures."

"Yeah, we did, and when you meet your mate, you can tell me how that goes, because I'm telling you, *you* won't be able to keep your dick zipped up either."

Eli snorted. "Okay, so why exactly are you calling me during your post-coital bliss?"

"She's fucking dead to the world, E. Did you get that, or did you think I was bragging about my prowess in bed?"

"No need to shout, I got you. Tell me what happened."

Caelan winced and shot a look at Tieran. She was still out even though he was shouting. "Christ. I don't even know. She came, I came, then bam, she's gone. Her eyes rolled back, her head lolled to the side, and her body went all rigid. It was like some kind of seizure or something. It took me almost a full minute to shake her out of it."

"Then what?"

"She starts pushing me away, telling me to leave. Panicking almost."

"Where is she now?"

"Bed." He had to stare hard at the blanket draped across her chest to make sure she was still breathing. She hadn't moved yet.

"Damn."

"What do you mean, 'damn'?"

"Cael, another file came through the fax a little while ago. A buried one someone went to a lot of trouble to hide. I was kind of hoping she'd tell you about it first. When you put her name in the system, it alerted someone in Florida."

"So?"

Tieran shifted on the bed, the first movement she'd made since he laid her there. He reached over and re-covered her with the dislodged blanket.

"So she was involved in a serial rapist case down there when she was younger."

"Fuck. No." Not his mate. Please God don't let that have happened to the woman he'd just made love to. The woman who'd shown no inhibitions in letting him fuck her.

"No, not that," Eli spat. Caelan could almost see Eli's hand dismissing him and let out a breath of relief. "But she was almost instrumental in putting the bastard behind bars."

"How are you *almost* instrumental?"

"She's psychic, Cael. She has visions, sees things somehow."

Caelan shot out of the chair and stared down at his mate. Is that what had happened? Had she had a vision of some sort as he ejaculated deep inside her pussy? It appeared they both had secrets, which should make his a tiny bit easier for her to accept.

A cold blast of air pressed against his back. Caelan jerked around, looking for a possible source. It wasn't the first time he'd been bombarded by an unexplained sensation inside Tieran's home. Drafty fucking house, he decided when he couldn't come up with a source. He turned back to Tieran. Her face was drawn tight with whatever was troubling her.

He found himself rubbing unconsciously at another set of goose bumps attacking the bare flesh of his arms. Had she had some sort of vision? About him? If not, then what?

He moved to stand by the window where he saw a man walking a dog on the sidewalk. The dog lifted its head and stared at Caelan, its tail wagging ferociously, before letting out a bark in greeting.

"You still there, Bro?"

Caelan cleared his throat. "Yeah."

"The police didn't believe her. She took a lot of heat, so much that her parents moved back here, where her grandmother lived. Florida police eventually arrested the man she'd told them about, but they couldn't find her and closed the case without talking to her again."

"Son of a bitch. Then maybe she already knows I'm a shifter."

His breath puffed out in a neat white cloud, frosting the window and making him drop the phone. It was seventy fucking degrees outside! And not much cooler in the house. No way should he be able to see his goddamn breath!

"Cael. Cael?"

"What?" he hissed, picking up the phone and putting it back to his ear.

"Cael, if she is even halfway able to see our Mate Killer, and he somehow finds out, she's as good as dead."

"I'm aware of that. Fuck! E, I need you to bring me some things. It looks like I'm going to be here awhile."

"What?" Eli sounded surprised.

"Would you have me leave her here unprotected?" Caelan growled. What was his brother thinking?

"No. Jesus, that didn't come out right. Maybe you could just get it over with and tell her about us. Then get her the hell out to the ranch where you know she'll be safe."

Caelan sighed. "She's not ready for that yet. Besides, I have a feeling she had a vision and that's why she's unconscious."

"Do you know that for sure?"

Why did Caelan detect wariness in Eli's voice? "What in the hell is wrong with you, E?"

"Nothing," he insisted, but Caelan could practically hear him squirming in his seat. "It's weird, ya know? I wonder what kinds of things she can see."

"You got something to hide, Bro?"

"Hell yeah. What if she *sees* one of us shift, goes ape-shit and tells someone?"

If they weren't separated by the phone, Caelan would slap Eli upside the head. "That's one of the reasons I'm not leaving, and short of kidnapping her, I can't make her leave the one place she probably feels the safest. Besides, as you've already pointed out, normal people tend not to believe the spouting of a psychic."

"You're right," Eli said. "I don't know what my problem is. What do you need?"

After requesting the items he wanted, Caelan flipped his cell phone closed. He climbed onto the bed next to Tieran. Her body relaxed into his arms. He combed the sweat-dampened hair off her face and kissed her temple.

He tried to shrug off the nagging suspicion there was something wrong with his twin. When this was all over, he'd have to sit down with him and find out what had been bothering him the past couple of weeks. Eli was becoming increasingly agitated about something and Caelan wondered if it had anything to do with Nikki Taylor.

He inhaled. Since the moment he'd smelled Tieran's scent at the bar, he'd been worried about putting her in danger. Now, because of her special abilities, the threat level had increased tenfold.

Caelan buried his nose in the crook of her neck. It was too late to turn back.

She was already carrying his child.

🐾 🐾 🐾

Tieran tried to focus through the pain holding her brain in a vise. What happened?

The last thing she remembered was the screaming orgasm Caelan had forced on her as she sat on her counter.

"Forced, Tulla?"

"Yes, forced. I didn't ask him to do that to me."

"You're right. I believe you begged. Are you saying you didn't like it?"

"Gramama! I am not having this conversation with you. And please tell me you did not watch because that would just be way too creepy and I would definitely have to disown you." Tieran shivered.

"I most certainly did not watch. Not after he stuck his tongue down your throat anyway, but oh how it made me remember

being so young. Your grandpa could turn me on like a light switch. We used to go at it no matter where we were."

"Oh my God, stop! Do not talk to me about you and Pawpoo. That is so...eew. Go away, my head is killing me."

"Think, Tullabelle. Think about what else happened on the countertop. It is important you remember."

Well, let's see. She'd had her legs wrapped around Caelan's lean hips as he'd buried himself inside her pussy one last time. She'd felt his release in hot spurts against her womb.

She'd felt his release in hot spurts... Oh, good God. They hadn't used a condom. How could she be so stupid!

"Forget about the condom, Tulla, what's done is done. Focus on what happened next."

Forget about the condom? Had she really just said that? Holy shit. What else had happened then? Must have been pretty damn big for her grandmother to tell her not to worry about the fact they hadn't used protection.

It hit her like a sledgehammer between the eyes. A vision. She'd had a vision of the woman from the newspaper. The one who'd caused her eye to twitch earlier. The one who'd been nearly eaten by a wolf-like beast.

Tieran gagged and prayed her Doritos stayed down because no way would she make it to the toilet.

And where exactly was Caelan?

"Right beside you, Tulla."

She groaned silently and hoped he was asleep so she could get out of bed unnoticed.

"I thought I told him to leave."

"There are things you don't know yet, Tieran. Listen to him. Please."

"Whoa, must be serious, you said please."

"It is life or death, Tulla."

"Whose?"

"Yours."

Tieran shuddered. Gramama had never steered her wrong. She guided without telling Tieran what to do, pushed when a vision was serious enough to warrant attention, but didn't normally interfere with Tieran's decisions. She trusted her granddaughter enough to do the right thing.

Then again, Tieran had never encountered a situation that might lead to her own death.

"He is not going to go away, Tieran, and he is not like most men. Trust him enough to tell him what you just saw."

"You're asking a lot, Gramama. You, of all people, know what happened the last time I trusted someone."

"Yes, but Caelan is different. You'll see."

Fine. She'd think about it. If her gramama thought Caelan was a good man and could handle Tieran's visions, maybe she would tell him. It would serve her grandmother right if she had to do a lot of consoling tomorrow for getting her granddaughter's heart broken again.

And besides, why on earth would the man be interested in a wolf attacking a woman?

Tieran started to roll to her side but her head spun crazily, making her stomach dip and threaten an upheaval. Puking after a vision happened more times than not. She couldn't wait to see how Caelan would handle that. Peter had looked at her in horror the three times it had happened in his presence.

The third time he'd actually accused her of having morning sickness and not telling him she was pregnant. She'd still been making a disbelieving fish face at him when he stormed out spouting horrible things about her. She'd never seen him again.

She sucked in a deep breath when her belly swayed and waited for the sensation to pass. A few seconds later she was good to go.

What must the man be thinking watching her at her finest? On top of this, he probably thought she was easy. She'd given in to him with a minimal amount of resistance. Might as well go find a corner to work.

She blinked her eyes slowly open knowing even that slight movement could cause another revolt. Caelan had to be asleep because he hadn't moved or spoken since she'd woken several minutes ago.

"*Aaaaaahhhh.*" Her scream echoed through her small house, mixing with the loud thump her body made as she landed in a twisted heap on the floor. She tried to get up but got tangled in the blanket wound around her legs and torso.

She would never make it! It would tear her apart like it had the poor woman.

She sobbed and scrambled again.

The huge dark-furred beast hung its head over the side of the bed, resting on its paws.

"Oh shit, oh shit, oh shit."

Its eyes sparkled a yellow-brown, not two feet from her face. Its tongue slurped along one jowl, and its teeth, sharper than ever-fucking hell, snapped together when it swallowed. Then its mouth dropped open again.

It panted little shallow doggy pants and cocked its head to look at her. Her heart pounded as it tried to force its way out of her rib cage and make its own run for the door.

"Nice doggy," she breathed. "Good boy. That's it. Staaay, staay." She inched backward toward the door, untangling the blanket as she went.

The wolf thingy tilted its head in the other direction and she stopped moving. Its ears pricked upward. Wasn't that the universal doggy sign for "I'm pissed"?

It's going to pounce, it's going to eat me, and I'm going to die. Please God, don't let me die. Not like this. Not in the same agony as that woman did.

"How could you not warn me?"

"I did, Tullabelle."

"You did not tell me there was a huge beast about to eat me. I would have remembered something like that!"

"Look closely, Tulla."

How could she not? The massive thing sat back on its haunches on her bed, still panting like a puppy. His tail wagged behind him, thumping against the mattress. When it jumped from the bed, Tieran screamed like she'd never screamed before.

Two padded steps and it was on her, literally, covering her body with its larger...furry one. Its belly hair tickled her bare belly and she nearly peed on herself. She bit her lip to prevent herself from moving and possibly scaring it into mauling her. Her chest heaved with each breath. Play dead. No, no, that's a bear thing, she thought insanely.

She went cross-eyed looking at it as it leaned forward and pressed its big, black, wet nose to hers. She screwed up her face. It was going to rip her face off first, she knew it!

"Tulla, would you stop thinking so much and look?"

"Fine. You want me to look at the thing about to devour me? I'll stare it down with the best of them!"

She focused on its eyes and her breath caught. God, they were the same as...no. No, they weren't the same as Caelan's, but...no. Impossible. They couldn't be. A man could not turn into a-a thing.

"You see things."

"So what? No. No!"

Her head spun again, swirling her stomach with it. The effects of one of her visions usually lasted for hours. Adrenaline appeared to have no effect on them whatsoever.

A long, pink tongue poked out of the thing's mouth and licked her lips, attempting to taste them. Wouldn't that be fabulous if she barfed all over both of them?

Resigned to the fact she couldn't get away with it standing over her, she collapsed onto her back and silently begged her stomach to settle. She wished if it was going to eat her, it would just do it and get it over with.

Caelan...no, *it, it* sat on its haunches. With a doggy whine, he licked her cheek. She should be screaming her head off, not feeling the sudden sense of calm wrapping around her. Caelan made her feel the same way. Like he could protect her from anything.

What was she thinking? It was not possible for a man to become a wolf.

That went over well. At least she wasn't screaming anymore. He leaned in to lick her cheek again and ended up sticking his long wolf's tongue in her ear when she turned her head. He let out a low whine.

"Gross." Her hand came up and wiped at her ear, then pushed hesitantly at his muzzle. "Get off me."

Caelan consented, giving her the space she seemed to need. He padded to the bathroom since she probably wouldn't be receptive to what he really wanted to do—shift into a human and sink his cock into her tight pussy again. While in his wolf form, her scent was even more enticing.

Caelan shook himself like a wet dog, his jowls flapping. He loved doing that.

The tile on the bathroom floor was icy beneath the thick pads of his paws. When he turned, Tieran was still lying on the floor, sprawled in the tangled mass of her blanket, staring at the ceiling. If the rise and fall of her chest was any indication, her breathing was becoming more regular.

He expected nothing less than the reaction she'd given him. There wasn't another human woman alive who wouldn't be running for their safety right now. Of course, she was probably more receptive to his differences because of her own.

He nosed the door partway closed and concentrated on shifting. His fur shrank and disappeared, tickling him as it did so. Joints and bones popped painlessly and with practiced ease as they returned to their human positions. She didn't need to watch the actual shift just yet, there'd be plenty of time later.

Caelan rotated his head, working out the last few kinks, and walked, naked, back to her. She still hadn't moved, except to close her eyelids, and for that small show of trust, he'd be grateful. Not that she'd have had time to get away in the few seconds it took him to shift, but she could have tried.

Her brownish-pink nipples were beaded tight and he longed to take one in his mouth and suck it.

His shaft grew, the purpled head bobbing against his abdomen when he reached down and stroked it.

"Do not even think about touching me with that thing again."

He laughed and met her gaze. Her features were filled with a mixture of anger, fear and lust. The lust was apparently winning because the spicy scent of her arousal bombarded his nose, filling his senses with her essence.

"I think you'll be begging for it in a few minutes. Your pussy is already creaming for me."

He bent down and scooped her up off the floor, ignoring her startled squeal, leaving the blanket behind. Her skin was warm, soft and way too tempting against his. Tieran sighed, as if accepting the impossible, and snuggled into him. She traced a fingertip around his puckered nipple.

Caelan growled deep in his throat. "I wouldn't do that, my own." He laid her on the bed and loomed over her, silently begging her with a look not to be scared.

He didn't need to beg. Her big eyes met his with no trace of the fright she'd gone through just minutes ago. He snorted softly. She really needed to lose the contact because it wasn't hiding the different hue of her eyes. Not up this close anyway, and certainly not from him. She could have red eyes and he wouldn't care.

"I know I saw two of you last night at the bar."

"You did." He took one of her nipples into his mouth and sucked hard, drawing the bead along his tongue, and heard her breath catch. "Eli and I are twins." He switched to the other breast, laving that nipple with the same attention.

"Is he a... Oh, God."

With two fingers, he penetrated her slick channel. Her body bowed off the bed. Caelan knew exactly what she wanted to ask. He could have saved her the trouble, but he wanted to hear her say the words. He scissored his fingers, caressing the delicate inner walls of her pussy, reaching for her G-spot.

"Is he a what?" He added the featherlight pressure of his thumb to her swollen clit and circled the swollen bundle of nerves.

"Don't stop, don't stop!" Her head tossed from side to side on her pillow.

He chuckled. "I told you you'd beg."

"Don't be an ass," she hissed, grinding her teeth and trying to move against his hand.

He threw his other arm over her belly to keep her still.

She whimpered and blew unsuccessfully at the sweaty bangs plastered to her forehead.

"Is he a what?" he prodded.

"You're torturing me."

Caelan flicked lightly on the nubbin. "And I love the sweet pout on your lips. While that might get you what you want from me most of the time, it won't work right now. Is. He. A. What?"

"A werewolf!" she yelled, her eyes shooting flaming daggers at him. "I swear to God, if you don't let me come..."

"I prefer to think of us as shape-shifters," he answered calmly, ignoring her sworn retribution.

Her eyes widened with incredulity. "Did you, or did you not, just turn into a wolf? Which I might add," she paused and stroked herself on his fingers until she nearly purred, "is very freakish, and I'm not sure why I'm still lying here."

He nodded. "Yes, I just turned into a wolf," he parroted and kissed her pouting lips.

"Then that makes you a *werewolf*."

He nibbled around her chin. "Werewolf has such a negative connotation, don't you think? It makes me think of a seven-foot-tall, hairy man with sharp teeth and a snout. *I* was clearly a wolf."

She shuddered beneath him and he wondered what she was thinking.

"Oh, my God." She squirmed on his impaled fingers, looking for relief he wasn't ready to give. "What does it matter what you're called? You turned into an animal!"

66

He shrugged. "We all have our little quirks." He circled her clit again and grinned when she moaned and bit her lip. "Besides, while you were knocked out, I learned that you have your own secrets."

Caelan looked Tieran in the eyes as he slowly slid his fingers in and out of her cream-coated passage, drawing out the tension. Her vaginal walls gripped him in a matching rhythm.

She swallowed, giving herself away. She turned her head, but not before he saw a tear slip out of the corner of her eye. She was trying to pull back from him, to shut him out both physically and mentally, but her body wouldn't let her. He wasn't going to give her an inch. They would hash all this out right now and get it into the open. No secrets.

"You have some *freakish* ESPN ability?" he mocked, turning her own word back on her.

Tieran's sudden burst of laughter at his deliberate misnomer quickly became a moaning pant as he continued to piston his hand between her legs, increasing the pace.

"Mind telling me what happened right before you passed out?"

She jerked her head, squeezing her eyes shut. "No. God, just give me this one day."

That sounded ominous. What the hell did she mean, this one day? He intended to give her the rest of his life, even if she didn't know it yet. Caelan bent over and pressed his mouth to her clit. He'd set her straight later.

"Oh, shit." Her hands tangled in his hair.

He lapped at her creamy center, swirling his tongue everywhere his fingers weren't.

"I can continue this torture all afternoon," he taunted, making sure his lips tickled her sweet clit. "Or you can tell me what happened and I can make you explode."

"Jesus," she panted, trying to get closer. "I had a goddamn vision, all right? Please, please let me come," she screeched.

"What about, sweetheart?"

"Do you think we could...have this conversation...another time?" How could he do this to her? Tieran pressed her heels into the mattress trying to gain some sort of purchase between the arm holding her down and the fingers burrowing with delicious abandon inside her, but not deep enough. Where did this sudden, uncontrollable, wanton need for him come from?

"As long as you don't try getting out of it later, my own."

"Whatever. Just please, I need your cock inside me. Now!" She tore at his shoulder with her fingernails, scratching at his slick skin, urging him to roll onto her and slide inside her. Instead he retracted his fingers from her drenched pussy and flipped their bodies. She found herself suddenly straddling his hips and her head spun dizzily. His engorged cock stood proud mere inches from her sheath.

"Take it, baby." He cupped both her breasts, his thumbs and forefingers tugged and pulled at their stiffened peaks.

Tieran dropped her chin to her chest. She was about to fuck a werewolf. Again. She was insane. With want and need, and goddamn if she didn't fuck him now, she was going to die. She lifted herself and hovered just over the head of his penis.

She glanced down at his cock between her legs and suddenly wanted to taste him, to slide her tongue up the thick vein running along the underside of it. Insane, she thought again. She had never given Peter head, had never once been tempted to, but with Caelan she wanted it all.

She grasped his length. Her fingertips didn't even touch around the circumference. How had she even been able to take him?

"It fits, my own, you know it does," he whispered, reading her mind.

She ignored his strange endearment for like the tenth time and returned her gaze to his face. Did he have the same ability as her? Could he hear her thoughts? The questions must have shown in her eyes because he answered her.

"No, I can't read your mind. Take me. Ride my cock."

"Uh-uh," she said and surprised him by leaning over and capturing his length between her lips.

Caelan's thigh muscles clenched rock hard. "Jesus Christ. Warn a guy before you do that, will ya?"

Tieran nodded, which only forced his penis farther into her mouth. His hands fisted in her hair, tugging her forward and gagging her the closer he got to touching her throat. Backing off, she dragged her tongue up the velvet soft underside, along the thick vein, all the way to the top.

His hands tightened in her hair, urging her back down but she stayed where she was. She lapped at the head, licking the salty pre-come from the slit. He hissed. When she looked up the length of his torso, his head was thrown back.

Good, she thought. Payback for his teasing her earlier. With one last lingering suck, she sat up, grinning at the pained look on his face. His chest heaved like he'd run a marathon. She'd definitely remember this as a way of bringing him to his knees.

He swallowed, his body relaxing minutely as she guided the thick mushroom-shaped head to her entrance and lodged it just inside. Lowering herself partway, she sighed in relief as he filled her. He wasn't the only one affected here.

69

It was like coming home. They were perfect together. He would ruin her forever for other lovers. There'd never be another.

Tieran set off on a slow and sensual rhythm of sinking and rising.

"More," he grunted and grabbed her hips in a tight hold, forcing her further down on his cock, stretching her tender vaginal muscles. "Take all of me."

She impaled herself on him, sitting all the way down until their pelvises touched. She ground her clit on the base of his penis and saw stars.

"Oh, Lord. Mmm." Tieran tried to form a coherent thought but came up short. He lifted her until he was almost entirely out, then slammed her back down again. Apparently he wasn't satisfied with the way she was moving. "Yesss," she hissed, not caring as long as he did it again.

In another dizzying tumble he had them reversed.

"Fuck it, I can't take slow and easy right now." He thrust into her, pushing her knees as wide as they could go.

It was sweet, sweet torture. She felt his hand between them and cried out when he uncovered her clit so his pelvis would rub against the bud with each thrust.

A climax ripped through her body. She writhed beneath his punishing assault, which didn't end with her orgasm. He pushed through it, scraping raw nerve endings.

"Stop, stop. I can't take another one." Her head thrashed back and forth as he pressed the tip of his cock against her supersensitized G-spot.

"You can."

"No," she cried, her face wet with tears.

"Yes." Caelan was relentless in his pursuit.

The headboard banged against the wall. She fisted the sheet in her hands and tried to hang on as the sensations built again.

"One more for me, my own." He thrust into her to the hilt one last time, his body rigid, his jaw ticking as he ground his teeth together.

The spurt of his come on her womb triggered a second orgasm. Too much. It would kill her. She fought him as he released his load deep inside her. Her inner tissues tightened around his cock, milking him, taking all he could give. There was nothing left to do but ride the wave firing through her clit and taking her breath away.

He collapsed onto her, breathing hard and dripping sweat. Tieran took his weight, enfolding him in her arms. She kissed the column of his neck, her pussy still throbbing around his length.

At least she hadn't had another vision. After that first time, she'd been scared to death it might happen every time he came inside her.

Bad. That would be so bad, because he was so good. Maybe good enough to suffer through a vision as often as they fucked, because she imagined this was only the tip of the iceberg for them.

Chapter Four

The sun was just beginning to set by the time they made it out of the bedroom. Caelan eyeballed the meager contents of Tieran's refrigerator looking for anything that would knock out some of his hunger. For food anyway. Besides the literal mountain of Mountain Dew, one of which she was chugging like water at the table behind him, and a few condiments, there wasn't much.

"So what happens now?" she asked.

Screw it. He'd order a pizza. Or three. If tonight went anything like this afternoon, he'd need nourishment in the morning too. He closed the refrigerator door with a thump and faced his mate.

"Now we talk about your ability. And we stay away from each other, because if I touch you, I'm going to fuck you."

Crossing her legs, she groaned and threw her already empty green can toward the trash. In that direction, at least. It bounced off the wall about two feet away and clanked to the floor.

He quirked an eyebrow at her. His feisty mate was prone to clumsiness. The corners of his lips twitched. It would be his pleasure to follow in her footsteps, protecting her from life's little accidents.

She shrugged as if to say it was a normal occurrence for her and she didn't care.

"Talk." He made his prompt a command by stabbing a finger in her direction.

"Anybody ever tell you you're like a dog with a bone?"

He snorted. "A wolf, my own, much better than a dog."

"Whatever. Did you know that shape-shifting is a category of psychic ability?"

"No shit? Then why did you have such a hard time believing me?"

"Because it's just really weird, and actually, I've never heard of anyone doing it for real."

"Hmm," he acknowledged. "I happen to think what you do is really weird too, so I guess we're even."

"I'm not weird," she muttered.

"Quit diverting the subject and talk." He picked up the phone book and searched the pizza listings for something in the area. "But first, I'm ordering a pizza. What kind of toppings do you like?"

"Are you implying I have nothing in the house to eat?"

"That's exactly what I'm saying." He grinned. "You have crusty, old mustard and something that may have been considered Chinese at one time. Uh-uh. Won't cut it for me, baby."

She sniffed. "There would have been more, but I believe it's still scattered around my foyer." She stood, displaying those incredibly sexy legs beneath his T-shirt she was wearing, and Caelan's dick stirred. "Pepperoni."

He cleared his throat and turned away from the sight of her. "That's it?" Damn it. Nothing like a cracking voice to give yourself away.

"What else is there?" she asked, as if pepperoni was the only logical pizza topping.

"Oh, I don't know, hamburger, green peppers, sausage, onions..."

"Did you want me to kiss you later?"

"Abso-fucking-lutely." Dropping the phone book to the counter, he grabbed her shoulders and tugged her close. "You'll kiss me now." Her lips were cool beneath his and tasted of the soda she'd just downed.

She ground her mouth on his, darting her tongue in and out before pulling away breathlessly. "You said no touching."

"Then don't tempt me, my own."

"All right, damn it. You've been calling me that all day. Where the hell does it come from?" She had her head tilted and was looking at him like he'd grown horns.

He hadn't meant to let the endearment slip out the first time, but it had and now he couldn't stop saying it. She was his.

"What?" Maybe if he played stupid he'd get out of having to tell her what she was to him.

Her lip curled. "You know what I'm talking about, my own." She reopened the fridge and popped the top of another can of high-octane sugar. Caelan imagined the one-celled embryo in her womb shriveling up, and winced. "What's wrong?"

Caffeine probably isn't good for our baby.

"Nothing." He picked up the cordless phone and nearly dropped it. It felt like a block of ice in his hand. Ignoring the strange phenomenon, he dialed the phone number for the pizza place with the biggest ad and placed an order.

"Are you going to answer me?" Tieran asked when he'd hung up. She slid the can of soda onto the table, so close to the edge he reached over and pushed it back before it took a nosedive.

"Now who's the dog?" He had to stall her, to lead her in another direction. He wasn't prepared to tell her all the ramifications of being his mate.

"I thought you said a dog was beneath you." Tieran crossed her arms in front of her, plumping up her breasts.

He salivated. Like a dog. A wolf, like a wolf, damn it. "What were we talking about?"

She dropped her hands to her sides with a slap. "Quit staring at my breasts and you might remember." Her voice grew as sickly sweet as the smile on her face. "My own."

He cleared his throat. "It's just a wolf thing," he fudged.

"What kind of wolf thing?"

Goddamn, but the woman was tenacious. And he loved her. He'd never believed the elders when they'd told him that finding your mate meant instant true love. At least on his part. Humans, of course, had a bit harder time of it.

"It's what we call our mates," he muttered.

"What?"

"Our mates. It's what we call our mates." Caelan ground his teeth together. It was coming, he could feel it. First she'd laugh, then explode, then try to throw him out the door. Key word here—try. She could try to throw him out, but wouldn't succeed. Not with the Mate Killer, her psychic abilities and their baby growing in her belly.

"That sounds so...permanent."

"It is," he granted.

She dropped her head back and he swore he saw her mouth form the words, "why me". Then her head cocked to the side and damned if she didn't look like she was listening to something nobody heard but her. She sighed and tucked her chin to her chest, looking resigned, to say the least.

"Something tells me you're not going to go away. Why don't you tell me about this whole mate thing?"

Caelan paused for a moment. He wanted to kiss her. No laughing, no gawking, no, "Are you fucking crazy?" remarks, just pure help-me-out-here, and make-me-understand. He cleared his throat.

"No, I'm not going anywhere. Especially not now." He stepped closer, turned her around so her back was to his front, and covered her belly with his hands.

"Why not now, Caelan? What's happening?"

He blew out a breath, vibrating his lips against the side of her neck.

Tieran pulled out of his grasp and moved around him. She kept her wary gaze on his face as she dropped into a chair. Her elbow knocked into the soda can, nearly tipping it over.

"I am a shape-shifter. One of many," he said when she quirked an eyebrow and looked at him like she wanted to say, "duh". "There are communities of us all around you. We live and work and play amongst humans who are none the wiser."

"How is this possible, Caelan? You're talking about an entire race of peop—what are you again?"

"Shape-shifters."

"Shape-shifters. How is it that no one knows about you? Scientists would have a field day."

Caelan winced. She was absolutely right. "We've kept our anonymity for centuries by simply hiding in plain sight. We hold the same jobs and positions as humans, eat the same food, pay the same taxes. The only difference—"

Tieran snorted.

"Okay, so it's a huge difference. On a full moon, many of my kind shift into wolf form."

"Many of you? You don't all do that?"

"Yes," he said, pulling out a chair next to her and sitting so he faced her. "But here's where humans come into play. Generations ago, it was discovered that if a shifter mated with a human woman, their child had the ability to control the shift. Half-bloods can change forms whenever they want, like me. Full-bloods cannot. It's once a month for them, no matter what."

He watched her swallow and let the information sink in. When she lifted her gaze, it was full of questions.

"So by mating you mean..."

"I mean finding the one woman in the world who is your other half and claiming her."

Tieran's hand flew to the spot on her neck where he'd bitten her. Her eyes were wide, shocked.

"Yes, I claimed you. And I'm not sorry, and I can't take it back."

Her breath hissed out. "That's what my grandmother meant."

"Your grandmother? I don't know your grandmother."

"No, but she knows you," she muttered.

"Oh stop, you're making me blush, Tullabelle."

Tieran snorted. *"As if that's possible."*

"Explain," Caelan barked.

Tieran jumped in her seat. At least now he was the one confused for a change. The skin on her neck pulsed where he'd bitten her. How do you explain something that can't be explained?

"I think he explained his side rather well, wouldn't you say so?"

"Well, what the hell am I supposed to say? Caelan, it's like this. I talk to my grandmother. Oh, and by the way, she's been dead ten years. That ought to go over really well."

"Again, Tulla, the man just told you he is from another race of people. You don't seem to be having too hard a time believing him."

Yes, but apparently the public didn't know about his abilities. The few times she'd told others about hers, things had ended very badly. She was still uncomfortable sharing that part of her life. To make matters worse, Peter knew about her visions, but she'd never told him about being a medium with her gramama. The visions were more than enough to make him run.

Except Caelan didn't seem to care that she could see things.

"In case you hadn't noticed, Caelan is still here. The man can handle anything you dish out. Trust me."

"Hello? Did you go away?"

"No, I..." The doorbell intruded. "I better get that." She let out a breath with an audible whoosh and all but launched herself from the chair. She darted toward the front door, and heard him bounding after her.

"Tieran, wait." His foot came down on a box of food still in the middle of the foyer.

Out of the corner of her eye, she saw Caelan stumble. His arms windmilled as he tried to catch his balance. She started to take a step back toward him when the doorbell pealed again.

"Hold on, would you?" she muttered. "Why is everybody always in a hurry?" She braced her feet shoulder width apart and grabbed the doorknob with both hands but paused for a split second to look back.

Caelan finally caught himself with a hand on the desk. "Don't open the..."

Tieran yanked the protesting door open.

"...door," he finished with a curse she chose to ignore.

"Oh look, it's the clone." Her voice sounded dry as dust even to her own ears. And why shouldn't it? She was faced with two shape-shifting werewolf...beings, one of which had claimed her without her consent. She would not think about how earth-shattering the idea of him claiming her was.

"No need to be snotty, Tulla."

"Goddamn it, Tieran. Don't you ever fucking open this door again unless you ask who it is first." Caelan grabbed her by her shoulders and swung her around. He shook her as if scolding a child for not looking before crossing the street. Her teeth clanked together as her jaw snapped shut.

"Just who in the hell do you think you are?"

"Your mate." His roar made Tieran flinch beneath his hands.

"Well, I didn't ask to *be* your mate, you big oaf," she shouted back.

Their noses touched, their breathing turned heavy, their eyes dilated.

He kissed her hard, relinquishing his bruising hold on her upper arms and hugging her closer to him. Her tongue tangled with his, exploring his mouth in a parry and retreat dance. Their lips melded, sealing in the moans coming from both of them.

"Break it up, you two."

Caelan pulled his mouth off Tieran's and steadied her before turning to his brother, leaving her wondering what had just happened.

"Eli."

Eli grunted. "Who else did you think it would be?"

Tieran stuck her head around Caelan's arm and answered for him. "The pizza man."

Eli's gaze roamed over her face then took in her bare legs beneath Caelan's T-shirt as she stepped out from behind his overprotective twin. He poked his nose up in the air as if he smelled something and grinned a huge wolfish grin.

No, not wolfish, stop thinking about wolves!

"They aren't going to go away, Tulla."

Eli slapped Caelan on the shoulder. "Congratulations, Bro."

"For what?" Tieran swept her gaze between the twins. Eli's eyes twinkled with pure delight, Caelan's were narrowed and dangerous. She'd have missed the tiny shake of Caelan's head had she glanced away one second earlier. Eli's smile faltered and he dropped his hand.

Eli cleared his throat and tried to be surreptitious in looking around the room. "What happened here?"

Damn, she really needed to get this place cleaned up so she could get on with her life without rehashing this particular story again. "I was attacked by..."

"He's already fucking found her?" Eli's explosion drowned out the rest of her sentence. He grabbed the door and slammed it shut, only to have it bounce back and smack him in the ass. Tieran jumped back and out of reach of the suddenly angry man who'd just entered her home. She couldn't stop the laugh that bubbled up. It was too funny to watch a grown man struggle with the complexities of a piece of wood.

"...the door."

"By the door."

Caelan and Tieran spoke at the same time. She covered her mouth with her hand, deciding it was better not to let the man think she was laughing at him. He appeared ready to spit nails.

Then it dawned on her. What did Eli mean by...? "Who is 'he', and why is he looking for me?" Tieran tried to walk between the brothers. There had been enough space for her to fit without her accidentally touching Eli, except he took a step at the same time. She dodged him by practically tripping over herself and backing up to the door. Eli reached out, a surprised look on his face, and grabbed hold of her arm to steady her.

A streak of pain shot through her temples. She hissed and fought the instinctive need to grind her palms into the throbbing veins at the sides of her head.

Pictures flashed in her mind like a warped movie. An old warehouse, a cracked, overgrown, weed-filled concrete lot, a sign, half-hanging from its post, the letters faded beyond recognition, and woods. A man got out of a pitch-black sports car and walked toward the building. His gait was purposeful, but his eyes were wary. He jerked his gaze over his shoulder at the rumble of another engine and turned around just before he got to the rusty-hinged set of double doors adorned with a brand-spanking-new, shiny padlock. "Dane Christian?" There was a flash of metal through the air and darkness.

"Hello? Jesus, where the fuck did you just go?" Eli asked.

The pain subsided as quickly as it had attacked. Tieran sucked in a breath and tried to focus. She sagged against the door and braced her hands on it, scratching at the wood with her fingernails. She prayed for mercy and waited for the churning of her belly to diminish. Only then did she attempt to put all of her weight on wobbly knees.

"Nowhere. Nothing's wrong," she lied as calmly as possible, fumbling for the knob and slamming the door shut with the aid of her butt. A fine sheen of sweat had broken out on her upper lip. "Twist the knob to close the door." She leaned against it, wrinkled her nose at them and crossed her arms over her chest like nothing strange had happened. The vision had lasted scant seconds. She could easily downplay what they'd seen without giving herself away. Later she'd worry about whether she needed to assimilate what she'd seen, which wasn't much.

"Bullshit, nothing, Tieran," Caelan barked. She startled, dropping her hands to her side. "One minute you're fine, the next you look like someone rammed a spike through your heart."

Eli glared at her. Clearly he held the same opinion.

"You had a vision, didn't you? Just now, when Eli touched you. He triggered something, didn't he?" Caelan demanded.

Arrogant...

"No, I did not," she answered succinctly. "I...stubbed my toe is all. When I tripped going past him. Hurt like a sonofabitch."

Both men stared at her like she'd grown devil's horns. As if on cue they focused on her feet. No redness, no bouncing on one foot. They didn't believe her toe-stubbing story any more than she would.

A look passed between them. One of those, "she's deranged" looks. See? That's why she never told anybody. They always ended up seeing her in the same way. A wacko who needed a padded cell. She'd thought Caelan might be different, especially because of what he could do.

The door shook with a pounding from the other side, vibrating the length of her spine.

"Shit!" Tieran jumped forward and threw her arms around Caelan's waist, vision forgotten. His arm whipped behind his back and when he brought it forward, there was a gun cradled in his palm. How had she not noticed he was carrying a weapon?

"Because you were too enamored to notice, Tulla."

"Who is it?" Eli's voice was loud and commanding.

"Pizza."

Tieran groaned into Caelan's chest. She'd gotten so distracted by the door mishap, Eli's mysterious words, the vision, and now to top it all off, she'd forgotten all about their dinner.

"Ooh, good, I'm hungry." Eli rubbed his hands together and Tieran's head swam at the abrupt change of his mood.

🐾 🐾 🐾

Caelan stared at her mouth with such intensity he was giving her a complex. Tieran licked her lips and found the object of his scrutiny. The spicy tang of tomato sauce bombarded her tongue. She wiped at her mouth with the back of her hand, making sure she got it all.

"So, you do that freaky werewolf thing too?" she asked Eli.

Caelan groaned and dropped his head onto the back of the couch in the living room where they'd gone after devouring the pizzas. She gave him a snide look. He should have known she wouldn't let this subject go for very long. Caelan took a long drag off the beer Eli had brought in. Thank God the man had stopped at the grocery store for a few of his "essentials" before coming here. There still was no food in her house. Whatever gifts she had, teleporting objects wasn't one of them. If she wanted to eat tomorrow, it was either go to the store later tonight or go out to eat in the morning.

With a grimace and a shudder, Eli glanced away from the pictures he was studying on the wall. "I prefer to think of us as shape-shifters."

"That's what I said." Caelan sat up and leaned forward, resting his elbows on his knees.

"Do you, or do you not, turn into a wolf?" she demanded.

Caelan smiled. The smug bastard.

"Yes." Eli lowered himself onto the loveseat across from Tieran.

Ugh. That's the same answer Caelan had given her. "Then you're a werewolf."

She watched Caelan mouth the words with her and nearly gave in to the temptation of kicking him in the shin.

"Werewolf has such a negative connotation." Eli's voice was whiny and slightly offended.

"Oh, for God's sake." Tieran slapped her jeans-clad thighs and stood. She put her hands on her hips and glared at both of them. "I am in a serious déjà vu."

"What'd I say?" Eli blinked in innocence.

"The same exact thing your brother did. You guys turn into wolves, you're werewolves. End of discussion. Now tell me what you were talking about at the front door. Something about somebody finding me already?"

Caelan sighed, the sound adding to her irritation for some reason. She wasn't the one who'd brought it up, they had. The least they could do was fill her in. Especially with Eli's earlier angry reaction at the door.

"A couple of mates from local packs have...died in recent weeks," Caelan answered, albeit reluctantly. She couldn't blame him, not really, especially when she couldn't bring herself to come right out and say what she'd seen in her vision.

"Died how? Car accidents, disease?"

Eli cleared his throat. "No. They were murdered."

Tieran sucked in a breath. Knowing now what she did about Caelan's abilities, she had a very bad feeling that the wolf she'd seen killing that woman wasn't a wolf at all. Her face blanched.

"By who?" she whispered, unable to conceive either of these two men as a cold-blooded killer. But oh God, the one in her vision had looked so much like Caelan had on her bed. Since Eli was identical to his twin in human form, was he also in wolf form? Did the whole group of them look the same? Her heart thumped wildly with the implication.

"We don't know, my own. We're pretty sure he's a shifter like one of us though. No, we're positive."

Tieran's knees buckled and she found herself sitting on the couch. She *had* witnessed the killer. The last time she'd had a vision this momentous had been down in Florida. She could not go through something like that again.

"You won't have to, Tullabelle. They will understand."

"That's what momma said about the police."

"Oh, honey, Caelan's not like them."

"But what if he is? You weren't there, Gramama. You can't know how they made me feel." She swallowed. Jesus. Somehow, she'd already fallen for Caelan. It would rip her heart to shreds if he rejected her. *"Why is this happening to me?"*

"Because you're his mate, Tulla."

"You okay, Tieran? You look like you've seen a ghost." Caelan took hold of her hands. She wanted to laugh hysterically. No, she hadn't seen a ghost, just spoken to one.

The physical connection of his thumbs rubbing her knuckles brought her fully back into reality. She blinked when Eli suddenly spun around, his gaze jerking from one corner of the room to the next. What the heck was he looking for?

"Where the hell did that come from?" Eli demanded.

Caelan snorted and rose to stand next to his brother. "I was beginning to think it was just me."

"What are you guys talking about?" Totally bewildered by their actions, she switched her gaze back and forth between them for some clue.

"Don't tell me you didn't just feel that cold air." Eli pointed an accusing finger at her.

She sucked in a breath. As if she'd been the one to bring forth whatever delusional wind...

She groaned and turned her face toward the ceiling. Damn the woman for meddling.

"Gramama!"

"What?" her grandmother answered.

"Don't pull that innocent crap on me."

"What the hell is going on, my own?" Caelan took a step forward.

"Why? Why are you talking to them, Gramama?"

Tieran waited for a response. *"Hello? What, now you leave?"*

"Tieran," Caelan growled.

"What?" she snarled. Sighing, she collapsed back into the soft, worn fabric of the sofa she'd spent many a night on as a child. "It's my gramama."

"Your grandmother is here?" Eli sat, looking ridiculously large and out of place on the floral print love seat. He also looked thoroughly confused. Caelan stayed standing, his arms across his chest, emphasizing the hard muscles of his pecs.

Oh, don't do that. Her mouth watered and her pussy clenched.

How could she possibly want him again?

"No," she said carefully.

"Then she has a particularly drafty old house? It's seventy degrees outside, and not the least bit windy." Eli's right eyebrow hitched upward. He didn't believe her.

Damn. She really thought she'd gotten out of having this conversation. Having it with a lover who didn't seem too upset about the fact she'd wigged out on him earlier was one thing. Talking about it in front of a stranger was another. Didn't matter that the stranger was identical to the lover.

"Anyone ever tell you you're stubborn?" Caelan asked.

She bit her lip and waved him off. "All the time." Nearly every time she mentally communicated to the meddling woman who, right now, seemed to have something up her sleeve.

"Oh fine. I'm a medium. With my gramama anyway, not everybody, and I'm glad because that would be just way too weird. I mean, can you imagine having a bunch of dead people talking to you all the time, asking you for things, telling you what they wanted you to do, who to talk to, explain to their loved ones why they're gone, all the while hounding you wherever you go because you can't go anywhere without having a dead person hanging over your shoulder. They know who you are and what you do and it's..."

"Take a breath," Caelan shouted. "God damn. Ask one little question." He sat on the coffee table in front of her and took hold of her hands. "Just tell us about the cold air."

87

"Oh, that."

"Yeah, that." Eli grabbed his beer off the table and settled back in his seat, flipping his feet up on the coffee table. He appeared ready to stay all night if he had to.

"It's my gramama's way of talking to you. You can't hear her but the air gets cold." She pulled her hands free and twisted one in the air. "Or sometimes objects do."

"Explains why the telephone felt like an ice cube," Caelan prodded.

She nodded. "Yep." Pacing to the window gave her something to do, so she peeled back the curtains and peered out toward the street. Two dogs were sitting in the darkness, lit by the glow of the street lamp, tails wagging, tongues hanging out. One cocked his head and she got the strangest feeling he was studying her.

"Get away from the window, my mate."

"You know, we really need to talk about that," she muttered, ignoring his softly issued command. "This is the weirdest thing. There are these two dogs—"

Her feet flew out from under her, making her tummy flip as she went down beneath Caelan's crushing weight. Thank God he had the sense to wrap his arms around her, protecting her from what would have been a rough landing. She fought to catch her breath through her squished lungs.

"They're just dogs, Cael, it's fine," Eli announced.

She'd already told him they were dogs, she thought crazily. Tieran blinked slowly, trying to refocus on her upside-down world. Eli was staring out the window. Caelan's chest vibrated along her arm with his fierce growling. He nuzzled her throat to a more open position and his sharp teeth rasped her neck.

She jerked her head away, suddenly very aware of her surroundings. Who wouldn't be when their lover was planting more than a love bite at a very vulnerable spot?

"Ouch, get off me." She squirmed and tried to dislodge him, but instead the action caused him to bite down harder. When she stilled, his jaws loosened. Her pulse beat a wild tattoo just below where his tongue lapped at her neck.

"Caelan!" When Tieran wiggled again, he bit her again. Any harder and he'd puncture her jugular. She submitted, giving him what he obviously wanted.

Submission? Bullshit. She'd turn into the tooth fairy before she submitted to him.

"Yet there you are, lying so still beneath your wolf-man, Tulla."

Ah hell. Her gramama was right.

Her lungs deflated on a huge sigh. Above them, Eli chuckled. Finally the razor-sharp teeth were removed from her skin.

"The next time I tell you to fucking do something, by God, you better do it." Caelan's growl was laced with deadly menace, but she detected something else too. Nervousness? Anxiousness?

His tongue flicked out, lapping at the wound he'd inflicted, making her forget everything. He smelled so good. Like sweat and man and sex from their earlier romp. She looped an ankle around his calf and pulled his leg between hers, fitting his thigh snugly against her pussy. Finally! Maybe she could relieve some of the tension throbbing at her clit.

"Mmm." She wrapped her free hand in the soft locks of his hair and angled her head to give him better access. Not that he needed it. He was doing just fine on his own.

His mouth moved to her earlobe and sucked it. She imagined it was her nipple he had embedded in that wet heat. She wanted his hands on her. Wanted to feel him tugging and pinching the sensitive beads. She lifted her hips and rubbed herself on his thigh. It wasn't enough! There were too many clothes in the way. She needed his fingers, his tongue, or better yet his cock, inside her, filling her. Not where it was, poking into her side.

"Man, you guys are hot."

"Oh shit." Tieran yanked herself free from Caelan and raised up on her elbows, her chest heaving with each breath. What in the hell was happening to her? She'd certainly liked having sex before, but until now, having it wasn't a requirement. Not a need that festered like an infected wound. She'd never craved it like she did with Caelan. And she'd never lost control in a way that everything around her disappeared.

Her cheeks flamed. Eli stood above them, watching as she and his brother went at it on her living-room floor like two randy teenagers.

Caelan couldn't resist smiling as he rolled more firmly on his side and propped his head on his hand. He palmed the small, cotton-covered breast furthest away from him, flicking at the nipple. If Eli hadn't interrupted—for Tieran's sake, 'cause it damn well wasn't for his—Caelan would have fucked her right here on the hardwood floor.

"Stop it." Tieran slapped at his hand. "Your brother is watching."

He shrugged. "So?"

Her eyes widened, her face drained of color and she gulped. "Please don't tell me you guys do that...that...sharing stuff," she hissed.

Caelan snarled; Eli burst out laughing.

"Nobody but me will ever touch you," Caelan growled.

"Sweetheart, I'm not ready to die." Eli reached a hand down and pulled Caelan to his feet.

"What does that mean?"

"Wolves mate for life." Caelan winced at his gruff attitude, but goddamn, share her? Never. He helped her off the floor and guided her to the sofa. He needed to sit and have a drink after nearly having his heart ripped out. When she'd said dogs, he'd immediately assumed she wasn't looking at dogs, but wolves. Rogue wolves on the prowl and looking for another kill.

Eli scratched his head and sat across from them. "What it really means is that as a Prime's mate, you are the alpha bitch. The only way I'll *ever* get to touch you is for me to fight Caelan to the death and take over the pack. I'm really not all that intrigued by the prospect."

Tieran turned away from Eli. "Did he just call me a bitch? 'Cause I really don't think he's known me long enough to make that kind of presumption."

Caelan choked on his mouthful of beer, spitting it across the room. "Only you," he said when he could breathe again, "could make that kind of statement and totally ignore the part about him killing me." He threaded his fingers through hers and gathered her closer until she was tucked under his arm.

Her scent was driving him crazy. If he didn't get inside her soon...

"Don't you have a meeting with Mr. Christian, E?" Caelan shifted on the sofa, pulling away from temptation for the few seconds it would take to throw his brother out the door. He stood to do just that.

He had some business of his own to take care of. The sexual variety, but there would be no negotiating involved.

Eli looked up and grinned. "Here's your hat, what's your hurry?" He slapped his hands on his thighs and stood also, extending both arms above his head in a long stretch.

"Exactly," Caelan answered with a nod. "Call me later with the details."

"Aye, aye, captain." Eli gave a two-fingered salute, his face glowing with mischief as he turned to look at Tieran who rolled her eyes.

"Are you guys always so rude to each other?"

"Always," they agreed in sync.

Eli turned back to Caelan. "Do I have long enough to use the john before you kick me out the door?" He spun on his heel and left the room without waiting for an answer. His chuckle followed him down the hall.

Caelan barely refrained from growling. Instead, he curled his hands into fists and with supreme effort, sniffed the air without looking like he was sniffing the air. Tieran's essence permeated the room, aroused, musky and ripe for his taking.

She gasped when he fixed his gaze on her tight, beaded nipples beneath his T-shirt. He licked his lips, eager to suck them.

"Do you mind?" She crossed her arms over her chest, covering the delicious peaks from his view, and tapped a slim, bare foot.

The wolf in him howled.

The man in him groaned.

They were caught in a snare where time seemed to stop. In four long strides, Caelan crossed the room to stand in front of her, oblivious to everything around them. He grabbed both her hands and guided her to her feet.

"I need you." His nostrils flared when the tip of her pink tongue poked out along her bottom lip. He wrapped a hand in her hair and pulled her closer until their mouths touched.

She moaned and angled her head for a better fit. Her hands came up, one twisting the fabric of his shirt at his chest, bunching it up and exposing his abs, the other gripping at his shoulder. Tieran pressed her body more firmly against his, straddling his thigh and grinding her pussy on him.

Caelan burrowed his free hand under her shirt. He cupped the precious weight of one breast and rubbed his thumb over her nipple until her body jerked in his arms.

At what sounded like a gunshot, they rocketed apart.

"Holy mother of God!" Eli's muffled yell sounded from behind the hallway bathroom's door.

Tieran stumbled backwards, her eyes wide, her lips red from Caelan's form of punishment. He reached out and caught her before she could fall, then stormed past, his gun already in hand.

"What the hell was that?"

"Stay here," he said pushing her back.

She ignored his command and chased after him down the hall.

"Jesus Christ. A little help here!" Eli yelled.

The intense sound of rushing water reached their ears the closer they got. Caelan shouldered open the door and his feet flew out from under him. He landed on his ass in a growing puddle of water with Eli above him trying unsuccessfully not to laugh, his hands shielding his face from the assault.

Her faucet had become a fountain. Caelan groaned, both his pride and ass bruised. This is what he got for trying to help out his dunderhead brother.

Chapter Five

"Oh, now that's a real shame. Get the men some towels, Tulla."

Tieran cringed at her grandmother's mock-sympathetic tone. *"You did this?"*

Water sprayed out in spectacular geyser fashion where the faucet had once been. Eli did a poor job of covering it with his hands while Caelan disappeared beneath the sink to try and shut it off. By the time the water stopped flowing, both of them were soaking wet and breathing heavily. From her vantage point outside the door, Tieran remained relatively dry.

She pursed her lips in an attempt to keep from laughing at the dripping men filling the small space of her bathroom.

"Don't you dare laugh," Caelan grumbled, a big drop falling from the tip of his nose.

Tieran snorted and covered her mouth with her hand. She cast her gaze to the floor, staring at the black and white tile beneath the water. The shag bathmat was waterlogged, having absorbed a ton already, or they would be standing in a half-inch of water.

"What the hell did you do, E?" Caelan ground out. His face was as red as a beet and Tieran was tempted to lick the trickle that ran down his chin. Her tummy did a little flip-flop just looking at him. His shirt was plastered to his chest and his hair stood on end. In a word, he looked yummy.

"What did *I* do?" Eli demanded. "It's this freaked-out house, I tell you—"

"Hey, I take exception to that fact." Tieran stopped just short of stomping her foot. Eli's slander of her home broke through her thoughts of throwing Caelan down on the floor and having her way with him.

"That's right. Fact," he said, stabbing a finger at her. Caelan growled low in his throat and Eli immediately curled his finger into his fist, dropping it to his side. His cheeks reddened beneath his tanned face. "Sorry."

At least he had the gumption to apologize, even if he wasn't really sorry at all, and his brother had prompted it. Twins, equal, yet there was clearly a division in the hierarchy here. She remembered them talking about Caelan being some kind of Prime.

Tieran cleared her mind and took a deep breath. Who was she kidding? Her house *was* "freaked out". Had been since before her grandmother had moved in forty-five years ago.

"Hey, now I'm taking exception."

"For what? Your house is weird. Always has been, always will be. Get over it."

"Tieran Annabelle Jones, my house is not weird."

"Oh yeah? What about the front door? The space in the closet that doesn't like clothes? Oh, and let's not forget the lamp that turns on and off with no explanation."

"Hmmph. The door is old, for Pete's sake, the rod is crooked, and the lamp has a short in it."

Tieran snorted. *"The only thing with a short in it is you."*

"Tullabelle!"

"Gramama!"

"Hello? Earth to Tieran."

She jerked her head up. Caelan was waving his hand in front of her face and snapping.

"What?" She felt her cheeks flame with embarrassment. They probably thought she was a fruit loop, the way she kept going away. Of course, they did turn into wolves...

"Where'd you go just then?"

"Hmm?" She nibbled on her lip and picked at an imaginary hangnail.

"Tieran."

She jumped, startled by the reprimand in Caelan's voice.

"Do not keep things from me, my own."

"Keep what from you?" Geez, did he think he owned her? Besides, she'd already told him who she talked to when she "went away". Weren't they listening? They had to have been. Part of their makeup was supersonic dog hearing, wasn't it?

She shrugged. "Look, it's no big deal about the faucet. These little 'things' that happen are the story of my life. Forget about it."

Eli cleared his throat. "I would, except it didn't happen to you this time. It happened to me, and things like this," he grumbled and waved his hand at the mess surrounding them, "don't happen to me. Ever. Period, end of story."

"Yes, but you're here, in my house, with me. My...whatever you call it...rubs off on you by association." She propped her hands on her hips, satisfied with her rebuttal. They didn't need to know her gramama had somehow caused the disaster. She'd get to the bottom of that later. There had to be a reason behind her grandmother's intrusion.

Eli ran both hands through his hair, making the ends stick up in wet spikes all around. "I've got a meeting to get to." He pulled at his drenched shirt. "Looks like I'm going to need to borrow some of those clothes I just brought you, Cael."

"Clothes? What clothes? Why did you bring him clothes?" Oh goody, the babbling idiot was back.

"We'll talk about it later. Among other things," Caelan muttered as he easily pushed by her and headed for her bedroom.

Eli dropped two towels from the bar onto the floor to sop up some more of the water. Acting like a human mop, he did a dance on the towels. At the same time he peeled his shirt up. The muscles of his abdomen rippled as he stretched the clinging fabric over his head. Tieran's gaze riveted on him and her jaw fell. They really were identical, perfect pieces of flesh any artist would be thrilled to get their hands on.

She itched to rub her fingers over his belly then shook herself. This was Eli. Not Caelan, Eli. She had no business thinking of him like this. Not twenty minutes ago she'd been grossed out by the thought of them sharing, and now she was lusting after her mate's brother.

Tieran groaned at her use of the word mate. They'd brainwashed her, pure and simple. In less than twenty-four hours, Caelan had somehow convinced her brain she was his mate. His powers of persuasion were incredible.

"Caelan did not brainwash you and you know it. Deep down inside you feel connected to him, Tulla. Be honest with yourself."

"You be honest, Gramama, you aren't standing here lusting after your mate's brother. Geez, there I go again. Do you see what I'm up against?"

"Yes, Tulla, I do. The big picture, not how afraid you are of getting serious with Caelan, but how much your lives are about

to be impacted. Trust. It will all come down to trust. Trust in each other, Tieran. Never forget that."

"Here, put these on." Caelan threw a pair of jeans and a white T-shirt at Eli, who caught them in one hand. Somehow in those few seconds, Caelan had managed to change his own clothes.

"Thanks, Bro." Eli's hands slid the length of his torso before reaching for the zipper on his pants.

"You gonna stand there and watch, my own?" Caelan's chest rumbled against her back when he came to stand behind her. His hands rested on her shoulders, his thumbs rubbing lazy circles on her nape. Then his insanely sharp teeth bit into the crook of her neck making her catch her breath.

Mortified, she turned her cheek into him, dislodging his mouth. "Crap. I'm sorry, it's just...you're both... God, you're exactly the same." She shivered.

Eli spun around, giving them his back while he worked on getting the wet material of his jeans off.

Tieran gasped. A long, thin, pink, puckered scar marked his left shoulder blade. A sense of déjà vu slid over her. Where had she seen something similar? The answer, just on the tip of her tongue, eluded her.

Eli looked over his shoulder, one eyebrow raised either in question or concern. "Something wrong, Tieran?"

"No, I...your shoulder. What happened?"

"A fight." He grinned, reminding her of what he and Caelan were. Wolves. "Don't worry, sis, I won."

"Hey." Caelan lifted her face with a thumb under her chin. "Let's get out of here so E can get changed. We'll clean this up later, okay?"

Tieran nodded, gaze still glued to the scar, but couldn't speak.

"Find your own way out of the house, E."

Caelan's low growl was so palpable she felt it. Eli chuckled behind them, making her stomach churn. She took one last glance at the scar as Caelan led her away. Her eye twitched.

"No, please. Not another one."

"'Fraid so my dear."

Suddenly her body felt heavy and weak. Her legs wobbled and threatened to crumple. A second vision so quickly following the previous one might leave her incapacitated for a lengthy amount of time.

"Whoa, baby, I've got you." He scooped her up, snuggling her against his chest.

"I'm going to have another one," she whispered.

"Another what?" His strides ate up the hallway and before she knew it, he was laying her on the bed and leaning over to place a soft kiss on her temple.

Shit, she hadn't meant to say that out loud. Too late now. He'd needle her all night if she didn't tell him. What she should be doing is getting rid of him. One time was enough for him to see her in action.

Instead, she found herself saying, "A vision."

"Christ. How do you know? What can I do to help?" His fingers brushed the bangs off her forehead, his words agitated.

An unidentifiable emotion clogged her throat. Not since her gramama had been alive had anyone ever been there for her during an episode. The comfort felt good, too good. It overrode the roiling of her stomach and her common sense. She couldn't believe she was about to tell him this. To leave herself vulnerable to the pain and suffering he could so easily bestow upon her.

The front door slammed, echoing through the house, but she barely heard it.

"It killed her," she rasped and her heart felt strangely lighter. Like a weight had been lifted off her.

Caelan's heart skipped a beat. What other "it" could she possibly be talking about? When Eli had first told him about her clairvoyance, naturally it had run through Caelan's mind that she might be able to help uncover the identity of their killer. He didn't know how her ability worked and he didn't care. But he was certain he didn't want her involved. Not now, with her carrying their child.

Tieran's eyes were unfocused, yet she stared straight ahead, seeing something he couldn't, her face a pasty shade of white.

It took everything in him not to shake her and demand she tell him what she was talking about. He sucked in a deep breath, forcing his wolf to back down and let her go at her own pace since she was obviously locked in her own kind of hell.

"It was so big. She never had a chance." Tieran idly scraped her fingernails on the sheet. "She was looking for someone named Micah."

Surprised, Caelan narrowed his eyes and a shiver passed over his spine. The way she talked made it sound like she'd been there when it happened. Her visions were a lot more involved than he thought. Fuck.

The pictures he'd seen of Micah's mate were gruesome enough on paper, he couldn't imagine seeing it in his mind as she apparently had. Damn, he wished he knew a way to shield her somehow.

How did she live with this?

His skin tingled on a cool draft of air. Caelan searched the darkening room for any evidence of a breeze, then remembered what Tieran had said earlier about her grandmother.

Was it her, trying to communicate somehow? Goose bumps crawled up his arms, providing his answer.

"I'll keep her safe," he vowed silently.

"I know you will."

Caelan jerked at the barely audible words he swore he heard. Not possible! He was imagining things he wanted to hear. That was the only plausible explanation.

"It jumped at her from the woods, tearing at her clothes and skin. There was so much blood," Tieran murmured. Her face paled even more. "It had a scar on its shoulder, like Eli." Her voice shook with what sounded like anxious confusion and her brows drew together.

Now they were getting somewhere. At least he could tell everyone they were looking for a shifter with a noticeable scar. "That's good, Tieran. Those kinds of things give us a place to start."

Her gaze sought his for the first time since he'd laid her there.

"You don't understand," she pleaded. "It was on the same shoulder." Her words were hushed, her eyes sad, but clearly she was trying to tell him something.

Her implication set in like a bomb dropping. Caelan lunged to his feet. She thought Eli did this? The idea was inconceivable, ludicrous.

The only thing keeping him from ripping his clothes off, shifting and loping off to have a minute alone to lick his wounded pride was the look on her face. She obviously hadn't been thinking along these lines the whole time. In fact, in retrospect, she hadn't been anything but normal in Eli's presence until he'd taken his shirt off in her bathroom. Now he knew the reason for her sudden intake of breath.

"You can't be suggesting that Eli could do something like this. The scar is a coincidence, Tieran, that's all." If he sounded harsh, he couldn't help it.

A forlorn look crossed her face. Nodding, she turned her head into the pillow. "You're right."

Damn it! She made him feel like he'd kicked her puppy and crushed any confidence she might have been building up to confide in him. Caelan knelt down and tilted her face with a forefinger under her chin.

"You are my mate, and as such I am bound to keep you happy." He tapped her nose when her eyes widened a second before she squeezed them shut and tried to turn away from him again. "Don't close your eyes." Seconds passed and he growled in frustration while she decided whether or not to obey his quiet command.

Finally she did. Her eyes were liquid with unshed tears.

"Okay, that didn't come out right." He laced his fingers with hers and kissed the knuckles along the top ridge. "What I mean is, I will never do anything, on purpose, to hurt you." He moved, trailing his lips up her arm, pausing to swirl his tongue in the crook of her elbow, gripping her hand tighter when she started to pull away.

"You are my heart," he continued, working his way over her shoulder and along her neck. She shivered when he nipped at the delicate skin of her throat. "My soul." He bit gently on her earlobe. Tieran angled her head, giving him better access, and moaned. "My mate."

Caelan caressed his way up her belly with his free hand and palmed one of her perfect breasts. The nipple stabbed into his palm through her T-shirt.

"But I cannot, in good conscience, allow you to go on believing Eli had any part in what you saw. He didn't do it," he whispered rigidly in her ear.

She whimpered and twisted beneath him. Warm lips met his.

"I'm sorry, Caelan. I'm so sorry." She sniffled and brought her hands up to frame his face before pressing her mouth more firmly onto his.

A feeling of pure desperation thrummed through Tieran's body. A desperation to obliterate the notion of Eli and the beast being one and the same. To destroy the idea he may have had anything to do with murdering defenseless women.

She was desperate to postpone the inevitable vision looming on the horizon. But most of all, she was desperate to get closer to the man pressed on top of her. To feel his hardness penetrate her body and take possession, to be marked again by his teeth, branded by his kisses.

She needed this more than anything right now. Needed him. She would never be able to look at another man without feeling Caelan's lips on hers, his teeth sinking into her skin, his cock embedded in her pussy. He had woven a spell around her, declaring for the entire world to see that she was his in every way possible.

His tongue invaded her mouth, plundered its depth, taking without mercy. She threaded her fingers through the hair at the nape of his neck, dragging him into firmer contact with her body. It wasn't enough, would never be enough until he was inside her, seated to the hilt, making them one whole instead of two halves. One whole, when yesterday she'd been happy with hiding away from men for the rest of her life.

The bed dipped when he crawled over her and straddled her torso. His hands rested on either side of her head, supporting him so he didn't crush her. He tasted so good, like a flavor she would crave for the rest of her life. She dueled with his tongue, parrying back and forth between their mouths, and lapped at his elongating teeth, mesmerized.

Tieran slid her hands down his shoulders, smoothed the length of his upper arms, then back up and under his armpits. He jerked and grunted against her mouth when she hit a ticklish spot along his side.

She gently scratched the spot again. Caelan jackknifed above her and trapped her roving hands at his sides with his arms. A smile played at his lips and she pouted.

"You don't play fair, my own." He tsked, wiggling a finger at her.

She took advantage, pulling her hand from its confinement, and walked her fingers up his rib cage.

"Why can't I resist you?" she whispered.

His eyes seemed to glow in the dim light of her bedroom. The teasing smile faded into a possessive snarl.

"Because your body belongs to me, and it knows it, even if your mind wants you to think differently. This is the way things are between mates. Your senses will grow stronger, they will detect me even when you can't see me. A part of me will be with you, always."

His fingers cupped her breasts and pinched the distended nipples. Tieran arched her neck at the twin sensations zinging straight to her core. She ached to feel his hands on her skin, instead of through the cotton covering her body.

"When you smell me, immediately your body will prepare itself for my cock. During your heat, you'll not be able to resist me. In fact, you'll beg me to fuck you. Fucking will be the only thing that will keep you sane during those intense times of the month. It will ease the hunger inside you, take the edge off, but not for long. Soon you'll need me again."

Oh God. He was killing her. His hands kneaded her small breasts and her womb clenched. So far he hadn't touched her pussy with any part of himself, but her clit was furiously aching. He slid her T-shirt up, uncovering her bare breasts, and she bent her neck to see herself.

The tips stood proud and large, beaded into tight points. A reverent fingertip caressed one.

"Me, Tieran, no one else will ever be able to satisfy your body, nor will you want them to."

She swallowed. The fierce, determined look on his face said he would kill anyone who even tried to get near her. Then his head swooped down and he strongly sucked a nipple into his mouth, dragging the bud deep inside and drawing it along his tongue.

"Oh, Christ, oh, oh God." She slapped at his biceps, his shoulders, anywhere she could reach, and dug her heels into the mattress. It was too much. It wasn't enough. Her womb seized into a tight ball of nerves, contracting over and over again until she thought she would explode. When he turned his attention to the other nipple, she did.

The orgasm slammed through her body. Her legs and arms went rigid. Her toes pointed, her hands fisted in his T-shirt.

And still he lapped at her, finishing her off, bringing her down off her high, soothing her until she sank into the mattress, boneless.

Caelan gathered her weak body to his chest and peeled off her shirt. Then he rose up on his knees and stripped his own shirt over his head. Tieran's chest heaved with the exertion of her climax as he laid her down again, but her eyes were softly closed and a sweet smile touched her lips. When he abruptly stood on the bed, her eyelids fluttered open to watch while he ripped open his jeans and shed them.

His steely erection bobbed as he balanced on the squishy bed, a tiny drop of come clinging to the broad head. Tieran levered herself up on her elbows and her pink tongue darted out to lick her lips. Caelan's cock jumped in response.

"You keep looking at me like that, you're gonna get more than you bargained for," he hissed.

For long, excruciating seconds she stared at his rock-hard penis, her chest rising and falling with each heavy breath.

"I don't remember bargaining for anything," she whispered, and lifted a seductive gaze to his face with a slow perusal that missed nothing on its way up.

Un-fucking-believable. Did she even know what she did to him?

She started to sit up but he stopped her by kneeling again, sandwiching her ribs between his bent knees and forcing her to lie back. Her mouth formed a perfect "O" in surprise. His cock twitched in anticipation of penetrating that sweet circle of lips.

"I need to feel that warm mouth of yours wrapped around my cock."

"Yes." Her small hand reached out to wrap around the base of his dick and he sucked in a breath. The tips of her fingers didn't even touch.

For long, painfully frustrating moments she discovered him inch by inch. She swiped her thumb across the glistening bead of pre-come seeping out and smeared it slowly around the head before sliding her hand back down his shaft and starting the exotic dance all over again.

The glide of her fingers and palm on his flesh was pure heaven. Caelan groaned and threw his head back, fighting the need to howl. His incisors lengthened further, begging to mark her again for everyone to see and know who she belonged to.

With a fist in her hair, he lifted her head to the swollen tip of his cock. "Lick me," he growled.

Her tongue tentatively flitted out to lap at the underside of his erection. Caelan dropped his chin to his chest and watched Tieran with hooded eyes. So damn good. She tasted him, worked her way down the length of the heavy vein underneath, then around the side and back up to the top. When she flicked at an ultra-sensitive spot, he nearly shot his load early.

He groaned and gripped her hair tighter. "Jesus. Stop," he gritted out. "I can't take any more." Two fucking licks and he was about to go off like a Roman candle.

The little minx doubled her efforts, slurping at him like he was an ice-cream cone, and then her mouth closed on him, drawing him deep and sucking for all she was worth.

Son of a bitch! Every ounce of blood in his body surged to his groin. The perfect sucking motion made him lose control. His fingers released her hair of their own accord. It was a good thing too, because his legs wouldn't support him anymore. He collapsed forward, catching himself at the last second with his hands above her head and lodging his cock deep at the back of her mouth.

Caelan eased out just enough to keep her from choking but damned if she didn't pull at his cock like someone was taking a sucker away from a two-year-old. He pressed back in again, knowing he shouldn't, but knowing if he didn't he'd die.

Tieran moaned around him, swallowing whenever she had the chance and tying his balls in knots.

"Jesus, baby, you gotta stop. *I* gotta stop," he amended when her eyes widened as if to say, "I'm not doing anything!"

He slowly extracted himself. Not easy to do when she followed his movement, holding onto him for dear life. Finally she let go, scraping her teeth gently across the slick head.

"Don't fucking do that again, my own," he growled. "I'm trying not to come all over you." He slid down her body and rested his sweaty forehead on hers. With supreme effort he drew breath into his lungs until the pounding in his dick subsided enough for him to move. One more touch and he was a goner.

"Sorry," she said, breathing heavy herself. A smile tugged at her lips.

"Yes, I can see how sorry you are."

"It was good then?"

Caelan looked at her, incredulous that she even had to ask. He launched himself backward and Tieran squeaked. Good. He liked to think he could keep her off balance sometimes.

"Time to get rid of these jeans, my own." He attacked the button and zipper and yanked both the jeans and her underwear over her hips and off her legs, throwing them on the floor and leaving her drenched pussy open for his touch.

Lowering his head, he swiped the length of her labia with the flat of his tongue. He heard her breath catch and caught her hips in his hands when she lifted off the bed. Sweet and spicy. Inhaling, he flooded his senses with her essence, and that of their unborn child nestled inside her womb.

With his palm, he rubbed a small circle on her belly, encircling the tiny embryo that would one day be a person. Tieran sighed and laid her hand on top of his.

Did she know? Was it possible? He mentally shrugged it off and tugged her swollen clit between his lips.

"Caelan." Her back arched and her thighs squeezed at his ears. With one last deep kiss to her pussy, he backed away. Before she could gather her wits, he flipped her onto her stomach, startling her with his quickness.

"I've waited long enough to have you this way, baby." He lifted her hips with one arm and stuffed a pillow underneath her with the other, effectively propping her ass in the air. The perfect position for a true wolf mating which would allow him access to the slope of her shoulder and neck, where another one of his bites would mark her for all time.

"You are a truly beautiful woman." He spread her thighs and settled between them, lining up his cock with her glistening entrance and spreading the moisture pooling there with the tip.

Tieran snorted. "That's what they all say," she mumbled into her pillow.

Caelan jerked, his dick slipping off her pussy and along the crack of her cheeks. She squealed and squirmed around his shaft. Not even the sensation of her squeezing him could disperse the hot-blooded jealousy rearing its ugly head.

"Who's they?" he demanded. He'd kill the motherfuckers, rip their throats out with his bare hands. Not because of the beautiful remark, anyone with eyeballs could see that, but because they'd gotten to touch her first.

And then you'd be no better than the killer you're looking for, his brain taunted him, taking over his emotions. He loosened his bruising grip on her thighs.

She let out a breath. "Nobody, Caelan. It was a figure of speech."

"I'm sorry, my own," he said leaning over her and kissing the nape of her neck, "but you're mine and I don't want to ever think about anyone else touching you." He shifted his hips, gliding his cock over her crease again. "One of these days I'm gonna fuck this sweet ass of yours, baby." She tensed. "I'll make it good for you, working my fingers in and out of your tiny hole 'til it's stretched and ready for my cock. Think about how good it'll feel." He rasped his teeth over the nape of her neck.

Tieran moaned and leaned back into his groin. "Please, Caelan, I need you."

Caelan slipped a hand under her and palmed her mound. "So slick, sweetheart." He slid his fingers through the puffy flesh of her labia, spreading her cream, then circled her swollen clit.

"Oh." She widened her knees and ground her pussy on his fingers, rubbing herself back and forth. "Now, Caelan, do it now. I'm so—oh crap," she panted when he pinched the distended bundle of nerves. "I'm going to come."

"Not yet, my own." He pulled his hand away and guided his cock to the ripe, wet opening. Slowly he pushed in, savoring every millimeter of her vagina gripping him until he was seated to his balls. Her inner muscles clenched and unclenched, teasing him.

"Move," she begged.

Caelan bit into the soft skin where her shoulder met her neck, holding her in place when she began to writhe, forcing her into submission. He smiled when she stilled.

Keeping his teeth planted on her smooth shoulder, he started rocking gently into her. He wanted to draw this out, take her to the edge again and again, and drive her into begging for release. One of her hands came up and sharp fingernails dug into his ass. He growled and stopped moving, telling her without words to remove her claws.

At first she sank them deeper and he envisioned them making small crescent shapes on his butt. "Don't stop. Jesus, God, go faster, something," she screamed. He bit down on the flesh in his mouth, warning her to be still, that he was in control of this session, not her. After several seconds she relented with a whimper.

His lips curved as he resumed his slow torture.

Sweat beaded his forehead. Her torture was his too. His balls contracted, drawing energy to force an explosion of seed. Caelan released his bite and licked along the wound he'd inflicted.

"You are mine," he growled and slammed into her, driving his cock against her womb. Tieran grunted with the force.

"Whose are you?"

When she didn't answer he placed a hand on the small of her back and reached with the other one to her clit. The bud was tight as a pebble. With one touch she jerked and tried to rub against his finger. He wouldn't let her and held her in place. There was no space for her to move between the pillow underneath her and his hand on her back.

"Whose are you?" he demanded, sweat dripping on her cheek as he leaned over her.

"Yours," she cried. "Yours."

His cock jolted at her acceptance. He pulled his hand off her clit and released her back to hold both her hips. The slaps of their bodies echoed in the small bedroom, mirroring the sucking sounds coming from her pussy as he drove himself in and out of her body.

"Make it stop," she shouted and fisted a hand in the comforter.

"Never, Tieran. This is...too good...never want...to...stop." He thrust into her one last time, her tight pussy wringing every last drop of come and milking him with her own convulsions.

Caelan collapsed on top of her and buried his nose in the silkiness of her hair.

"Oh, God. Oh. God." She twitched every few seconds around his length sending tiny lightning bolts of sensations through his cock.

He never wanted to leave this spot.

"Get off me, I can't breathe."

Caelan laughed and relaxed with a whoosh. He was thinking about how he didn't ever want to move and she blurted out something as mundane as not being able to breathe. Damn. He rolled to one side, disengaging from her as he went and gritting his teeth as her vaginal walls tried to suck him back in. See, her pussy didn't care that her lungs couldn't get air.

He pulled her to his chest, spooning her and wiping the hair off her face. If what she'd said earlier about having another vision came true, she was probably in for a long night. He sighed and closed his eyes on the memory of her subtle accusation.

Caelan caressed the new mark he'd given her with his thumb and placed a gentle kiss on the red welts forming there. Her breathing slowed and her body melted into his as she drifted off into a sated sleep.

She had submitted to his dominance. His heart swelled with fierce pride for his mate even as his brain warned him that their relationship would never be stable until she accepted that Eli wasn't the one responsible for the deaths of those women.

On top of all this, he still had to worry about her becoming a victim herself. Somehow he had to keep a lock on her ability. If word got out, it would draw attention to her like a moth to a flame. Any shifter would be able to smell that she'd conceived as well. If the killer was after alpha mates, then Tieran already had a target painted on her back. With her gift, she didn't need any help attracting attention, which is exactly what their baby would do.

With both arms he gathered her closer, cradling her tightly to him, their bodies sticky in the aftermath.

No one would ever get to his mate.

Not without going through his dead body first.

Chapter Six

"You've got to be kidding me." He slapped the steering wheel with his open palm and guided the coasting vehicle to the side of the road. The dash was as dark as the rest of the interior of the small car. A strong whiff of leather assaulted his nose when he shifted in the driver's seat. He was going to be fucking late for his meeting with this Christian guy. Gravel crunched under the wheels on the shoulder of the two-lane desolate highway.

Night had completely set in around him, adding to the already dark shadows of the woods bordering both sides of the road. They called to him, whispering in the wind to shift and go for a run. He stared into their inviting depths and wished he could.

An image formed in his head of a lithe, nubile body. He pictured her wearing a T-shirt and panties, and stretched out under a sheet on her bed. Blood flooded his groin. His cock jumped against the button-fly of his jeans.

Goddamn, what he would give to sink into her pussy. To feel her tight heat grasp his cock and hear her cries as she came long and hard around him. Someday soon, she would. Lately, whenever he was near her, her scent drove him crazy. It teased him, making his dick twitch.

As it stood now, he could hardly sleep for wanting her and his cock sported a perpetual hard-on. He'd tried to ease it with other women to no avail. His body only wanted its mate. His heart did too.

He pressed the heels of his palms into his eye sockets. Up until now he'd never had one problem with his Mustang GT. His baby had run perfectly, was fine-tuned whenever he had a spare moment, buffed to a sparkling black shine every weekend. The damn thing was only a year old, anyway. He cursed his luck and unclipped the cell phone from his waistband. With his thumb, he flipped it open and glared at the screen.

No fucking service. "Son of a bitch," he bit out, throwing the offending phone into the seat next to him.

In the middle of nowhere, no phone service, with a car that chose tonight to dick around. His plans were royally screwed over. He grabbed his mini-flashlight from the glove box, flicked it on and glanced at the TAG Heuer watch circling his wrist. Ten-fifteen. They were supposed to have met at ten. The scar on his shoulder suddenly blazed with pain. He gritted his teeth against the searing sensation ripping through his upper arm and covered the six-inch puckered line with his empty hand. He'd received the injury one night when another shifter who thought he was better than everybody else had challenged him. He still hadn't forgiven the wolf who'd given it to him. With a sly smile, he remembered giving as good as he'd gotten. Little fucker still pissed people off, despite his rank in the community.

"Christ." The pain wrenched through the years-old wound again. The flesh had been flayed open by the teeth of the wolf and hadn't healed the way wolves typically heal. It had taken longer and been more painful than any other injury inflicted upon him. Why in the hell was it acting up now, when it hadn't bothered him for ages?

He turned the key and hoped his car's electrical short circuit, and his phone's, was due to some anomaly in the area.

The only sound that greeted him was a soft whir, whir, of the engine failing, not the usual mind-blowing, deep-throated roar that accompanied his specialized exhaust system. His championship thoroughbred had been turned into a whinnying, wobbly-legged foal. A fact that was completely incongruent with an electrical malfunction.

"Damn it." He pushed open the door and slammed his hand down on the roof of his prized possession. No cars had passed him in the few minutes he'd sat on the side of the road, no sign of life.

This wasn't the way tonight was supposed to go. Instead of finishing his job, it looked like he was going to get his run in after all. He toed off his shoes and yanked his pants off, pissed at the turn of events.

Again, a beautiful face swam into focus, making his cock thicken. Fuck soon enough, he needed her now.

He fisted his hands at his sides and screamed his frustration into the dead night.

Why was he putting himself through this hell? Why not just come right out and take her, make her understand how much he needed her, wanted her, craved her, body and soul? Fuck.

She'd hate him, that's why. Be scared to death of what he was.

"Son of a bitch. Be the alpha that you are and make her see." He resisted the urge to howl.

He still had time. She wasn't going anywhere. When all this was over, she'd still be here and then he'd be all over her.

Stripping off the rest of his clothes, he dumped them in the backseat along with his keys and slammed the door shut. He'd bring his spare set from home when he came back to get it later. Hopefully the car would still be here. It burned a hole in his gut to leave his baby vulnerable in the middle of nowhere. An owl hooted in the distance, reminding him that the only things in these woods were himself and the wild animals. One of which, he was about to become.

He tugged on the door handle one last time and then initiated his change. The woods called to him again. His nude body transformed, popping and stretching to accommodate his wolf's shape, fur taking over his skin. When it was over, he lifted his head and howled. A plethora of other animals responded by scurrying into hiding.

He loped off into the trees, thankful his wolf's senses would pick up a trail for home far better than his human self.

Tieran woke up gasping. Her visions were getting stronger. Always before she saw the event as an outsider. An observer looking in. That's how she'd been able to tell the Florida police what the rapist had looked like. His features, not his thoughts. Lately, she'd been morphing into the person she was "seeing". She knew everything the person was thinking and feeling, but had no clue what they looked like.

She shivered beneath the covers. It was a truly eerie feeling to know what someone else was thinking. At least nothing had happened this time, other than a man turning into a wolf. Right, because that was a normal, everyday occurrence.

Tieran settled into her pillow and listened to the thumping of her heart. The steady cadence of Caelan's breathing next to her said he was still sleeping. A dull throb ticked away at her temples, but strangely, her usual nausea was absent.

No way could she go back to sleep now. Reading was an option, but she might wake Caelan with the light. The soreness between her thighs announced she was not ready for another round with the insatiable, gorgeous man lying in the bed next to her. Sleeping with her, for God's sake! One day and the man had practically moved in with her. If the world would stop spinning for even one minute, she might be able to make heads or tails out of what was happening in her life.

She sighed and her tummy grumbled its presence. A snack would be nice. Fortification for all the calories she'd burned today. His stamina at lovemaking could run circles around any aerobic workout those Hollywood types could dish out. She'd taken more naps today than she had since she was four. Her stomach rumbled again and she rubbed a hand over her face.

In order to have a snack, one must have food on hand. She could go to the store. It wasn't that late and the trip might help make her sleepy. Yep, a midnight raid of the grocery store it was.

Thirty minutes later, Tieran flinched when the apples she'd just bagged bounced off the wire basket of her shopping cart. She hated bruised apples. For a second she thought about dumping them back into the bin, but nixed the idea. With her luck, someone would see her. Her ears heated with the embarrassing image of getting caught putting her fruit back.

"Coward." She sighed and glanced around to make sure no was looking and guessing what she was contemplating. The produce area was empty.

Not surprising, considering it was the middle of the night. "Normal people don't grocery shop at this time of day—night," she muttered. Oh, goody. Now she was talking to herself.

Perhaps she was here at exactly the right time then, because she was nowhere near normal on the weirdness scale.

Sticking her tongue out on a gag, she passed the heaping pile of disgusting smelling oranges. The cart made a repetitive, very annoying squeak and thump with every revolution of its flat-on-one-side wheel. She never even glanced at the other good-for-you stuff. Bananas and apples were about all she could handle. All the rest might look good in her fridge, but it would go uneaten and rot there.

"Maybe Caelan would like some, Tulla."

"Maybe Caelan doesn't live in my house," she responded defiantly.

"Tsk, tsk, Tullabelle. The man had clothes sent over. I don't think he's going anywhere anytime soon."

"Dead people are not allowed to tsk, Gramama. And I didn't give the 'man' permission to move in with me. For God's sake, I don't know anything about him. Besides, he seems like a meat kind of guy, I don't see him going for the roughage either."

"How could you not know anything after all he's told you? He is only trying to protect you."

From what? she wanted to scream. She caught herself just in time.

"Can I help you find something?"

Oh, good Lord. A stock boy was staring at her, hefting a crate of mini-carrots. She shook her head and practically sprinted from the produce section. Or would have if the cart had been capable of rolling in a straight line. Instead she veered to the left and had to muscle the thing back on course before it took out the potatoes.

Her body ached in places it hadn't for a long time. The memories of all the times Caelan had fucked her left her panties damp. He certainly had stamina. What a waste of time she'd spent with Peter. Obviously *he* didn't have a clue when it came to sex. Good thing Tieran hadn't known then what she was missing. Or maybe it was a bad thing.

Had she known how good sex could be, she would have dropped Peter on his ass before he ever got the chance to hurt her like he had.

"Peter's a weasel."

Tieran choked back a grunt of laughter. *"I believe you've said that before. On more than one occasion."*

"Well, it's the truth."

She stared at the meat. Her mouth pooled with saliva. That was weird. She wasn't usually turned-on by meat. Okay, so Caelan had a piece of meat that made her whole body spasm. She smiled. Ooh boy, the things he could do with his meat. A giggle escaped her lips at the same time her stomach growled again.

"Man, I must really be hungry."

What kind of meat did wolves eat, precisely? Steak, hamburger, roast? A roast sounded good. She could make one of those. But then she'd have to go back and face the produce boy to get some carrots and whatever else goes with a roast. She opted for the ready-made hamburgers. If Caelan was still around tomorrow night, they could have them for dinner.

Awkwardly pushing the reluctant cart up and down the aisles, she added several other items. Doritos, a case of Mountain Dew, hamburger buns, pickles, pre-packaged potato salad, which she had to go get from the deli section, and a six-pack of Bud Light.

"Nope, better get the twelve-pack." She shoved it under the cart. No reason for the beer to touch her soda and contaminate it.

Turning the corner at the frozen foods aisle, her skin prickled. Tieran whipped around at the sudden sensation of being watched. She half-expected Caelan to be standing there glowering at her for having left him in bed without asking permission.

A flash of movement caught her eye and then was gone, beyond the corner of another aisle. Uneasy, she shivered. Had someone followed her then jumped down the aisle? Or was she imagining things, spooking at nothing? With her last vision prominent in her mind, who could blame her?

"Don't go look." She forced herself to continue her shopping if for nothing else than to get the hell out of there. Her belly grew queasy.

She grabbed a box of fettuccine Alfredo out of the freezer and threw it into the cart. The box tilted to one side and slid to the bottom of the stack. She had to laugh at the innocuous box that had been the start of her crazy-ass day. Maybe this time she'd get to eat the damn thing, she thought, still smiling.

Done. She'd pay for her groceries and leave. If she asked they would probably lend her the produce boy to walk her to her car.

Tieran couldn't help but look down the aisle where she'd seen the momentary glimpse of movement. Whoever it was, was gone now. She blew out a breath, angry with herself for jumping at shadows.

At least her trip had helped with her temporary insomnia. She was more than ready to go home and slip into bed against Caelan's naked body.

🐾 🐾 🐾

He dragged in a long breath. The grocery store had been too close a call. After missing his meeting, he'd come back here just in time to catch Caelan's new mate leaving. He'd thought about taking care of her right then, but didn't. He would save her for last and savor the look on Caelan's face when he did so.

She'd already conceived. Caelan must be beside himself thinking about his mate carrying the next little Primelet in her belly.

It would be his pleasure to rip the whelp from her womb before it had a chance to live. No one would stop him from becoming Prime. Not even a single-celled embryo.

It should have been his position all along. He was the stronger shifter.

The house was dark. Enough time had passed for the cunt to be back asleep. Dumb motherfucker. Didn't Caelan give a shit about his mate? So many things could have befallen her. Especially now with a killer on the loose. Reminded of the pack's feeble attempts at finding him, he laughed. No one would ever suspect him. Ever.

Tomorrow he'd call and reschedule the meeting. Same time, same place. The trap was set and things would have gotten taken care of tonight if he hadn't had to bow out. It was the perfect plan to pin everything on a red herring. While everyone was sitting around scratching their asses, he would have plenty of time to move in for the ultimate kill.

Right now he was going to have a little fun with the Prime's mate.

He'd sensed her in Elizabeth's mind as he'd torn her apart. No fucking psychic cunt would take away what was rightfully his. Not when he was this close.

He itched to storm into her house and be done with it. Instead, he forced his feet to remain still, and reminded himself that the Prime was in there with her.

His cock hardened in his jeans. He soothed it, rubbing his palm over the length. Maybe he'd fuck the cunt before he killed her. Better yet, he'd do it in front of the Prime and then kill them both.

No. He liked his plan for their demise. He wouldn't alter it now.

From his hiding place in the shadows across the street, he centered all his energy into the house and waited for the fun to begin.

🐐 🐐 🐐

Tieran's eyes flew open. What had woken her? Again. Her gaze flashed to the open bedroom door. There it was. The tiniest of creaks. Not her front door then, because opening it was paramount to setting off a nuclear explosion. She was still surprised she hadn't woken Caelan when she'd gone to the store earlier. Or when she'd gotten home.

What then? Had Eli come back? She glanced at the clock, glowing a red one-o-four. Geez, she'd only slept about an hour since getting back in bed. At this rate, she'd be lucky to get a full five hours in tonight.

Another sound. A footstep? Her heart pounded ferociously. Nudging Caelan's still form, she leaned over and whispered, "Wake up." He didn't move. She shook his shoulder. "Psst." Nothing. Christ, what did she have to do?

There was another creak, louder and closer this time. Someone was definitely in her house. No time for subtlety. She punched him. He never flinched. Jesus, he gave new meaning to the term sleeping like a rock.

Apart from screaming like a banshee, what could she do? *The phone, you idiot!* Tieran crawled over Caelan's seemingly lifeless form, wincing when the bed squeaked. She froze, sure that whoever it was outside her bedroom could hear all the racket she was making. She turned to the door, expecting to see someone there.

The floorboards groaned in the hallway. So not in the doorway yet, but getting closer. She scrambled to the nightstand, ignoring the noise. Dialing 911 would at least alert the operator to her location, even if she didn't get the chance to talk. If nothing else, she knew they would send a policeman to investigate.

Holding it close to her chest to try and hide the glow, she pushed the buttons and set the phone face up beneath the bed. Her dust ruffle would contain the small light.

With both hands, she shoved on Caelan's back. "Come. On," she grunted, terrified. The man was immovable. She'd never get him off the bed. Why didn't he wake up? As a last ditch effort, Tieran yanked the comforter up from where it bunched at his torso until it concealed him from head to toe. She had to do something to try and protect him. If the intruder wasn't blind, then he'd have to be a moron not to see Caelan's form under the covers.

She squeezed herself into the crevice between the nightstand and bed and heard the operator droning on through the phone. Scooping it off the floor, she breathed, "He's here."

"Ma'am? Ma'am, stay on the line."

Like she was going to hang up? she thought, hysterically.

Tieran sensed a disturbance in the room. Hugging her knees to her chest, she tucked herself into a ball and held her breath until her lungs burned. With her chin down and her face buried in her knees, she couldn't see anything. The hair on her nape prickled and she knew he had entered the room.

"Wake up, wake up, Caelan," she chanted silently. Any second he would, launching himself off the bed and coming to her rescue at the last possible second. After she kissed him senseless, she'd choke him to death.

A warm puff of air ruffled her bangs and she jerked. Oh, God. This was it. A horrible sense of foreboding flooded her body. She was going to die. Her whole body shook in absolute fear.

Tieran raised her gaze a scant inch, sweat beading on her forehead. Its lips were curled back, exposing the razor-sharp teeth that would rip out her throat. She tried swallowing but her mouth was dry as cotton.

Its low snarl reverberated through the otherwise silent room. Ever so slowly, she backed her head away, as if those few more inches gave her any leverage. Its yellowed eyes glowed back at her as he followed the movement. Her breathing became desperate pants.

It barked, lunging at her and snapping its teeth where her nose had been. She screamed and buried her head in her arms, expecting to feel the vicious shredding of her forearms.

Caelan flung himself upright at the ear-splitting scream, his heart pounding as he readied for an attack. Christ. There was nothing. The house was dark, as quiet as when he'd first gone to sleep. No trace of anything wrong. Except the woman next to him. He laid a hand on Tieran's shoulder. She was scrunched up tight, her arms covering her head in a defensive position, and her breath bellowing out of her lungs. Her pulse raced beneath his fingertips where he placed them on her neck.

A nightmare. It was only a nightmare. Or worse, a vision.

"Tieran, wake up. It's me, baby." Jesus, she was nearly catatonic, trapped in some kind of hell. "Shh. Everything's okay," he murmured.

He curled up next to her and wrapped his arms around her, pulling her sweat-slickened, naked form to his chest. She reeked of fear-induced adrenaline. Caelan attempted to soothe her with his fingers and his words. Finally he felt her relax a fraction.

His heart soared. Subconsciously, her mind and body trusted him. The rest would come later. He continued rocking her until the last of the shudders subsided and she whimpered.

"Must have been some bad dream," he muttered into her hair.

"Caelan?" she whispered.

He rose onto his elbow and rolled her to her back, taking sharp notice of the way her pupils were dilated. Even in the dark room, he could see how big they were.

"Yes, baby." He nuzzled her cheek with his lips and kissed down her jaw. She swallowed and ducked her head, dislodging his roaming mouth.

"It was him. He was here, in the house."

Caelan inhaled deeply, and pushed her wet bangs off her forehead. "He's gone now," he consoled. Had never been here, either. There were no foreign scent markers whatsoever.

"I heard something," she continued, oblivious to his reassurance, "and I couldn't wake you up. I had to crawl over you and squish into the space between the table and the bed." Her gaze searched the room in a wild fashion.

"I called 911." She jerked up, rapping his chin so hard he bit his tongue and fell back onto the pillow. Then she was laying over him.

He twisted to see what she was looking for. There was nothing out of place that he could see. Even in the dark, his enhanced wolf's vision picked up the clock, lamp, book, phone and picture of Tieran and someone who could only be her grandmother. They were all there. Everything looked untouched.

He felt her breasts rise and fall with each harsh breath and her skin was clammy against his abdomen.

"It was the one who killed the last woman. I know it," she insisted. "Same hair, same eyes, same teeth, same sc..." Shuttering, she laid down again, this time pulling his arm over her chest and snuggling into him.

She had to be exhausted.

"It barked at me and I screamed."

"I know you did, baby," he said absentmindedly and buried his nose in the crook of her neck. Barked? What the hell? He thought she'd been rattling off the traits of the burglar in her nightmare. Of the human kind. So, did she have another vision, or had the one about Micah led her to have a bad dream?

"Why didn't you wake up? Why didn't you protect me?" The censure in her voice broke his heart.

"You were dreaming." Please God, let this have been a dream. He felt her hot tears on his cheek and laced his fingers with hers. No way would he have slept through a real attack. Hell he would have sensed any intruder long before they got to her. Even in a dead sleep. But he couldn't fight something that wasn't real.

"Where's Eli, Caelan?" she whispered.

How the fuck should he know? He tightened his grip on her body. Why the hell did it matter? He forced himself to answer her, dreading her response. Eli should be the last person on her mind right now, so why was he the first?

"He had a meeting, remember? He's probably home by now. Why?" he asked when he really didn't want to.

"Are you sure?"

Why did he smell a renewed sense of fear? He couldn't be positive where Eli was, but he assumed Eli would go home after a meeting that late at night. Then again, this was Eli they were talking about. He may have hit a bar somewhere and picked up a woman, or he could be at Derek's, his best friend's house. God, please let him have done one of those things. Then Caelan wouldn't be outright lying about the whereabouts of his twin.

Caelan cleared his throat. "I'm not positive. I've been here with you, so I wouldn't know exactly where he went afterward. I'm not his keeper either. He comes and goes as he pleases, and trust me he pleases all the time."

"Call him."

It hit him then. She thought Eli was the wolf that had barked at her. He did some barking of his own then. "No!" He pulled away from her and rose on his elbow. "Damn it, Tieran, I'm not gonna call him. He'll call me in the morning to tell me how things went tonight. You still think it's Eli? How can you not trust me?" he demanded, wanting to hear the words straight from her mouth.

"Because you didn't just see what I did," she cried, turning over and giving him her back. God, how did he do this to her? Stir her into such a tizzy that she blurted out the first thing in her head. She never should have said anything.

"You have to stop thinking that Eli is responsible for whatever it is you've seen." He laid a hand on her upper arm and rolled her until she faced him once more.

Damn him for making her feel like this.

"Why should I?" she screamed, startling him with her vehemence. "You have to understand where I'm coming from here, Caelan." She swiped angrily at her wet cheeks. "The only

129

thing I can do is tell you what I see. I can't help it if you don't like the answers."

Caelan wrapped his arms around her shaking body and gathered her close to his chest, holding firmly when she tried to push away. She hated that despite the fact he pissed her off, he still had the ability to make her feel safe.

"Shh, baby." He stroked his hand over her hair. "You're doing your best. That's all I can ask." With a hand cupped under her chin, he lifted her face and forced her to look at him when she didn't want to. "But you have to understand where I'm coming from too. Eli is my twin, my other half, and he is not capable of the maliciousness of this killer."

Tieran sniffed and flicked her gaze away from him, searching the deeply shadowed room. She half-expected the beast to jump out at her again. Another wave of chills wracked her body. Her heart said Caelan was right. Eli was too much like his brother to have killed a woman in cold blood. Her brain said screw your heart, there are too many damn coincidences not to think of him as a suspect.

Tieran shivered and sank into his warm strength. She was too tired to think right now.

"Just hold me. Please." They could talk in the morning, but no more tonight. She felt his sigh and his fingers dug into her hip. Caelan wasn't happy with her putting him off again.

"I'll hold you whenever you need me to, sweetheart." He snuggled closer than she thought possible. "Please tell me what happened. I promise to listen."

Tieran sighed. He would, too. He wouldn't like it, but he'd wait until she was done before listing his reasons why she was wrong.

"Please, my own," he whispered, nibbling on her earlobe. Warmth pooled in her belly.

She could honestly say with Peter, she'd never once felt inclined to talk to him about her visions. Sometimes they inadvertently came out, much to his chagrin, but she'd learned not to involve him. After the Florida debacle she hadn't gone to the police again either.

Caelan, on the other hand, somehow made her want to spill her guts. She wondered what kind of hold he had on her that put her in some kind of trance-like state *making* her talk to him.

"What did you see, Tieran?" His tone was almost hypnotic and she felt herself slipping under his spell again. It was a damn strange weakness she had with him.

"A man in a car. It died and he had to pull it off onto the shoulder," she heard herself say.

"What did he look like?" His voice was as soothing as the fingers he gently combed through her hair.

She shook her head. "I don't know. It was almost as if I was inside his mind."

Caelan stiffened around her. "Is that normal?"

"No." She swallowed. Not at all, and she really didn't care for the way her gift was starting to evolve. "Before I met you, I was always an observer. When that wolf attacked that lady, I was her. I felt her terror, her pain, her...loss." Absentmindedly, she smoothed a hand over his bunching biceps. "I can describe the wolf because I saw him from her point of view, but other than the fact I saw her in the paper, I have no clue what she looks like."

"Okay, let's try it this way. What did he see?"

Tieran searched her memory for details. As with most of her visions, not all the pieces fell into place. Oftentimes, something would happen much later that triggered tidbits of information to the forefront.

"There were woods," she remembered. "He wanted to go for a run. And there was a woman. He kept picturing her and leering at her. No, not leering, but...lusting for her."

Caelan's fingers tightened in her hair and she winced. She wondered if he was thinking the same thing she was. If this was his killer, he already had another victim in mind.

Gradually his hand loosened its hold. He took a deep breath. "What kind of car was he driving? You said it broke down somewhere? Are there any landmarks, something that might lead us to where he's parked?"

"No, nothing but woods in both directions. And asking me to tell you what kind of car it was is like asking me to sing the Greek National Anthem. It ain't gonna happen. The best I can do is something black and sporty. Sorry, I don't always remember everything I see right away. It will probably float in and out all day."

"But maybe you could ID it if you saw it again?"

She shrugged. "Possibly."

Now it was his turn to sigh. "What else?"

"Nothing, Caelan." Thinking about it too much right now would probably bury her deep in headacheville.

She yawned so big her jaw popped. He held her face in his hands. It was amazing how much she could see despite how dark the room was. She liked to sleep in pitch black and normally she wouldn't be able to see her hand in front of her face. So why was he so clear in front of her?

"You'll tell me if anything else comes to mind?"

She nodded. He tucked her head beneath his chin and squeezed her to his chest.

"Fuck. I hate doing this to you. If I didn't need all the help I can get, I'd help you get through the pain and not make you bring it up again."

"'S'okay," she mumbled. Her eyes welled with tears. Where had he been all her life?

He gently rocked her through her quiet sobs until her eyes grew too heavy to keep open and she let the darkness of sleep consume her.

Chapter Seven

Caelan added a third pancake to the stack and slathered it with butter before covering them in warm syrup. He eyeballed the golden discs for a second then poured another dollop. Perfect. The pancakes were anyway, Tieran's ass would be his for a spanking whenever she appeared.

He'd gotten up this morning intent on making her something to eat and had been shocked to see the newly stocked refrigerator. Dumbfounded, he'd stood there for several minutes, the cool air washing over him and his heart pounding at the implication of just where the food had come from.

He'd let her continue to sleep out of the sheer goodness of his heart. What he'd wanted to do was storm in there and demand she tell him what the hell she thought she was doing going out in the middle of the night for groceries. A twinge of pain in his hand made him realize he was gripping the syrup bottle to the point it was about to burst.

"What the hell have you done to my kitchen?" she growled from the doorway, mirroring his grumpy mood.

Tomorrow, he'd remember that she was obviously not a morning person. Caelan smiled despite his anger but kept his back to her so she wouldn't see.

"It's called making breakfast, my own."

"I don't eat breakfast," she grumbled.

He heard the scrape of a chair and had to laugh at her "humph" when she plopped onto the seat.

"Have fun on your little late-night expedition, Tieran?" he asked, still not bothering to turn around. If he did, he was liable to snap at her. Literally.

"You've got food, don't you? Be happy."

He curled the corner of his lip. Damn her smart-ass mouth. "The food could have fucking waited until this morning." *When I could have gone with you to watch out for your stubborn behind,* he added silently.

"But then you wouldn't have had anything here to make whatever it is you've made, now would you?"

Caelan finally turned, the pancakes in one hand and a huge pile of sausage and bacon in the other. Tieran's face faded into a sickly shade of green when her gaze landed on the food he'd made for her. Her lips curled in distaste and she jerked her gaze out the window.

"You need to—"

She threw a hand in the air, palm out to him and her head shook violently in protest. When she faced him again, her eyes were wide, her cheeks puffed out. Her eyelids lowered like a curtain a second before she bolted from the chair and raced out of the kitchen.

Caelan sighed and set the plates on the table. He knew a shifter pregnancy could be hard on a human but he sincerely hoped this didn't last too long. Her body would need protein to maintain the life growing inside her. How could he get meat in her if she started throwing up every time she looked at it?

The sound of violent retching filtered down the hall. He went after her. It was his fault she was like this anyway.

"Do you mind?" she cried, spitting into the toilet.

"Nope." He wet a washcloth with cool water and filled a glass, then plunked himself on the floor next to her, willing to be there for her whether she wanted him to or not.

Tieran yanked the washcloth out of his hands and wiped her face with it. She took the water from him and guzzled it down like a lifeline to a desert survivor. Defeated and weak, she dropped the glass to the ground with a clunk. Caelan was surprised it didn't shatter, but she seemed unfazed.

"Better?" He caressed her shoulder with his lips and rubbed her lower back.

She nodded but he heard the small sob break free. "Why do you have to be so nice?"

He was shocked. Why wouldn't he be? She was his mate, his other half. Hadn't he already told her it was his job to make sure she was happy?

He sighed. "I hate to say this, but you might be like this every morning for a while. Something about our DNA makes the human mothers of our children ill."

Tieran glared at the ceiling and sucked in a breath, holding it for more than he was comfortable with. He waited for her to deal but wasn't prepared for what came out of her mouth.

"Dear God, why? Why are you doing this to me? Is there one man out there you haven't made stupid?" A second wave of vomit erupted from her throat.

What the hell, he thought, stunned beyond doing anything but watch his mate throw up again. She sat back and wiped her face with the washcloth. "I'm not stupid," he mumbled. Jesus. He scrubbed a hand over his face. He sounded like a pouting five-year-old.

"Peter also accused me of being pregnant. Imagine being accused of the same thing by two different *men!*" She laughed. "One day. I've been with you for one day. Okay, one night too, but not feasibly long enough to be showing signs of pregnancy this morning!"

An eyebrow raised, he twisted to refill the water and handed it to her so she could wash her mouth out. She squeezed her eyes shut and her cheeks puffed out. Apparently her stomach still wasn't happy.

She cocked her head, working something out in her brain. "How did you get the sink fixed?"

He smiled. "Worked on it while you were out cold this morning." He shrugged. "Wasn't a big deal. The faucet was loose I guess." His smile faded. Tieran's cheeks puffed out and a green tinge took over.

"Christ, baby, I can't stand to see you like this."

"Then leave, goddamn it!" she spat out.

She was the most stubborn... He leaned into her shoulder and spoke in her ear. "When are you gonna get it through that thick skull of yours I'm not leaving?"

She turned on him so quickly she nearly took out his nose with her forehead. "Maybe when you stop saying such asinine things." He jerked his head back. "Women don't suddenly become ill the second they conceive, if they've conceived in the first place, which, thank God, shouldn't happen with us since I'm not at the right time of month for something like that."

Caelan snorted and folded his arms across his chest, a smug smile on his face.

"I got news for you, toots, you're carrying my child, I can smell it on you. I could yesterday. Hell Eli could. And when you meet the elders of my pack later today, they will too. You can't hide something like this from a wolf, baby. It's all out there in the open." He flicked his fingers like he was counting. "Fear, joy, anxiousness, mate status, conception. Get used to it," he growled.

She sat there, stunned. "What are you saying, Caelan?" she whispered.

Before he could formulate an answer, Tieran shouted into the air, "Oh, stay out of this, Gramama."

Great. That's all he needed was for her grandmother to be here with them.

"I'm saying, my own," he said softly, "that you are carrying my child. You have been since the first time we made love."

Her hands clenched and she looked as though she wanted to punch him.

He watched her indignation flare. "Just how long were you going to wait to tell me this, Caelan?"

He pulled her between his spread legs, draping her knees over his thighs until his hardening cock pressed against her pussy. She gave in with little resistance.

"Soon, baby. When you'd at least gotten the chance to accept being my mate before I threw in, 'oh and by the way, how do you feel about being a mother?'" His lips brushed her forehead as he spoke against it.

Tieran buried her head in the crook of his neck. He loved the feel of her in his arms. A tiny spark jumped in his heart when she cradled her tummy with both hands.

"Are you sure?" she murmured.

Caelan chuckled against her hair. "Yes, my own, I am definitely sure. Your scent is positively ripe with conception." He covered her hands with his own.

He was sure she had a thousand questions but she didn't utter even one.

He lifted her head with his finger under her chin and kissed her nose. "I love you. I will answer all your questions, but not now."

"How? How can you love me when you don't know anything about me?"

"I'll be the first to admit, I don't know how it works. It has something to do with the mating, swapping DNA, marking you." He shrugged. "I don't know. But I can feel you in my soul, and when we're apart, you'll feel it too."

He hugged her close then pulled her head back to look into her eyes.

"We'll get through this together." He helped her stand, steadied her when her wobbly knees wanted to give out and patted her butt. "Take a shower. We can talk over breakfast. Oh, and brush your teeth. I haven't had a good-morning kiss."

He walked out, laughing and dodging the washrag she threw at him with a furious look and an even angrier curse.

"I wouldn't kiss you now for all the money in the world," she shouted and slammed the door.

He could still hear her as he walked to the kitchen, his heart a little bit lighter now that she knew about their baby.

🐈 🐈 🐈

"What the hell happened, E?"

Tieran stopped outside the kitchen entrance. Caelan was staring out the window, talking on his cell phone. He grumbled something unintelligible and raked his fingers through his hair. It was shining wet, suggesting he had taken his own shower while she'd been taking hers.

"So it just fucking died on you? Why didn't you use your cell, call for someone?"

Tieran's breath caught in a tight ball in her throat. She closed her eyes against the wave of anxiety that threatened to swallow her whole. After dropping his little pregnancy bombshell, she hadn't been able to think about anything else. Even the vision had eluded her. Until now. She'd told Caelan what she'd seen and now he was hearing it straight from the wolf's mouth, so to speak. Now maybe he'd believe her.

Caelan grunted and took on what could only be described as an annoyed stance. He shifted his weight to one foot and propped his hand on a hip, all the while shaking his head. He was either pissed off again, or agitated. She couldn't tell from where she stood behind him.

"Well, did he call this morning, try to make some contact, or did we lose him altogether?"

He turned, giving her a feeling he'd sensed her standing there. His eyes smoldered under half-hooded lids as he raked her figure from head to toe. Cheeks superheated, she lifted an eyebrow when he finally met her gaze. He waved her into the kitchen, moving toward her at the same time. It was all she could do not to slap him.

"You got damn lucky then, that he still wants to see us. I sure the hell wouldn't," he pronounced, pulling out a chair and lowering her onto it with a tug on her wrist.

What's next, she thought, a bib? How could he be so calm? His brother had just said his car broke down, just like in her vision and Caelan acted as if it were no big deal.

"Perhaps what you saw was no big deal, Tulla. After all, you only saw a man whose car died on the road. Happens all the time. And he didn't kill anyone."

"No, but he thought about a woman," Tieran said, even as doubts flooded her mind.

"You're right," her gramama agreed. *"He thought about one. But at no time did he think about hurting her. She was just there, in his head. You cannot condemn a man for thinking about a*

woman. That's pretty much all they have on the brains. Big and little."

Crapola. Was her gramama right? Was she reading too much into this particular vision? Seeing trouble where there wasn't any?

The stack of pancakes was back—a new one, thank God— passing in front of her face along with a monstrous plate of sausage and bacon. Where the meat came from, she had no idea because she didn't keep them on hand and they had not been in her basket last night. Her stomach rumbled loud enough to make Caelan look over at her in surprise, a smug smile splitting his lips.

Bastard.

She didn't eat breakfast, ever. If she did it was a Mountain Dew and something snacky. And speaking of Mountain Dew... She stood, scraping her chair on the linoleum in an irritating fashion just to irk him, and headed for the refrigerator. Caelan stopped her as she reached for the handle and thrust a tall glass of orange juice in her hand. She stared at him, gagging on the smell alone and wondering where the vile stuff had come from because it was the last thing she'd have in her house.

He smiled, tipped her mouth closed with his forefinger and turned her back to the table, patting her butt to get her marching. The phone never left his ear as he listened to his brother on the other end.

Infuriating bastard!

"*He's only trying to do what's best for you, Tulla.*"

"*He doesn't have any damned idea what's best for me, Gramama. I've only known him for a day and a half, if that. And disgusting orange juice does not constitute what's good for me.*" "Like you need reminding of that fact," she mumbled.

Aggravated, she slammed the juice down on the table, sloshing the liquid on her skin. Gross. She hated OJ. She hated oranges. And tangerines, and tangelos, and hell, she hated orange Jell-O. Who the hell was he to think he could tell her what to drink?

"Do you need any help picking up the 'Stang?" she heard him say and she whipped around to face him.

A 'Stang. Short for Mustang. The word hit her hard and the black car swam into view. A tidbit floated back to her. The man had said something about his Mustang never letting him down before. Then it *had* been Eli. But who was the woman? And more importantly, was she in danger?

"Don't say a word," he mouthed, pointing at her. Caelan covered the mouthpiece. "I know exactly what you're thinking."

She stood there openmouthed as he turned around and continued his conversation.

The cool stickiness on her hand dragged her back. Tieran stomped back over to the fridge, wiping her hand on her jeans to remove the vile substance. She'd get her own drink, thank you very much, and yanked the door open. She could almost hear the angels sing as a heavenly light beamed behind her stash, illuminating them like a halo. Sweet nectar of the gods.

Hmph.

Caelan's hip brushed hers when he slid next to her at the open door. He crossed his arms and gave her an annoyed look. She shrugged and mouthed, "Fuck you." Two could play this game. How many times did she have to tell him she was not a child, damn it.

With a flare of his nostrils, he growled. She heard Eli say, "What the hell was that for? I told you I'm meeting him tonight." Tieran wasted no time removing herself from Caelan's reach and settling back at the table to the twenty pounds of food in front of her. The can's top popped with a hiss. She tilted it to her lips and guzzled a good portion before coming up for air.

Aahh. Blew orange juice out of the water any day.

"It wasn't directed at you," he sighed, still staring at her like he wanted to wring her neck. "You going today?"

Tieran wondered where he was going. Earlier he'd mentioned to her that she'd be meeting some elderly people but God only knew when that was. She could barely remember anything the way they fucked non-stop.

"So I'll meet you there. Why don't you bring Nikki," he said, grinning.

Tieran jumped at the sudden rough bark of laughter.

"I'm just kidding, E." Caelan paused and glanced at her with a twinkle in his eye. "No don't tell them about her. I need to be the one to do it, although they'll probably smell her on you since you were in the house last night."

Smell who? Not me. She glared at Caelan. He returned her look with one filled with intense heat.

Her pussy flooded. Unbelievable. Would this happen every time he looked at her? Tieran averted her gaze to stare at her pancakes. There was no way she could swallow even one bite around the sudden lump in her throat or the quiver in her belly.

The cell phone snapped shut, startling her.

"Do you plan on ingesting those pancakes through osmosis?"

"I told you, I don't eat breakfast," she grumbled in a tone that was whiny even to her own ears.

"And I'm telling you, the protein is good for a human mother carrying a shifter's child."

Jesus. Again with the good-for-her crap. Tieran slumped over and thumped her forehead on the table. "When I want a

143

man's advice on what's good for a woman, I'll let you know." Damn but he could turn her into a brat like no one else. She hated feeling like she no longer had control over her life. This was payback for having walked into the blasted country bar the other night when her instincts had shouted at her to stay out.

"Stop bitching, Tulla, and eat the meal the man prepared for you. I've seen you chow down with the best of 'em, why are you being so prickly now?"

Tieran grimaced. *"Stop bitching, stop bitching."* If she really were pregnant with some werewolf baby, it sure the hell was way worse than PMS. That explanation was the only one she could come up with as a reason for her attitude.

Caelan pulled out the chair next to her, plunking the St. Louis Post Dispatch down on the table in front of him.

"Hey, why aren't you eating, Mr. It's Good For You?" Shit! She was going to glue her lips together. Nothing coming out of her mouth today was normal.

"I already ate," he said, ignoring her barb. "While you were taking a shower."

She groaned and rolled her head on the table so her heated cheek rested on the cool Formica. "Where did you get all this stuff anyway? I know I didn't have any of it."

"What stuff?" he asked, sounding deliberately obtuse.

"Don't play ignorant with me. The sausage, the orange juice." She shivered. The stuff was absolutely horrid.

"Your neighbor." His gaze never strayed from the paper. "I went out to get this and she was out there too. I believe she heard me grumbling about your lack of breakfast supplies. She offered me some from her rather impressive stash."

How busy he'd been, Tieran thought. Cleaning the messes in every corner of her house, fixing faucets, cooking breakfast, borrowing from her neighbors. What had she been doing? Apparently taking the world's longest shower.

"She thinks you're certifiable, by the way." He lifted his cup of coffee to his mouth and sipped.

Tieran jerked upright. "That batty old woman next door thinks I'm crazy? She waters her rocks!"

Caelan smiled and finally turned toward her. "Calm down, Tieran. I'm kidding. I just love it when you get so riled up." He leaned over and brushed his lips against her ear. "Makes me hot," he whispered, sending shivers down her arms.

She snorted. "Everything makes you hot." Picking up her fork, she stabbed the stack of pancakes that were quickly turning to a syrupy mush and took a bite.

Oh, my God, they were good. Buttermilk with a touch of cinnamon, buttery, syrupy. Yum. She cut into them again and eagerly shoveled another forkful into her mouth. She'd never had pancakes this good.

"I beg your pardon."

Tieran could almost envision her grandmother standing with her hands on her hips, and smiled.

"You can beg all you want, these are the bomb."

With uncharacteristic voraciousness, Tieran grabbed a sausage, something else she never much cared for, and dug into it. The spicy flavor exploded on her tongue. Two swallows later, the round disk was gone and she reached for another one.

When she'd devoured half the pancakes and five sausages, she sat back and groaned, one hand on her stomach. What a pig! Then she realized Caelan hadn't made a sound in all the time she was stuffing herself. She glanced at him out of the corner of her eye.

The smug bastard was tilted back, his chair on two legs. His lips were pursed and there was a definite gleam in his eye. "Feel better?"

Tieran brought a finger, sticky with syrup, to her mouth and sucked it between her lips, licking it clean. She ignored the low rumble from Caelan's chest. Served him right.

Suddenly he leaned forward, the chair thumping on the ground, and yanked her hand to his mouth. His tongue swiped over the finger she'd just cleaned. "Don't tempt me, my own."

"Heaven forbid," she quipped.

Caelan trapped her hand under his, resting them on his thigh, then went back to reading his paper.

Something caught her eye as she reached for the remainder of her soda. A picture in the upper left corner of the newsprint, depicting a woman, her hair flapping in the wind as she smiled at the camera. The caption underneath read "Missing".

Her eye twitched. She groaned and dropped her head back on her shoulders. "Not another one, please," she pleaded silently. This was by far the busiest couple of days she'd ever had.

🐐 🐐 🐐

Nicole Raine Taylor was wreaking havoc on his libido. The little minx didn't even know what she did to him. Eli glanced over the rim of his coffee mug to watch her slow progression across the kitchen floor. Ten o'clock in the morning and she was just now getting out of bed. She was wearing her glasses, something he didn't see very often, and her jet-black hair was mussed from a long night smashed into a pillow. Her bare feet slapped on the tile floor and his cock jumped to attention.

Oh, he had it bad when her fucking feet gave him a hard-on.

Eli wished he could have gotten out of coming here, but Derek was driving him back to his 'Stang. He couldn't very well tell the man he didn't want to go to his home first, and since his best friend was doing him a favor, he was stuck. Derek had been leaving some lucky lady's bed this morning when Eli had called. So now here he was, sitting in Nikki-Raine's kitchen, waiting for Derek to take a shower.

Eli skimmed his gaze up the length of her legs to the boxer shorts she wore. Men's boxer shorts. He jerked his head up, snarling before he could stop it.

One of Nikki's eyebrows shot upward. "Did you get a good enough look?"

"Who the hell's trunks you got on there, Nik?" he demanded, ignoring her question. Fuck no, he didn't get a good enough look. He'd have to strip her naked and spread her out on his bed in order to do that.

Her other eyebrow rose to meet the first. She eyeballed what she was wearing. Those damn pink painted toenails lifted when she rocked back on her heels.

"Hmm. I don't remember his name."

Eli saw red. He'd put his fist through the bastard's face for touching her.

Christ. If he didn't get this business done soon and claim her, he would go insane or take her before it was safe. He didn't want to put her in that kind of danger. Things were too tense right now. His brother didn't know Nikki-Raine was Eli's mate yet. He hadn't told anyone. Especially not Derek. And if he didn't want Caelan to know and add one more worry to the pot, he'd have to keep it quiet for a little while longer.

No matter how much the little witch tempted him.

"Geez, calm down, E." Nikki laughed. "I bought them for myself." She brushed by him, rubbing her damn apple scent on his clothes.

Great, now he'd have to smell her all day. And probably suffer this steel rod of an erection until he showered later.

"I am an adult, you know."

"Every damn male for a hundred miles can see you're an adult," he muttered.

She opened the refrigerator and pulled out a bottled water and a yogurt. "Between you and Derek, I'll probably never get a man."

You won't need another man once I get my hands on you, he vowed. She was the one woman in the world who had the ability to tie his dick in knots. All the rest were superfluous to him, no matter how much he tried to look like he was playing the field.

Nikki turned to him, taking a long drag on the water. The smooth column of her throat worked, making him wish it was his cock she was sucking on instead of the fucking piece of plastic. With her head tilted back and her eyes closed, Eli admired her beautiful body. Her small breasts pushed against the stretchy fabric of her tank top, the nipples poking out in twin beaded points.

Imagining how soft her flesh would be and how perfectly they would fill his hands made his mouth water. He reached down and adjusted his swollen cock so it wasn't pressing quite so painfully into the button-fly of his jeans.

Taking one last swallow, Nikki set the bottle on the counter. Her tongue darted out to capture a drop of water on her upper lip and Eli groaned.

"I swear," she continued, "if you guys don't stop scaring off my dates, I'm gonna move to another state."

"Like hell you will," he growled.

She stared at him, a bewildered look on her face. Who could blame her for being confused? He'd never talked to her like this before. In the past he'd always been able to keep up his big-brother act. Now, every time she was around, his wolf came closer to the surface. Closer to revealing itself, when Eli wasn't ready.

"What on earth has gotten into you, E?"

You have, he nearly snapped, but held his tongue. There were too many things to hash out between them, but now wasn't the time.

Derek stomped into the kitchen, breaking the static tension between her and Eli. "All right, let's get this done."

Nikki turned to rummage through a drawer.

"Yo, E," Derek said, snapping his fingers, "You ready?" He grabbed his keys off the counter.

"Yeah," Eli grunted.

"Where are you guys headed?" Nikki asked, sounding as if nothing strange had happened between them. She ripped the top off the yogurt and licked it clean. After dipping her spoon into the pink cream, she stuck it in her mouth, upside down. Her lips closed sensually over the metal. Eli almost came in his jeans picturing those lips taking in the head of his cock.

"E's 'Stang broke down last night. We're going to get it."

Nikki's eyes widened. "You're kiddin' me. Did you forget to screw something back in the last time you worked on it?" She smiled, twisting his gut into a tight knot, and spooned another bite.

"Yeah, and what the hell were you doing way out on 49 anyway?" Derek asked, and snagged an apple out of the basket on the table.

"Highway 49? That's pretty far out there. How'd you get home, E?" Nikki's voice was laced with concern.

Oh, I shifted into a wolf and ran home. Eli glanced over at Derek who grinned from ear to ear. Asshole. Derek knew exactly how Eli had gotten home last night. Apparently he was content to let Eli worm his own way out of Nikki's question.

Eli rubbed a hand over the back of his neck and cleared his throat. "Caelan," he offered as his only response and turned back to Derek. "Can we go now?"

"Yep." Derek laughed, slapped Eli on the back and led the way to the door.

Eli took one last look at Nikki. She'd already settled herself at the table, one leg crossed over the opposite knee, engrossed in the remainder of her breakfast.

She wouldn't even know what hit her when he was ready to make his true self known.

Chapter Eight

Caelan gritted his teeth against the silence filling the car. It had been this way since the moment they'd gotten in his truck a half an hour ago and the ominous mood was starting to grate on him. In fact, she hadn't spoken since eating breakfast this morning. And they still had a good thirty minutes to go before reaching the ranch.

Perhaps they should get this conversation out of the way before he brought Tieran in front of the elders. As his mate, she would attract a ton of commotion, making it difficult for them to speak again until they were on their way home. Unless she was still itching to give him the silent treatment, that is.

"Maybe if I tell you what I know, you'll tell me what you know?" he asked, breaking the silence. Tieran shifted in the seat next to him, releasing a puff of her peachy scent that drove him crazy ninety-nine point nine percent of the day.

She cleared her throat. "I haven't remembered anything new. Besides, I'm sure you don't really want me to tell you what I know."

Out of the corner of his eye, he could see her cheeks were red. Her hands were fisted in her lap so tight the knuckles were white and he wondered what was making her so nervous.

"Why wouldn't I?"

"Because the last time I tried to talk to you about it, you had a cow," she muttered.

For the love of... "Tell me again," he gritted out, "and I promise to keep my cow birthing in check." Then it occurred to him that she didn't want to tell him because she still thought Eli did it.

"Forget it. I'll go first. We've been hunting a man who's killed four of our mates."

"Probably more like six," she grumbled, "and you've already told me this."

"I'm going to tell you again and again until you get it through your thick skull how serious the situation is. What do you mean, six?" His fingers tightened on the steering wheel. She'd seen two more and not told him? Fuck.

Tieran dropped her chin to her chest. She picked at a fingernail and seemed to be having some type of internal debate.

"What do you mean, Tieran?" he asked again, trying hard not to lose his patience.

"That woman, in the paper this morning."

What woman? There'd been women all over the paper. Dozens of them.

"Her picture set off my little warning system. Since lately my visions have all been about your killer, I'm assuming this one is too. He's either already killed her or is going to."

"Jeeesuus Christ." The leather creaked beneath his fingers. "Why didn't you say something this morning?" Damn it. He'd thought he was getting closer to earning her trust. Apparently not. Whatever the little fucker from her past did to her, it destroyed her ability to rely on other people. It made him want to pull his hair out.

"All right," he said, biting back the words he wanted to shout when she remained silent. It wouldn't help. "So she's five. Who's the sixth?"

Tieran sighed deeply beside him. When she spoke he could barely hear her. "The one the man in the car kept thinking about."

Son of a bitch, she was one tenacious woman. He held on to his temper by a hair. "Right, but since we've already established that was Eli, then whatever woman he was thinking about doesn't count."

"We didn't discuss anything. You decided the little black car from my dream was Eli's Mustang, that doesn't mean I'm convinced, and why shouldn't she count?" Tieran snapped, jerking around in her seat to face him.

"Because," he ground out, "I can guarantee if Eli was fantasizing about her, he wasn't thinking about killing her. Unless it involved killing her with pleasure."

"What's that supposed to mean?"

"My brother likes women, Tieran. Too much to ever hurt one. He's the ultimate playboy. Hell, he tried to pick you up at the bar the other night."

"And what does that have to do with the price of beans in China? The fact is I had a vision about him thinking of a woman and so far everything I've seen has been about your killer. Tell me what you would think if you were in my shoes?"

The muscles in his jaw bunched. "God help me, you are the most stubborn... I knew there was a reason I didn't want a mate right now." He laughed. He couldn't help it. The whole situation was becoming one big clusterfuck and if he didn't convince her otherwise, she'd end up having his twin turned in for the murders.

"Do you know the elders in my pack have been pushing me to find my mate? But I said, 'no, not until we find the shifter responsible for this and bring him to justice.'" He pounded on the steering wheel. "It isn't safe for me to have a mate right now," he growled, his face heating in rising agitation.

"So what did I do?" he continued. "I went out with my brother to this bar. And lo and behold he spots a woman he wants to take to bed for the night. Surprise, surprise." He leaned closer to her and swung his gaze back and forth between her and the road.

"I had to physically stop my brother from going after a woman he wanted to fuck all because I decided to take a whiff of the female who'd given him a hard-on."

Tieran bit her lip and edged away from him. He continued to crowd her, keeping one hand on the wheel and one eye on the road. Her shoulders pressed up against the door and her eyes were wide.

"Do you know why I had to stop him, Tieran?"

She started to shake her head. "I have no idea why men behave like Neanderthals."

He ignored her remark. "Because I knew from the second I'd seen—no smelled—you, what you were to me. That's why I didn't let Eli come after you. To do so would have been paramount to giving my wife to another man for the night. It didn't matter that we hadn't met, or that you had no idea about being a mate-in-waiting for a healthy, red-blooded, shape-shifting Prime."

He watched her eyes grow even rounder and after sucking in a quick breath she nodded slowly.

"Dammit." He swung the truck off the road and slammed on the brakes, throwing the gear into park before the truck even settled. Tieran shrieked and lifted her hands to catch herself on the dash. Her seat belt locked, holding her in place. "I'm sorry," he said immediately, thinking he might have harmed her or the baby. She flung him off when he tried to touch her.

"He was honing in on the one woman destined to be mine, Tieran. Mine. Not his. *Mine*, and fate doesn't give a rat's ass that this is absolutely the most piss-poor time for me to finally find you." He was so close to her face now she had to feel his breath puff out on her lips with each word. His voice grew softer, calmer, and he begged her to understand with his eyes.

He cradled her face in his hands, forcing her to look at him. Christ, he just kept making this worse and worse. Even he could see that his words had cut her deep to the bone.

She hadn't asked for this any more than he had. In fact, if anyone should feel put out here, it was her. He'd known about taking a mate his entire life, she'd only known since yesterday. So fuck him for thinking that this was a piss-poor time to *finally* find her. If he felt so damned strongly about not wanting her, he should have stayed away.

Then maybe she wouldn't be having goddamn visions about men and wolves killing women. More importantly, she wouldn't be having these doubts in her mind about Eli and the fact he shared a few strange characteristics with both the wolf and the man from the car. The eyes of all three were the same, the scars, the hands. Jesus, she must be losing her mind to be connecting the smallest things the way she was.

When she realized he was still practically on top of her, his cheek nuzzling hers like he hadn't said that he didn't want her, she shoved hard at Caelan's chest with both hands, drawing on the element of surprise to push him away. "You know, Caelan, what you just said proves how shitty the whole idea of matedom really is. Excuse the hell out of me for not being a werewolf and knowing the laws of...wolvery." She shot him a look, leaving him in stunned silence and staring at her like he was wondering what had happened to her. Good. Maybe it was time for him to see things from her vantage point.

"It's not my fault that any of this is happening. In fact, it's yours, because I was going along just fine before you. Now I'm having visions left and right, and puking, and being accused of being pregnant, and...and forced to eat pancakes, when I don't want any goddamn pancakes," she yelled.

Several heated moments passed while they studied each other. Caelan's body seemed to deflate. He was the first to break the silence between them. "Don't get me wrong, now that you're here, I wouldn't change having you for anything in the world," he placated.

Damn. She wanted to stay mad at him, not forgive him.

He leaned over again, tugging at his seatbelt until it was as loose as it could be, and nuzzled her cheek with his. His deep breath tickled her ear and she breathed in his familiar scent. Whimpering, she sagged into him. The man could control her like no other. Even pissed at him, he made her feel safe, comforted. It wasn't an altogether good feeling to have no control where he was concerned.

"I love you." He wrapped his hands around her face and kissed her eyelids and the tip of her nose. "No matter how weird that sounds, it's the truth. If something happened to you, it would kill me." Caelan moved to her lips, tasting them and begging her to open for him.

When she complied, melting into his arms even further, he dipped his tongue inside her heated mouth and tangled it with hers.

Stop. They had to stop or they'd be fucking right here on the edge of the highway. She groaned and pulled away from where she really wanted to be and put herself at arm's length, or at least as far away as she could get within the confines of the truck. Her breath came in shallow pants and she knew her eyes must be glazed over.

He smiled at her. He knew exactly what he'd done to her.

"If we take this any further it might lead to our arrest."

At least she wasn't the only one thinking along those lines.

Touching her fingers to her swollen lips, Tieran cleared her throat and twisted forward in her seat. Damn but the man could kiss. Almost as well as he could compel her to talk about things she didn't normally. She hadn't realized before now what he was facing by having her as a mate. Of course, she hadn't truly come to terms with being a mate yet herself. Or having a baby.

She rested her hand on her flat belly. There couldn't be one there. Could there? A tiny spark of something flared to life inside her. What was it though? Hope, want, need? When was the last time she'd felt this way? Too long ago, for sure.

Caelan gunned the truck onto the highway while her thoughts continued to race. If everything he'd said was true, then despite his vow of love, she was an inconvenience to him right now. Should she leave him to whatever it was he needed to do? Maybe if she weren't in the way, he'd be free to catch the killer. She didn't want to be a detriment to him.

Her chest hurt with the thought of not being close to him.

"So, you gonna talk, or do I have to torture it out of you?"

Tieran smiled at Caelan's attempt to lighten the mood. She had to give him more credit than the Florida Police. So far he hadn't gone running around laughing at the mere mention of her abilities. He'd listened.

Yes, he'd jumped down her throat about Eli, but he still wanted to know more. The thought made her feel used. Doubts flooded her mind. Was Caelan claiming all this mate stuff just to use her abilities? Had he wanted to make her think she was pregnant just so she would stay with him?

Every uncertainty she felt with Peter came swarming to the forefront. No way would she go through that again.

"If there were any other way, I wouldn't make you go through it again, baby. I can see what it takes out of you."

Oh, good Lord! She'd said that out loud?

"Yes, my dear, I believe you did. You should feel ashamed of yourself for even thinking Caelan could be so callous."

Damn it, her gramama was right. Caelan hadn't known she was clairvoyant when he met her or, if what he told her was true, even before they made love in her kitchen. She sighed.

"Can you describe the wolf to me?"

Of course I can, she wanted to scream. Tieran swallowed back the fear and frustration choking her. Somehow she had to find a way to tell him what he wanted to know without adding her own opinion about who she thought the killer was.

"Which one," she grumbled.

"Either one." He sounded so harsh it was all she could do not to cringe.

"Doesn't matter. They were the same."

"Okay," he said clearly exasperated with her. "What did it look like?"

She sighed. "It was big and hairy and looked just like you did in *your* wolf get-up."

His fingers were so tight on the leather-wrapped steering wheel they made a creaky noise. She saw how frustrated he was by her less-than-forthcoming attitude.

"Anything else? Maybe eye color, fur color, size? Anything might help whether you think so or not."

If only he knew what she thought. Somehow Tieran didn't think "Have Eli change and I'll be able to tell you exactly what it looked like, scar and all" would win her any Brownie points. Besides, then they would have to go over the damn scar again. Maybe she'd get away with leaving that part out.

"Don't keep things from him, Tulla. Didn't we just have this conversation?"

"All right already." She cleared her throat. "It was dark brown. I can't tell you the exact shade because it was night and the only light out there was the full moon."

"Okay. That's a start. Compared to me—darker, lighter?"

Jesus, the dog with the bone was back and tonight's bone was pulling Tieran's teeth until she spit out the truth and nothing but the truth. Didn't he understand how hard this was for her?

Groaning, she rubbed both hands over her face. "The same," she mumbled into her palms.

"What?"

She felt him lean over and half-expected to find his hand cupping his ear when she looked up.

"I said," she huffed, "he looked like you. Same color eyes, same color hair, same pointy white teeth."

"My pointy white teeth are going to sink into your soft white ass later if you don't watch it, my own."

Tieran's butt cheeks clinched. Whether in anticipation or wariness, she didn't know, but the sudden image of his mouth descending on her upturned ass had her shivering. Her pussy creamed, making her squirm with delicious feelings in her seat.

Because they hadn't had enough sex in the last twenty-four hours.

"Look," she said, shaking her head to get it back on track. "Why can't you just go to your...elderly people, and tell them you're looking for a wolf with a scar on its shoulder?"

His silence nettled, making the air in the truck seem thick.

"I can't do that." A flash of pain swept across the normally happy-go-lucky features of his face.

Her stomach bottomed out. Why couldn't he? She tread carefully, searching for the right words. "So, you do think there's a possibility Eli is—"

"No, God damn it! Jesus," he spat.

His jaw clenched so tight, she wondered if he might break a tooth.

"I can't because if I made all the shifters take their shirts off and the real killer isn't there, then yes, Eli would be fingered. I won't do that to my brother."

Tieran dropped her chin to her chest. His absolute, one-hundred-percent faith in his twin was amazing. She could only hope things turned out the way he wanted them to.

🐺 🐺 🐺

Caelan groaned at the number of cars littering his driveway. After the conversation they'd just had, he wasn't prepared to face the elders. He certainly wasn't prepared to share her information about the scar. Somehow he'd have to do some discreet searching on his own.

Despite his overwhelming sense of relief at being back on his home turf, he found himself wanting to go back to Tieran's if for nothing else than to hide her away. Another round of fucking wouldn't hurt his feelings either. Today would be a tough test for any Prime's mate. Being a human and pregnant wouldn't help matters.

"This is where you live?" Tieran asked.

The awe lacing her voice filled his heart with pride. He and Eli had planned every bit of this house to their exact tastes. Starting with remodeling the original ranch-style structure given to them by their parents when they'd decided to move deeper into the woods.

"Do you like it?"

"It's beautiful. What's not to like?"

He shrugged. "Eli and I do."

"Eli?" she croaked.

Caelan dropped his chin to his chest. It would be damn hard for them to live here with her in constant suspicion of Eli. And live here they would. As soon as he could get her here. After last-night's midnight raid of the grocery store, now wouldn't be soon enough.

"Eli lives on that side." He gestured to the right wing of the house. "Has his own set of rooms, bathroom, kitchen, everything. My side is over there. Kind of like a duplex although we do share some centrally located rooms. The living room, a formal dining room, a game room and our office, so we do see clients here as well." Caelan jumped out of the car, noticing that Tieran hadn't moved to unbuckle.

Looked like the whole damn pack had shown up today, he thought, rounding the car to retrieve Tieran. His dad must have made some kind of announcement. He'd have to thank Eli for that later since Caelan hadn't spoken to his father yet.

He opened the passenger door. "Come on, my own, let's get this over with."

"Get what over with, exactly?"

He had to laugh. She looked like she was about to face a firing squad. "The elders. They have to formally accept you as the Prime's, *my*, mate. Has something to do with tradition."

She jerked her gaze to him, indignant as all get-out. If she were standing, he would expect her hands to go straight to her hips.

"And if they don't? It's a little late don't you think? You've already made me eat meat!" she yelled, as if her eating meat were the vilest thing he could do to her.

Damn but she was cute when she was mad.

"Don't worry," he soothed and leaned in to kiss her tightly pressed lips. "They'll love you." He licked along the sealed seam of her mouth until she melted into him and opened to accept his tongue. He slid home, rubbing against her velvet softness and tasting her until he'd had his fill.

Her hands came up to rest at his shoulders, his went to her waist, one of them working to release the buckle. Tieran moaned and shifted closer, angling her head to allow him better access to the recesses of her mouth. His cock demanded to receive some similar action.

Caelan lifted the hem of her shirt and dove beneath it to touch her warm skin. She flinched and squeaked against his lips when he tickled a sensitive spot. He migrated to the soft mound of her breast, irritated by the material covering it. Releasing the front catch, he freed the objects of his quest and palmed one. With his thumb and forefinger, he pinched the hardening nipple and rolled it.

Tieran moaned and tried to get closer, her eagerness overtaking any unease she might have had about meeting his people. Which is exactly what he was shooting for.

"Caelan, quit pawing your woman and get in here."

The deep voice boomed behind them and Tieran screeched, practically diving under the dash like she'd been caught naked. Caelan barked out in laughter.

"Dad," he said over his shoulder, shielding his red-faced mate while she tried to reconnect her bra. "Didn't know you'd ask the whole pack out today."

"With what's been goin' on, thought everyone ought to be here, get a good look at her so's they know who to protect."

He smiled at Tieran's upturned, still flaming red face. "You don't think I can handle her on my own?"

His father snorted. "Son, ain't no man alive can handle a woman on his own. She dressed yet?"

"Jesus, Caelan. What does he think I am, a prize piece of horseflesh? Is he going to check my teeth too?" she demanded. Finally done fumbling beneath her shirt, she sat up and swallowed. She finger combed her hair.

Caelan noticed the quick pulse at the base of her throat, which told him he had her totally rattled.

"I want you to remember my kiss whenever you feel nervous in there." He grabbed her hand and helped her down.

"Nervous? I'm not nervous. Why would I be nervous? It's just your family. I can be civil when the moment calls for it. As long as your family can keep their hands off me and their noses to themselves, I'll be fine. It's okay. I don't like big groups of people, but it's all good. I can—"

"Tieran!" He lifted her chin with the crook of his forefinger. "Take a breath, honey. Breathe," he warned again when she didn't do so quickly enough.

She inhaled slowly, her gaze meeting his and holding as if she were searching for a lifeline.

He cursed himself for not realizing how hard being around a group of people would be for her. If a simple touch could wind up with her having a vision, she was in for a world of hurt with his touchy-feely parents. He'd have to lay down the law in there. If it meant acting like an overprotective oaf in order to keep her secret, then he'd do it.

Especially with a traitor in their midst. Revealing Tieran's abilities would be like signing her death warrant.

She could slap him for putting her in this position. There must be twenty cars parked here. When Caelan had said he wanted her to meet some elderly people, she'd thought he was talking about his grandparents. Unless he had ten sets of them, an elder meant something totally different to him than it did to her.

The big man who'd spoken to them from the porch still stood there, grinning like a fool. The resemblance between father and sons was remarkable. Besides the few extra pounds on the older Graham, they were pretty much identical.

She took a deep breath. This was so not going to be a good time.

"Hello, there. 'Bout time my son brought you home to meet us."

Talk about getting straight to the heart of the matter.

"I've only known your son for a day. I hardly think he could have brought me any sooner." Somehow she managed to keep her hiss from sounding like a hiss. Man she was crabby. The man was only trying to be nice to her.

A deep belly laugh erupted from his mouth, startling her.

"Damn fine woman you found yourself, Son. The name's Liam."

Before she could blink, Tieran found herself engulfed in Liam's arms, squeezed in a tight bear hug she was neither prepared for nor used too.

"Put her down," Caelan growled.

Tieran was immediately released and steadied by both men.

"You don't have to be so rude, Caelan." *Thank you for intervening.* Liam's face was one of shocked curiosity. Caelan wrapped an arm around her waist, immediately putting her more at ease. She fought the temptation to rub her arms.

"This goes no further than us, Dad." Caelan ushered the three of them to the corner of the porch.

He wouldn't.

"Tieran is psychic. She can see things."

Oh. My. God. He would. He did. Her jaw dropped practically to the floor. She hadn't been thrown for this much of a loop since Florida. Not even Peter had said anything to anybody else. Of course, having a weird girlfriend would have been detrimental to his social status.

"She's seen our killer."

Shut up, shut up. Mortified, she backed away from the two men whispering so closely together. The urge to cover her ears was overwhelming.

"Sometimes even the smallest touch can trigger a vision."

She watched his dad's gaze flick to her around Caelan's shoulder.

"Son, I think—"

"I'm serious, Dad. I'm gonna need your help in there."

Tieran kept backing up, shaking her head against what Caelan was doing. Her head spun and her knees wobbled.

"That's all good—"

"It's real, Dad. And I'll do whatever I have to do to protect her. If that means leaving before we go in there, we will."

"If you interrupt me one more time, boy, I'm gonna have to show you what made me a good Prime."

Tieran stopped, one foot on the porch, one on the step below it, and swallowed. Caelan stood straight up. Even from the distance, she could see his ears were bright red.

"I don't think your mate is all too pleased with what you're telling me."

"And I don't care—" He spun around as if he'd just realized she wasn't with them anymore. "What are you doing over there?" He marched toward her, an annoyed look on his face.

"Tieran, my dear," Liam spoke up and headed over also, "let's go meet Caelan's mother. Judith will love you."

He took her arm and led her to the front door from which she was eagerly trying to escape. No way could she go in there. Not now. Not when his father knew her secret and could easily bring the world crashing down around her again. She'd gotten her life back since Florida, it wasn't fair to have it ripped away a second time. She pulled away only to have her hand gently but tightly held in the crook of his elbow and patted with tender sympathy.

Liam paused and turned to her. "It wouldn't faze me a bit if you could balance an elephant on your head, dear. Look what we can do. No one here will ostracize you for being different. My big oaf of a son shouldn't have told me the way he did, but it's better this way." The corners of his mouth turned up in a half-smile. "Relax, child. At least now I know what I'll be up against in there. A mob of elders just waiting to touch the Prime's mate." He chuckled. "And I get to be the one to swat 'em away." He leaned closer and whispered in her ear. "Your secret's safe with me."

What could she say to that? She nodded. It would be safe with him. With both of them. How she came to that decision, she didn't know, but Liam was right. She would need all the help she could get with all those people inside. Her eyes tingled with unshed tears. First Caelan and now his father. Two men who made her feel more comfortable in her own skin for the first time since her gramama left her.

"Oh, Tulla, baby, I never left you."

"No, not my heart. It's your shoulder I miss the most."

"Caelan's shoulders seem more than capable of handling whatever it is you need them for."

"I know they are," she admitted. The man might not be able to see the hand in front of his face, or in this case, the killer, but he would be there to support her, no matter what. That much was apparent to her now.

"Perhaps you should apologize to your mate," Liam growled over his shoulder, returning her attention to the two men standing sentry over her.

Tieran twisted to see Caelan on her left. He stood there, looking sheepish and repentant like a toddler who'd been caught misbehaving. His face was so forlorn she couldn't help but laugh.

He cleared his throat. "I'm sorry, my own." He stood a little taller.

She found it endearing. Perhaps this was a small deflation to his ego to admit he had done something wrong.

"No. I'm not," he said, changing his mind and his attitude in the blink of an eye. "You need the protection in there and there isn't anyone I would trust more than Eli or my father. I can't be with you every second, I want to know there's someone here to look out for you."

167

"And I'm a big girl." Damn but the man pushed her buttons.

"Right," he agreed. "A big *human* girl who has no idea what a pack of shape-shifters can be like."

He had her there. Her heart thumped when Liam reached out and twisted the doorknob in slow motion.

"Now there's an apology," Liam said from the corner of his mouth. "You need to work on tact, Son."

The door opened and Tieran felt like she was entering another world. Would they all be in their wolf suits? Was that a bark she heard? Suddenly she wanted to run again, but her feet were glued to the floorboards. Caelan gave a little shove on the small of her back and ushered her into his home.

The huge entryway was filled with men and women. Every single one of them stopped what they were doing and turned to the door in anticipation. Her breath hitched and her cheeks superheated in embarrassment. They were all looking at her. An agoraphobic's nightmare to say the least.

Caelan stepped around her and held her hand to his chest. His father stayed to her right, still patting her hand in the same soothing rhythm. The silence was deafening. There was nothing like being the center of attention.

At first no one moved. They just stared in awe at her as if she were the one who was part dog. Wolf, she amended quickly. To her right, an older man lifted his nose and sniffed the air. Once, twice, three times. He cocked his head and grinned.

"She is with child!"

As one, the group lifted their noses and gave a collective sniff. Abruptly, the foyer erupted with cheers and claps and God, was that a howl? Tieran tried to step behind Caelan's broad back and hide. He wouldn't let her, the cad. Instead, he stood there smiling like a loon. They were all psycho. She hadn't decided if the so-called baby was real or not, yet the entire crowd of people had decided it was based on one man's sniff.

"My mate," Caelan declared, holding their joined hands high.

God, could this get any worse?

Yes, it could. The crowd stepped forward as a pack. Literally. With a squeak, Tieran ducked behind Caelan again, this time jerking her hand from his hold and cowering from the crush of people. What a time to bring out the cowardice. They must think she was some piece of work. Liam pushed forward and held a hand up.

"As I know you've all surmised, your Prime's mate is human, and not used to our ways."

That was a huge understatement if there ever was one. Tieran noticed one woman separate herself from the crowd. She smiled and held both arms out.

"Perhaps if we refrain from all the touchy-feely, it might make Tieran more comfortable."

Tieran stood up straighter, tears threatening behind her eyelids at Liam's verbal support. Unbelievably they all took a step backward. Everyone except the woman.

"My father has an amazing talent for making people listen." Caelan chuckled.

"Hmm. It didn't seem to work with you outside on the porch."

His grin stretched across his profile. "That's because he doesn't scare me with his former Prime persona the way he does all of them."

"No, it means they have more respect for him than you do."

"Either way," he said with a full-out laugh now. He shrugged. "Mother."

The suave woman stopped before them. She had dropped her arms at Liam's announcement and Tieran found she instantly liked Caelan's mother. By all rights, the woman could have touched her any way she liked. Whether it meant a welcome-to-the-family hug or a you're-not-good-enough-for-my-son slap to the face.

Looking at the petite woman, Tieran wondered how she had given birth to the more than six-foot giants her sons now were. Judith, she remembered Liam calling her, winked at her.

"I'll save my *touchy-feely* for later." She turned and addressed Caelan. "She is beautiful, Son. Many congratulations to you too, Tieran. If you have any questions about what's happening, you can come to me. I know what you're going through."

She turned again and, reaching up, slapped Caelan on the back of his head. "You and I will talk later on how crudely you just introduced your mate. Shame on you."

Tieran laughed at the contrite look on Caelan's face. Apparently it wasn't only his father who had the ability to make his ears go red.

"Caelan, we must meet."

Tieran started at the voice spoken close to her ear. She hadn't even known the man was there. On closer inspection, it was the man who'd originally made the announcement she was pregnant. Must have made him feel important somehow. He was beaming at her like he'd won a million dollars.

Beside her, Caelan shifted his weight and sighed so heavily, she stumbled. He caught her with a quick jerk on the hand he still held, bringing her back to his side.

"Perhaps my mother would like to show you around. If I don't get this meeting out of the way, they'll hound me all afternoon."

He was going to leave her here alone? Cripes. Everyone was still looking at her. And then they weren't. Tieran did a double take. Caelan strode away with the elder, she guessed, and his mother laughed.

"It doesn't take them long to corral the Prime. You'll get used to it, my dear."

Oh God. She sounded just like her gramama. Warm and inviting. Like someone Tieran could snuggle up next to and tell her innermost secrets, just as she did with Gramama.

"I'm just going to go over there and get us some drinks before we start the tour, dear. Wait here?"

Tieran nodded without really thinking about what she was agreeing to. Her mind was a complete whirlwind. At least her heart was settling into a more agreeable pattern. Talk about being put on the spot.

She tensed. Eli was heading her way, weaving his way through the crowd, a determined smirk on his face. Her heart hammered again and sweat broke out on her upper lip. She'd been hoping to avoid him today if for nothing else than to not have to lie to his or Caelan's face.

She was not a good liar.

"You never were, Tulla, and you shouldn't be lying now. Bring it up, see what happens."

"Why don't you bring it up?"

Tieran cringed at her shortness. It wasn't her gramama's fault she was in this predicament. Well, wait a minute, yes it was her fault. She'd arranged the meeting between the two werewolves and Tieran. The older gentleman who'd carted Caelan off a minute ago waylaid Eli on his way across the room.

Time to make a getaway. She slunk down the wall to the opposite corner and was almost at the door when a nearly gentle hand clamped down on her forearm.

"Don't you know by now, we can smell you no matter where you hide?"

"I'm not hiding," she said, peeved, and twisted her arm out of his grip. The thunder of her heart would give her away no doubt. She felt the color drain from her cheeks.

Eli grinned at her obvious flustered look. "Caelan said you might try to run." He crossed his arms over his chest exactly like Caelan did when he was annoyed with her. "I never figured you for a coward."

"I'm not a coward," she said bringing her chin up and facing him head-on. Not that you could tell that by the way she'd hid behind Caelan's back earlier. "I was...looking for your mother. She's supposed to show me around."

He smiled. "Right. I believe my father intercepted her. Perhaps I could take you."

Her breath slammed into her throat, nearly choking her. *Not on your life.*

"What woman has the black hair and green eyes?" she blurted and cringed, mortified that had actually come out of her mouth.

Eli's eyes widened, then narrowed sharply. "What do you know about her?" he hissed softly, swinging his gaze from side to side. Who, or what, was he looking for?

"Did you see her? Tell me," he commanded when she didn't speak quickly enough. He shook her, making her teeth rattle. If she'd been a little girl, the look on his face might have been enough to make her pee in her pants. She was pretty sure she might anyway.

His lips flattened into a thin line and he stared at her arm where his fingers dug into her skin.

"Fuck." Eli slowly released her, caressing the red flesh as he did so. "I'm sorry, Tieran. I didn't mean to—"

"It's good, Eli." Not. It was downright spooky. Not to mention it made him look even guiltier than hell in her mind. "I'm just going to go out and get some fresh air." *And maybe run a few miles.*

She backed away from him and searched the crowd. One of his parents had to be out there somewhere. She felt safe with them. Damned if she knew why though. Caelan. He stood with two other men, gesturing to an open door on the opposite side of the room. If she could get his attention...

Tieran darted across the room, mindful to politely dodge the well-wishers every few feet or so. She thought she even smiled to several of them.

When she glanced back, Eli was gone. No, there he was, walking to the front door. His features were a mixture of emotion. Anger? She couldn't tell from this distance. He stopped at the doorway and faced her.

Gasping, she tapped Caelan on the arm. "I'm going to go out..." and what? What exactly was she going to go out and do? She didn't even know where she was. Then she remembered what she'd seen driving up. "...to look at the horses." She stumbled over the words in her rush to get away.

Caelan glanced over her shoulder and nodded. By the time she turned around no one was there. "Be careful, my own. The ground is pretty rough out there."

"Yes, uh-huh. Careful. Gotcha." Tieran backpedaled. Another one of his I'm-just-doing-what's-good-for-you moments she guessed. Whatever. She needed the space. Suddenly the confinement and noise of the entryway was too claustrophobic.

Besides, she needed time to assimilate what had happened with Eli.

If anyone thought she was running, so be it. Hell, they would be right.

Chapter Nine

Tieran jerked with a gasp at the fingers touching her arm from behind and her eye made a barely conceivable twitch. Odd. Normally it went crazy.

She shivered in the heat, a tingly feeling swarming her where his fingers made contact.

Whoever he was, the man's shields were thicker than the CDC's highest-level containment facilities. Not a scrap of emotion out of him. Because she didn't want to offend someone who Caelan might regard with respect, she slowly pulled out of his loose grasp. Her heart rate returned to normal as she turned to face him.

He didn't look familiar to her, but then there'd been a lot of people in the house. She would have remembered him though. Tall and dark-headed, he was very similar to Caelan and Eli. If she hadn't known there was just the two of them, she might have thought this man was another brother.

"Sorry." He chuckled insincerely. "You looked a little lost. I wondered if, perhaps, I might escort you back."

Tieran found the sophistication in his voice fake and wondered why he felt the need to hide his true personality. A warning trickled down her spine. She glanced back at the house. Fifteen minutes ago—God had it only been that short a time?—she'd wandered out here to try and escape the mob inside.

No, that wasn't entirely true. She *had* hated being looked at like a bug under the microscope by the multitude of bodies in the house, but mostly she'd come to get away from Eli. No way did she want another run-in with him.

There. She said it. She'd come out here to escape Eli so she wouldn't have to explain to him and Caelan why she just couldn't be around him.

Besides, it was peaceful out here, or had been until now, and she thoroughly enjoyed the view of the horses grazing in the paddock.

And now she knew what they felt like being watched the way she was watching them. The sudden interruption of her newfound solitude rankled.

"There's nothing between the house and here." She raised an eyebrow to punctuate her next statement. "How could I possibly be lost?"

She swore the man growled, but then a grin split his lips. "Well then I guess when I say lost, I mean lost in thought, not in actual direction."

Now that was about as clever and cool a comeback as you could get. Tieran didn't believe him for a minute. His touch might not have given anything away but there was definitely something off about him.

He reminded her of the tow-truck driver who'd spit tobacco on her car. Not in looks, because this man was classy, or nicely dressed anyway. The classiness came across forced. No, it was the attitude. She got the impression he felt he was better than everybody else and therefore also knew what was best for her so there was no need to let her make a decision. Of course, Caelan had been doing the same thing since meeting her, but she liked him. Okay, more than liked. She admitted it freely.

The man leaned in, invading her personal space and causing her to take a step back when she wanted to stand him down. He sniffed the air around her.

"Do you mind?" she asked, swatting toward his nose like he was one of the pesky flies the horses were constantly flicking with their tails.

"You've already conceived the Prime's whelp," he condemned, obviously trying to hide his complete disdain for her.

"I prefer to think of it as a baby, thank you," she sneered, surprising herself with the admission. At what point had she decided there really was one?

Now, when this disgusting man called her child a whelp.

The word itself made her cringe and the idea of him defiling what should be beautiful made her want to slap the smarmy look off his face. She'd been right to think she hadn't seen him inside. No one there could have missed the elder's announcement that she was with child.

His cheeks flushed and his eyes flashed. Looking down, she saw his hands fisting and unfisting. Apparently she'd ticked him off. Good, because he sure the hell was doing a good job of pissing her off. His hands opened one last time and relaxed while she stared at them. The renewed casual air drew her gaze back to his face.

"Of course," he said, smiling. His whole demeanor shifted one hundred and eighty degrees. "Humans do call them babies. Forgive me, please."

Tieran breathed a little easier. His apology sounded sincere and he *had* only asked to escort her to the house. Maybe she'd imagined how much of a jerk he was?

"No, I don't think you did, Tulla. Don't let your guard down yet."

"I haven't even introduced myself, have I? The Prime would kill me for being so rude."

She snorted softly. Killing him would be a wee bit of an exaggeration.

"Michael Hayward," he said, offering his hand. *"Detective Michael Hayward."*

Tieran couldn't bring herself to shake the proffered hand. She hadn't gotten anything from his first touch, but he seemed slimy somehow. Knowing he was a cop made him that much slimier. She half-expected him to pull out a set of handcuffs and charge her with being a human. Something she was sure he found despicable. Strange when he stood before her now as a human himself. Why the attitude about humans when you played at being one most of the day?

Most of their lives, actually. Caelan had only shifted one time since she'd met him. She didn't get the feeling he did it very often either.

She was glad when Caelan's voice gave her the distraction she needed.

"Tieran." Caelan stepped between her and the detective. He took her chin in his own, a furious wave of energy radiating off him. "I wondered where you'd gotten off too, my own." Despite his anger, his lips were soft against hers.

Something was wrong. Caelan knew exactly where she was. She bit her lip to keep from blurting that out.

She coughed. "Just admiring the horses, my dumpling," she murmured, playing along. His smile confirmed her suspicions.

"I was asking your mate if she would like an escort back to the house, Prime. With things the way they are right now, I wouldn't think you'd want her to be alone."

Oh, he was smooth, but why did he keep referring to Caelan as the Prime? She hadn't heard anyone else call him that today. Not even the elders. She could imagine him preening like a peacock behind Caelan who blocked her sight of him. Her initial dislike of him grew despite the redemption he'd made a few seconds ago with his apology.

Tieran's eyes widened at the barely perceptible snarl emanating from Caelan. He turned and acknowledged the detective for the first time.

"She's never been alone." Caelan pointed to a small stand of trees about fifty feet from them. "Eli's been watching her and so have I." Eli waved and Tieran gasped. She hadn't known he was there.

"How is the search going for the killer, Michael?" Caelan continued, ignoring the man's stunned look.

His face blanched then reddened. In anger?

He was quick to recover. "She knows then?"

"Of course," Caelan answered, grabbing her hand and holding it at the small of his back. "I don't keep things from my mate. Neither does she from me." His fingers tightened on hers. "Do we, my own?"

🐈 🐈 🐈

Night had fallen by the time everyone left the ranch. Tieran was tucked away doing kitchen duties with his mother. Caelan smiled. He'd bet money she wouldn't do it at her own house. At least, not until the dishes were piled high enough to fill the sink.

"What's the smile for, Bro?"

"Just picturing Tieran doing the housewife thing." Caelan stood up from his chair on the porch and listened to the cicadas calling each other. A wolf howled in the distance. Jacob Christoff by the sound of it. Another half-blood who lived just a few miles down the road.

Today had been a total bust. No one had seemed to spark anything in Tieran's mind. Damn it. He'd been counting on something, no matter how small.

"Michael seemed his usual condescending bastard self today. What the hell has crawled up his ass anyway?"

Caelan shrugged. "Wouldn't you be if you couldn't catch a killer on either of your own turfs? As a shifter or as a human cop?"

"I guess." Eli swiped a hand across the back of his neck. A gesture Caelan noticed more often when his twin was wound up about something.

Treading carefully, he asked, "You got somethin' you want to talk about?"

"No."

"How 'bout some pool later tonight." Shooting pool was a sure-fire way to open his brother up.

"Nah, I got something I gotta do." Eli pushed away from the railing where he'd settled his hips moments ago. "Besides, I rescheduled that meeting with Dane Christian again tonight."

"Any more indication what he wants?"

Eli shook his head. "Not really. Says he has a job I'd be perfect for."

Caelan raised a brow. "How does he know you'll be perfect for it? I thought you said a friend recommended you."

"Don't know, that's why I'm meeting him," Eli growled as if perturbed by the direction of their conversation.

Caelan cursed silently. What the hell was wrong with his twin? They'd never kept anything from each other. Maybe if he changed the subject back to a more familiar turf. Like their hunt. Whatever was eating him would all come out sooner or later. "You know anybody who's got a scar like yours, E?"

Eli's head snapped to Caelan. "No. What the fuck is this all about, Cael? First your girlfriend and now you? Why you all of a sudden so interested in a scar that's been there for years?"

Caelan held his hands up. "Back off, E. Tieran said the wolf had a scar and seeing yours the other night had her wanting me to take everyone's shirt off today."

"She thinks *I* did this?" Eli laughed incredulously. "That's just great. Accused by the Prime's new mate of murder. As if I didn't have enough to think about."

"What *are* you thinking about?" he asked, ignoring the dig on Tieran. "You've been preoccupied for several weeks, E. What the fuck's going on?"

"Nothing. You're just not the only one with problems." Again with the neck rub. "I gotta get going. I'll call tomorrow with the details."

Before Caelan could respond, Eli was gone. A chill raced up his spine. Why had his brother gotten so defensive over the scar issue? Christ, maybe... No! No. Absolutely not, no way in a hundred million years.

A lightning bolt lit up the sky, the charge sending another set of wicked sensations skittering across his nerves. A low rumble of thunder followed quickly thereafter. He hadn't known it was going to storm tonight. When a second bolt fanned out

181

through ominous-looking clouds, Caelan decided he didn't want to drive the hour back to Tieran's house in a storm.

His mother and Tieran were laughing about something when he entered the kitchen through the back door.

"Ladies."

Judith shrieked, Tieran gasped and both swung around to face him. Red streaked Tieran's face and her eyes were watering as she tried to contain her laughter. Her cheeks puffed out until finally she spit it out.

Caelan cocked an eyebrow.

"Son," his mother said somewhat short of breath. "Hoo. Sorry."

Yeah. He could tell how sorry she was when she swiped a hand over her own watery eyes and sniffed.

"We were just talking about...things." She turned to Tieran and both of them burst out laughing again.

"Oh yeah?" He straddled one of the stools lined up at the island. "Like what?"

Tieran returned her attention to the sink. "Your mom was telling me about when you were born and how she wondered for the entire nine months whether or not she would give birth to a dog."

"Wolf," he muttered.

"That too." She exchanged another look with his mother and they both doubled over again.

He waited them out.

"Ahem." Judith cleared her throat and straightened just as the sky lit up through the window above the sink. "I had this nightmare for months after you two were born that I'd go into your room and find two puppies there, yipping and bouncing up and down to get out of your cribs."

"That's great, Mom, scare her to death."

She spun around, a dirty serving spoon yielded like a weapon and a serious look on her face. "That's why I told her, Caelan. Nobody took me under their wing when I met your father. No one told me what carrying a shifter child was going to be like. And I was too...in shock...of what was happening to go to your father. Besides"—she glanced again at Tieran—"he's a man. What the hell would he know?" she said, grinning. Tieran's lips quirked.

Great. They were ganging up on him. A clap of thunder rattled a precarious stack of dishes.

"Wow." Tieran jumped toward him. "Maybe we should get going, Caelan."

"Uh-huh." He didn't move from his perch. Now it was his turn to smirk. Tonight they were going to sleep in his bed. After they fucked in his bed, anyway.

"What do you mean, 'uh-huh'?" Tieran balanced on one foot and put her hands on her hips. Didn't matter. This was one battle she wouldn't win.

"Storm's already here, my own. I'm not driving in bad conditions and endangering your safety."

"But I—"

"We're staying here, Tieran."

Her body deflated in defeat. Score one for the Prime, he thought and secretly smiled.

"He's right, my dear. The last thing you need tonight is to have an accident. There are plenty of rooms here, aren't there, Caelan."

He nodded. "Absolutely." *But the only one you'll be staying in is mine.*

"There, see?" His mother patted Tieran's shoulder. She still looked a little weary. "He can be thoughtful when he tries. Now, then, I'm going to head home before the brunt gets here."

"Thanks for all your help, Judith."

"You're very welcome, dear. Remember, anything you need. I know how bone-headed my son can be."

Thank God for his mother. He hadn't thought far enough ahead to think about these things. Of course his mate would need some guidance. Being human, his mother was perfect, and she was the one person willing to tell Tieran anything she wanted to know. He saw the bond already forming between them and his heart gave a little jump.

He stood and hugged the smaller woman. "You want me to drive you?"

"Oh, no, I think I can manage, Caelan. It's not even raining yet."

"All right. Call us when you get there so we'll know."

"I will." She wiggled her fingers at Tieran who smiled and waved back.

"I like your mom," she said when the door shut behind his mother.

He shrugged. "She's okay."

"Caelan!"

"I'm kidding, I'm kidding." He took her in his arms and pulled her close. "You held up well today."

"Yeah, so, what am I? A side of beef?"

He chuckled. "Mmm. Yum. Can I taste?" He bent his head and took possession of her lips. "Best beef I ever ate," he whispered against her mouth. Her hands slipped into his back pockets and his cock hardened. "God I want you."

"What else is new?" She tucked her head under his chin. "Caelan?"

"Hmm?"

"Is...Eli going to be here tonight?"

Damn it. He was thinking about making love to her and she was still worried about his brother. Honestly, based on their earlier conversation, Caelan was more than a little worried about his twin himself. Not about the murders, that was ridiculous, but about whatever was eating away at his normal, playful self.

He sighed. Might as well get this over with. "He lives here, Tieran. This is his home. What would you have me do, throw him out?"

She shook her head against his chest.

"Look." Caelan lifted her head with both hands. "His rooms are all on the other half of the house. You don't even have to see him if you don't want to." She would never know how much it hurt to say those words. It tore him apart for her to be afraid of his twin. Especially since the two of them had always been inseparable. What would he do if his mate and his twin couldn't come to terms with one another?

"I'm sorry. It's not fair of me to judge him, you're right."

"I know I am," he said to try and lighten the mood. "I'm always right."

Her eyebrows arched. "And on that note, I'm going to ask you to point me to the nearest bed. I'm exhausted."

"Not *too* exhausted though, right?" Caelan led her out the door, into the foyer and down the long hallway to his room. "We can play around, huh?" He looped his arm around her shoulders and casually flicked at her nipple with his thumb.

The nub immediately hardened and pressed against her T-shirt. "Oh, man, you don't know how long I've waited to touch you."

Pushing her back against the wall, he tunneled his hand beneath her shirt and devoured her mouth. "I can't wait."

Tieran returned the kiss just as hungrily. "I can't do this."

Her breasts were firm, the nipples taut under her bra, and he fumbled with the front clasp to free them. They filled his hands a second later, smooth and warm. He yanked the T-shirt up and bent to take a nipple between his lips. She arched into him when he sucked the first one deep into his mouth.

"Oh, God." Her head shook back and forth on the wall, her hands pressed against his shoulders. Something in her voice made him stop.

"What is it, my own?"

A slow tear tracked its way down her cheek. She sniffed once and tried to smile but he could see it was false.

"How can you make me want you so bad?"

He shrugged. "It's the same for me."

She patted his chest and this time a real smile tugged at the corner of her mouth. "I believe that, I really do, but while you can apparently go on for days, I can't."

Jesus. Now that he looked closely, he saw the shadows beneath her eyes. She hadn't slept well the night before and then she'd been subjected to his pack with no break. His mate was exhausted. And here he was about to fuck her in the hallway. Her chest still heaved from his foreplay, yet her eyelids looked ready to close any second.

He pulled her shirt down, covering her reddened breasts. "I'm an insensitive jerk, aren't I?"

"Pretty much." She yawned so big her jaw popped.

"Hey."

"You said it, not me." She dropped her forehead to his chest. "I just want to sleep. Just for a little while before I have another vision."

What the... "What the hell do you mean, 'another vision'?" He bracketed her face in his hands and lifted until she looked at him. "You know you're about to have another one and you didn't tell me?" If he was growling at her, tough. He meant what he said earlier about not keeping secrets.

Her eyes widened and searched his frantically. "I...I...God, I must have forgotten with everything that was happening."

"Wait a minute. Are we still talking about the woman from the paper this morning?" His heart settled back into a more normal rhythm. Of course they were. She hadn't had one today, and if it always followed the twitch then that's the one she'd have. No wonder she wanted to sleep.

Her mouth opened and closed like a fish. "No. Well, yes, technically I guess, but I'd forgotten about that. No. This afternoon when the detective"—she shivered in Caelan's arms—"when he touched me, it happened again."

Tieran jerked upright, banging into his chin. If she kept doing that, he'd end up with broken jaw. Damn. He tasted blood on his tongue.

"Do you think he did it?" Her voice was frantic and she dug her fingernails into his forearms, diluting the pain of his jaw but making his eyes water all the same.

He shook his head to clear it. What the hell was she talking about?

"Caelan. Do you think the detective did it?"

"No. Hayward's a detective on the case. You probably just picked something up from him because of that. He's been at all the scenes, knows everything there is to know about it, except who did it," he muttered, disgusted.

187

"Damn, you're right."

"Like I said, I'm always right." At least, he hoped he was in this instance. Michael Hayward could be a bastard in his own right, but he was a cop, first and foremost. He fought for the shifter side and kept their secret when it would be so easy to go wolf in front of other cops to hunt a lead. Not to mention he'd kept Caelan up to speed on the case every day.

Tieran's deep sigh brought him back. She yawned again, making him yawn too. Since his cock had long since wavered, it was time to hit the sack.

"Come on, baby, let's put you to bed." He led her to his room and stripped her completely before turning back the covers and sticking her between them.

She snuggled in. "Mmm." Her eyes were closed and her lips parted on her soft breaths before he could even get undressed. After switching off the light, he slid in next to her and wrapped his arms around her, holding her close. Burying his nose in the crease of her neck and shoulder, he inhaled her scent. Her body melted into his. God, he loved her.

Chapter Ten

She was scared out of her mind. The harsh light dangling precariously above her made sweat trickle off her forehead, between her breasts and down the length of her spine. Every few minutes a sob burst out of her and fresh tears would mingle with the snot coating her upper lip, making her entire face wet.

The man had pinned her arms behind the chair with some kind of plastic cording. Her hands were sticky with the blood oozing from where she'd tried to free her wrists so many times. Her shoulders burned in agony. She'd been sitting here for so long she'd already urinated on herself twice. Dropping her chin to her chest, she moaned as the crude gag bit into the long-ago cracked corners of her mouth.

The stench of her own bodily fluid made her stomach clench. How long had he been gone? A day, two? Completely disoriented, she had no idea. Maybe he wasn't coming back for her. Would she die sitting in this chair in a place no one would look for her?

Daniel. God she would miss him so much. Half of her soul was already missing without him near. The man had ripped her sanity to shreds the minute he'd stuffed her in the back of his car, a foul-smelling cloth pressed to her nose and mouth. The next thing she knew, she woke up here.

She cried out through the gag and rocked the chair from side to side. Anything that might give her a new position, a chance to escape. She grunted, pulling at the bindings at her wrists and ankles.

No use. She was too weak after so many draining hours.

She jerked her gaze up. A sudden scratching noise meant she wasn't alone anymore. Her heart pounded as she searched the cavernous, decrepit space the years had not been friendly to for the millionth time. Beyond the circle of light surrounding her, darkness impeded her vision.

There. From that corner filled with what looked like decades old crates. She heard it again, like a footstep on the dirt-ridden floor. She felt him watching her, waiting. A match lit up the shadows and then the glowing red butt of a cigarette cut through the darkness like an evil eye, taunting her.

She whimpered. How could anyone stand there and not care? What kind of beast was he?

She knew. Deep down inside, she knew she was about to become another victim of the man Daniel had talked about. He'd warned her so many times. "Stay close to me always, my mate." Oh, God, what had he done to Daniel? Killed him? No, he was still alive, she felt him in her heart. He was looking for her. The whole pack would be looking for her.

It would be too late, though.

After what seemed like an eternity, her tormentor dropped the cigarette. In the silence she heard him grind it out with his shoe, crushing the demonic red dot. He would come for her now.

Her attempted scream sounded more like a moan through her overused vocal cords and the fabric forced between her lips. Her head fell forward in hopelessness. A curtain of dull, greasy black hair that had somehow been left out of the gag swept forward, shielding her gaze. She was glad for that at least.

The man laughed, the sound exploding through the dark spaces and bouncing off the metal walls, mocking her with its repeat. Her spirit fell even further.

With a heavy, obvious tread, he walked toward her in slow deliberation. She promised herself she would not look at him, would not let him see any more of her terror. She failed. Out of the corner of her eye, she watched him approach. He swaggered toward her. Not drunk, but God, preening. A ball cap cast a shadow over his face, obscuring his features.

He stopped in front of her and reached out to her face, caressing her cheek with the back of his hand. A pathetic whimper escaped her. She looked down her nose, her eyes nearly crossing, her breath heaving through her runny nose. There was a strange mark on top of his arm, at the wrist, peeking out from beneath his watch. She sobbed at his horrible, gentle touch. With wild eyes, she stared back at him. Pleaded with him. Begged.

One corner of his mouth curled into a snarl. Her stomach rolled with a fresh batch of tears. His hand moved to tangle in the mess of her hair and jerked, forcing her to look up. He sneered at her as he stepped to her side.

There was a hissing sound at her ear. She grew lightheaded from fighting to breathe and imagining what he would do to her. The metal glinted, catching the light from the one bulb he'd somehow rigged in this shitheap of a warehouse that otherwise hadn't seen electricity for more than twenty years.

Her panic multiplied a million times when he held a wicked-looking knife above her face, making sure she could see the jagged edge of the steel blade. She cried out, squirming and pulling at the hair fisted in his hand.

"Things will be so much better when I've taken over," he rasped. He lowered the knife and used the razor-sharp edge to *caress her cheek. "We won't have this problem when I am Prime."*

Eyes wide with shock, she inhaled sharply at his implication. He smiled and pressed the cold metal to her exposed throat.

She fought him, screaming and jerking, even as he pricked the delicate skin.

Her whole body shook with great uncontrollable convulsions. An arc of red spurted in front of her as he shoved her head forward so she could see the damage he'd invoked.

Her heart thumped once. Twice. Her eyelids grew so heavy she couldn't hold them open and yet her body seemed to dance still. His laugh erupted in an evil howl, his eyes glittered a feral golden brown.

Daniel.

Tieran bolted upright in bed, her chest heaving as she fought the dream off. Her head swam from the suddenness of her movements. Predawn shadows cast a gray tint over the unfamiliar room and the curtain in the open window fluttered with the slight breeze.

She glanced around at her surroundings before remembering where she was. Caelan must have opened the window sometime during the night. She hadn't been kidding when she'd said she was tired.

With a shaky hand, she scraped back the damp hair clinging to her face and away from her eyes, trying to erase some of the disorientation that often clouded her memory after a vision.

"What is it, baby?" Caelan mumbled, reminding her that she wasn't alone. He rolled to his side next to her and settled an arm across her thighs. His fingers gently squeezed her hip, calming her a fraction, before his soft snoring announced he'd already fallen back asleep.

As soon as the rotation in her brain settled, her stomach took over, sending bile rushing up her esophagus then dropping back down again.

Damn it. Tieran threw a hand over her mouth and stared opposite her at what she remembered to be the bathroom door. She hoped to hell she made it to the toilet before she puked in front of wolf-man. The last thing she needed was for him to hover like a mother hen again.

Right now she needed privacy, not overbearing protectiveness.

"It's his job as your mate to protect you, Tullabelle."

"I can't imagine what in the world I need protecting from here in his bedroom."

"You will soon, Tulla. Keep him close."

Tieran snorted and looked at Caelan's arm draped across her lap. He couldn't get any closer than he was. Well, he could, had, but she wouldn't go there. God forbid her grandmother start spouting stories of her and Pawpoo again. She shivered with the sweat beginning to dry on her nude body, and eased out from beneath the muscular limb pinning her to the bed. She didn't even recall getting undressed.

Her feet tangled in the sheets. Doing her best not to disturb him, she fought her way out of them, her awkwardness making her even more clumsy. Finally free, she stood beside the bed. Caelan was now planted on his belly, his arm outstretched where she had been.

Tieran angled her head and stared at his broad hand. Palm down, the tops of fingers were sprinkled with dark hairs. She swayed on her wobbly knees. He was wearing a sporty, expensive watch. Why hadn't she noticed it before? And why did she care that she hadn't taken notice? It was a watch, big deal.

But there was something else. Tucked beneath the watch, a dark tattoo peeked out. She squinted, trying to get a closer look at its shape, but the watch was too much in the way. A watch that *he* had looked at when his car had broken down.

Did Eli have the same watch? She couldn't remember and her brain felt like mush.

Her tummy rolled again, this time coming closer to blowing loose. She pivoted and took off for the bathroom, stumbling on the discarded jeans she guessed Caelan had stripped off her the night before. Off balance, she slammed her toe into the leg of the bed and howled in pain.

"What the fuck...?" Caelan hurled out of bed, gun mysteriously in hand before his feet hit the floor.

"Oh shit, oh shit." Tears streamed down Tieran's face as she hopped around on one foot and held her throbbing toe in the other. The bouncing made her nausea return in force.

Forgetting the pain, she bolted for the toilet once again, landing on her knees in a semi-skid on the small carpet in front of the commode. She flipped the lid up and lost the contents of her stomach.

When the worst ended, she crossed her arms over the seat and rested her forehead there. Good God, when would this go away? Would she never live a normal life, free of the nightmarish visions plaguing her?

The water in the bowl whooshed and swirled away as she stared down at it. Her body felt like jelly, so unless she had passed out for a second and forgotten that she'd reached up and flushed, he was there, standing over her.

She groaned in defeat. What a mate she made. Naked and sprawled out on the floor next to the john, puking her guts out.

She heard the water run in the sink and the clink of glass on metal. Caelan crouched down a millisecond before he swiped her hair out of the way and placed a blessedly cool washrag on the back of her neck.

"Leave me alone," she begged. Puking in front of him once had been embarrassing enough, twice was downright mortifying.

He sighed. One of those chiding, exasperated, drawn-out sounds that made her want to scratch his eyes out.

He handed her a capful of mouthwash from next to his sink and she took it gratefully. After swishing her mouth out for long seconds, she spit into the toilet and sighed.

"You getting sick isn't going to run me off, my own. I wouldn't care if you grew horns and a third eyeball. It's my job—"

"Yeah, yeah, yeah. But I do, so get the hell away from me. Leave me to puke in peace," she mumbled and slid down to lay in the fetal position on the cold, tile floor surrounding the one area rug below the toilet.

"I can't." He swiped at her bangs so he could look into her eyes. She closed them and pressed her cheek into the floor. "You see, we're like magnets. Your pain is my pain."

"Oh, right. Don't give me that crap," she said weakly. She drew her knees more tightly to her chest and hugged them with both arms. "I'm going to die."

"No you won't."

"How the hell would you know?" she bit out, shrugging his hand off her shoulder when he reached for it. "Had many visions lately?"

Caelan nearly laughed at her defiance. She still didn't want to pin her nausea on their baby. "Not a one, but Tieran, I'm telling you, with most of our human mates, this goes away after a few months."

"Well bully for them, Caelan," she shouted and rose up shakily to kneel. She stabbed a slender finger through the air in front of his chest, coming close but never actually poking him. Though he knew she wanted to.

"My throwing up doesn't have a fucking thing to do with a baby," she continued, "if there even is one, which I haven't quite decided yet. This isn't something that's just going to—'poof'—disappear in a few months for me. It happens every goddamn time I have a stupid vision. Perhaps if your...your...*people* would stop killing each other, it might subside for a few days, but no—"

"What'd you just say?" Pissed, Caelan grabbed the hand she was waggling at him and dragged her closer until their noses touched. She'd been teasing with his mother last night about having puppies. No way did she think she wasn't going to be a mother. No way did she not think she was carrying his child. Not after the elders had pronounced her "with child". That's not what concerned him, she was just letting off a little steam and thought it might hurt him to say those things.

Tieran's wide, wild eyes looked everywhere but at him. She swallowed, confirming to him that she hadn't meant to say what she had. Her little mouth moved faster than her brain sometimes.

"What did you just say?" he gritted out. He grabbed her other arm when she tried to pull away from him and held it captive with the first.

"I'm not sure there is a baby," she lied breathlessly.

Caelan waved that off. "Yesterday, you were damn sure convinced. I heard you with Hayward defending our *whelp*, remember? There is one, deal with it. I'm not talking about our baby right now anyway. You didn't tell me you'd had another vision, but clearly your words say otherwise. Help me, by telling me what happened, or so help me God, I will turn you over my knee and spank the answer out of your sweet ass."

Their faces were so close to one another she gasped against his mouth. "I am not a child, Caelan."

"Then stop acting like one." With his free hand he held her head in place and sealed their lips together. He plundered her surprised mouth with his tongue, swiping the velvet softness of hers until she capitulated and angled her head for better access. His wolf growled to the surface, his cock hardened painfully beneath his jeans.

Fortunately his brain was still functioning or he'd have taken her right there on the bathroom floor. She was ready for him, he could smell it. He could work his hand between her legs and physically test for himself how wet she was, but that would make matters worse. They needed to resolve some serious issues, not fuck.

He pulled back as far as the cabinet behind him would allow, still holding her hands in one of his. Her eyes were glazed over, her lips were a puffy red, and her breathing was heavy.

"Let go, Caelan." Damn, why did he affect her like this? She licked her lips, tasting him and the minty mouthwash, and pulled at her captive hands. If she claimed he was hurting her, he would probably drop them in a heartbeat and caress them until the redness went away.

Who was she kidding, there wouldn't be any redness.

His jaw ticked, indicating that despite the heated kiss he'd just laid on her, he was still perturbed with her.

"I'm serious, Tieran, tell me about your vision. And don't bother trying to deny it, you've already given yourself away. If you know something else, I need to know. This goes beyond you and me, my own."

"Ooohh." If she could stomp her foot in this position, she would. As it was, her knees were starting to hurt something fierce from the hard tiles beneath them. "You and my grandmother. 'It goes beyond just you and me'," she mocked.

Frustration shimmered in waves around her body. Her head hurt, her tummy muscles were sore, and she was damn good and pissed about being led around like a puppy. Did they both think she was so fragile she might break in two?

"I need more descriptions, more clues, anything. Goddamnit!" he shouted, clearly frustrated. "We have nothing. Do you understand? Nothing. Except you and what you see. Is that clear enough?"

"Yes," she hissed, "and I've tried to tell you, but each time the only thing you've done is deny what I've said. 'It isn't Eli'. Well if it isn't, it sure as hell looks like him. If it weren't for the scar and the fact you've been with me all this time, I would suspect you too. Is *that* clear enough?"

Slowly rising to his feet, he pulled her up with him, his eyes narrowed with deadly intent. The little muscle jumped along his jaw again. Tieran stepped back and tried to convince herself she wasn't afraid of the big bad wolf. He urged her out of the bathroom. Her heel struck the threshold, making her trip. Caelan's strong hands reached out, grabbed hold of her upper arms and yanked her to him, crushing their chests together. Then he continued to practically reverse frog-walk her, turning the corner until he had her backed against the wall outside the bathroom door.

"And you say you're not a child. That's how you're acting right now. Maybe I should show you what happens to recalcitrant children when they misbehave."

Tieran had to swallow the semi-fear, semi-arousal threatening to choke her. The look on Caelan's face said he would clearly enjoy punishing her, making her more than aware of the tingling in her pussy. Her cheeks flamed as she thought about the ways he might do it. She pushed her legs together hoping to stem the flow of juices from between her now slippery labia.

"Does the idea of me punishing you excite you?" he growled. His lip curled, allowing her a glimpse of sharpened teeth and reminding her of them sinking into the flesh of her shoulder as he pumped his cock into her from behind.

Her knees nearly buckled. A slow throb pulsed in her swollen clit and in the wound he'd left with said teeth. Her head sagged against the wall when he insinuated his knee between her legs. The top of his thigh pressed infuriatingly at her pussy, sending tiny shocks of desire strumming through her body. Suddenly she didn't care who either of them was. She wanted him. No, needed him. Now. Questions and answers be damned.

His mouth bore down on hers, bruising her lips with their intensity.

Breaking the kiss, she whimpered, "Please make love to me." She raked her fingernails in a not-so-gingerly fashion over his abs.

Tieran made him so fucking hot. One minute Caelan wanted to strangle her, the next, he wanted to lay her out, spread her thighs as wide as they could go and slurp at her delicious pussy. He groaned when her fingers landed on a nipple and pinched the tight bud. His cock begged, wanting to plant itself in the sweet haven of her body and thrust into her until it exploded and spent its seed deep inside her.

He didn't have time to screw around right now.

Moving his lips over hers, he tasted and nipped as she moaned beneath his onslaught. He smoothed his hands everywhere along her heated body. Her skin was so soft. It quivered with his touch along her belly and she sucked in another breath. He liked that he could make her breathless so quickly.

Answers. No time for this.

The sleek gold ring at her navel snagged his wandering fingers. Holding her pinned to the wall with his upper body, he played with it, flicking the gem dangling from its hoop, and tried to insinuate his free hand between his thigh and her mound.

"Have to stop, my own. Need to talk." At least his brain knew what he needed to be doing, even if it couldn't form the sentences properly.

"Later," she panted. "Promise." Her head rolled back and forth on the wall and her hand took a direct route south from his nipples to his groin. She squeezed him until he thought he would go blind from the feel of her fingers wrapped around his length. He pulled her away.

"Gonna come before I want to." Great. Now he was fucking panting.

He dropped to his knees in front of her. Damn if she wasn't the prettiest woman in the world. Everything about her was beautiful. Her brain, her courage, her body. Her cunt was swollen and glistening with the slick essence of Tieran. With his palms on the inside of her thighs, he spread her legs then slid his hands upward to either side of her vagina.

Pulling back her labia, he opened her up and inhaled her scent. Fresh, feminine, peaches, his. God he was hungry. With the flat of his tongue, he licked her from back to front. A long, casual stroke that had her gasping and squirming on his mouth. He ended at the distended nub of her clit, which he uncovered further by pulling back the hood of skin still trying to shield it.

Circling it with the tip of his tongue, he teased Tieran until she slapped at the wall with both hands in frustration. When one hand came to fist in his hair, Caelan flicked at the bundle of nerves, setting her off like he'd touched her with an electric charge. She screamed. The muscles in her thighs bunched and quivered beside his head as she tried to keep them open for him. She was standing on her tiptoes and begging for the release he kept just out of reach.

He slid his tongue along her slit again, gathering up the copious amount of cream spilling out of her, then moved back to the point where her body would convulse like wildfire. He sucked the tiny bundle of nerves between his lips and her body slammed down on the soles of her feet.

With two fingers, he entered her tight passage. Her pussy walls contracted in an explosive climax that had her back climbing up the wall to get away from his still pillaging tongue on her clit. Caelan wrapped his other arm around her back to keep her from doing so. He drank his fill, bringing her down from her high and taking her back up at the same time. She collapsed inch by inch onto the floor and he eased her way to lay her down on the carpeted hallway.

A dreamy satiated smile lifted her lips as he fumbled unsteadily to guide himself between her legs.

She sighed as he pressed slowly into her and gripped the back of his legs with her heels.

"How do you do this to me? Make me lose all thought?" she whispered.

"The same way you do it to me, my own." He held her gaze while he withdrew, pulling out of her until only the head was lodged inside her, then slid back home. She gasped when his pelvis rasped along the clit he'd just shattered into a million pieces.

"I don't want to have another one, Caelan, please." Her voice wobbled.

At first he misunderstood her, thinking she couldn't stand another orgasm, but then he realized what she really meant. She didn't want to have another vision. She was scared and at least once already he'd somehow triggered one.

He held still, quivering as his body screamed for release. It would kill him if she rejected him for fear she would have another terrifying vision. Angling his head, he placed a kiss on her sweaty forehead and whispered, "What do you want me to do, my own?" *Please God, don't say go away,* he begged silently.

"I don't know." Tears collected in her eyes. When he leaned forward to swipe at them his cock slipped further into her pussy. Her eyes widened then closed and her hips lifted to meet his. "Don't stop," she breathed.

Hallelujah. "I'll help you through it, whatever happens, Tieran, trust me."

Her eyelids lifted slowly again. For a split second, her liquid gaze was almost sad, but then she moved again and the moment was gone.

Caelan pounded into her. She grunted with each of his thrusts, her breasts bouncing beneath him, and he bent to latch on to one of the nipples with a greedy mouth. Tieran threw her head back and bit her lip.

His balls tightened with every penetration and slapped against her ass. With one last drive, he coated her sheath with spurt after spurt of his seed and sank his teeth into the soft skin above her breast, marking her. He laved the small cuts with his tongue, offering the quick-soothing healing powers found in his saliva. A very faint mark would remain but heal fast, just like those he'd left elsewhere on her body.

Spent, he rolled off, disengaging himself when he wanted to stay buried in her forever, and lay on his back next to her. Or rather, tried to. Their bodies took up the width of the hallway so the doorjamb gouged into his shoulder blade with every hard breath he took.

He turned his head and looked at her, sprawled out, knees still spread far apart and breathing just as harsh as he was. The air was permeated with the scent of their lovemaking. She was absolutely the most beautiful thing on the planet. Caelan linked his fingers through hers.

"You okay?"

"No," she murmured, alarming him when her eyes scrunched up as if she were in pain.

"Another one?" He levered his body up until he was propped on his elbow and laid his hand on her belly.

"Uh-uh," she grunted. "Rug burn. On my ass."

Caelan barked out in laughter, glad to finally have his feisty mate back. "Don't tempt me to add my handprint to that fine ass of yours."

"I can't move." She groaned, trying to sit up.

Caelan jumped to his feet and pulled Tieran along with him, then held her until she got her bearings back.

"You haven't gotten out of talking to me, baby." He turned her towards the bed and sent her walking with a little shove between her shoulders, wincing at the red marks marring the soft skin of her butt. She really did have a bad case.

Caelan scooped up her pants from where she'd tripped over them earlier and handed them to her. "Since I don't see either of us going back to sleep, take a shower, get dressed again, then come eat. Whether you believe me or not, our baby needs the protein."

She sagged onto the side of the bed and without looking at him, nodded.

"I'll go fix us something."

Chapter Eleven

His head pounded like a drum. Eli groaned and wondered what the hell had happened. Must have been some night if he couldn't even remember it. Slowly neurons started firing in his brain. Something sharp poked into his cheek where he lay and his shoulders screamed in agony. He tested them to see why they were hurting so much and discovered he couldn't move them.

What the fuck? His wrists clinked behind him. Handcuffs. He opened his eyes a crack, wincing as an explosive fresh wave of pain took over his head.

"Well look who's decided to join the party?" The sneer came from a long way off, compounding an already colossal ache.

Eli inhaled. He was face down on the ground, handcuffed. Christ what had happened? Why couldn't he remember?

"You're going away for a long time, boy."

Eli wanted to tell him to fuck off, but didn't have the energy. He wanted to go back to sleep and had to fight the darkness closing in on him once again. With extreme effort, he forced his lids open. Dancing lights cut through his brain like a knife and Eli slammed his eyes shut.

A pungent smell wafted by his nose, making him gag and flinch to get away from it. The movement caused another dagger of pain to pierce his temple. He peeked again. Slowly the world, which had been dark when he'd gotten here, came into focus. It clearly wasn't night anymore, but sometime very early morning. A voice shouted, another responded, a short burst of a radio transmission, flashing red and blue lights. One of his eyelids was lifted open and an explosion of light blinded him.

"The son of a bitch is awake, can we go now?"

Eli recognized the voice, but couldn't place it.

"He needs to be transported to the hospital, Detective."

Why? Eli's mind was blank. Besides arriving at the warehouse and getting out of his car, there was nothing else.

"The only transport he's gonna get is in the back of a squad car."

Christ. He was being arrested for something and didn't even know what it was. He tried to roll over. The least he could do was get a better look at who he was dealing with. Maybe then he'd be able see why the dick sounded like he'd be more than happy to be the driver of said squad car.

"Whoa, man. Don't move until I get this C-collar on." A hand stopped him from moving.

"Fuck the collar, Pete. Just get him the hell to his feet."

The man, who he assumed was Pete, stood. Shiny black shoes filled Eli's vision. Come to think of it, his neck was starting to feel crimped. Whether it was from being in this position for so long or whatever had landed him face down licking the pavement, he didn't know. If the collar would keep him out of jail for another hour or two, he'd gladly don it. The hospital would at least give him the chance to figure things out.

"And your Lieutenant would screw your balls to the wall for not sticking to procedure. You want to lose him on a technicality?"

Thank you, Pete. Eli sighed and closed his eyes. They were getting heavier and heavier and now his stomach was starting to churn. Whatever it was that had brought him down, must have been a doozy.

"Besides the fact my name would also go on the report for not doing *my* job."

"He's fucking guilty as sin, Pete."

Jesus, the guy was a hard-ass. He tried to shift off a rock gouging into his left pec but the small movement left him wanting to puke.

"Maybe he is, that's your business. Mine is EMT and he's got a concussion the size of Texas. Unless you want him to die before he gets the chance to have his *fair* trial, then you better step back."

Good thing Pete was on his side. For the moment. Eli had the feeling he'd be facing the wrong side of a jail cell in about five minutes if not for him, and from what he'd heard so far, the detective would probably swallow the key.

"Ricky, let's get this guy rolled and loaded before he goes out again."

Pete's shout had Eli's head swimming. He wasn't moving, but it sure felt like he was. The ground beneath him swayed like a waterbed.

"You mind the cuffs, Detective?"

"Yeah I mind. We've been hunting this asshole for weeks. No fucking way is he gonna have the chance to get loose."

"Then hold the goddamn cuff in your hand and clip it to the rail, but I've got to roll him to get a better assessment. Do it now!"

There was a grunt above Eli, the distinctive pop of a knee cracking as it bent. His hands were roughly jerked back and up sending another tearing rip of pain through him so that he missed the click of his wrists being released. That did it. He puked.

"Son of a bitch."

"Damn it. Ricky, get his head and neck," Pete said in a hurried voice.

Two hands bracketed the base of his head just below his ears, and strong fingers outstretched to wrap securely around his neck. He was rolled quickly. Too fast, and Eli threw up again on the way over.

"Get the backboard," Pete shouted.

"Unbelievable. Do you think you can play this up any more, Graham? Face it, you fucking got caught."

A hard surface met Eli's back and then he was right-side up. A C-collar circled his neck before he could open his eyes. The fucking sleazy bastard. Did he think he'd stuck his fingers down his throat and forced himself to puke? And what had he got caught doing? And where did he know that voice from?

Eli reached up to wipe at something wet on his forehead and heard the cocking of a gun.

"Don't fucking move, Graham."

His arm was grabbed and laid back down.

"Easy there, man, I'm just going to start an IV."

A snap coincided with a sharp tug on his upper arm and a pinprick inside his elbow.

His eyelid was lifted again and he was re-subjected to the penetrating light. When his belly revolted another time, he puffed his cheeks out.

"Shit, he's going to blow again."

They rolled him back to the side, this time attached to the board. Only dry heaves wracked his battered body this time. "Stop moving me," he shouted.

Pete leaned over his now prone form, his hair brushing Eli's chin. "What was that?"

His shout must not have been quite the shout he'd heard in his head. "No moving," he said again, gritting his teeth against the pain, the nausea, and the whole idea of the bastard detective standing above them like he was about to grind Eli under the toe of his patent leather shoe.

Pete chuckled. "Just a little more, I promise. We're going to lift you onto the stretcher and load you into the ambulance."

"What...happened?" Not a car accident, because Detective Dick Boy wouldn't be here, the smug tone of arrest lacing his every word.

Eli squinted up at Pete as they lifted him. His face was a mask of concern.

"You don't know?"

Eli swallowed and shook his head once.

"Not fucking likely, Graham. Nice excuse though, one that's not gonna fly. What, did you hear us coming and had to come up with something quick? Bash yourself over the head, lay yourself out on the ground and pretend to be a victim?"

The detective leaned over him and whispered so only Eli could hear. "There's not a fucking thing the Prime can do for you now."

It was then Eli finally recognized where he'd heard the voice before. The cop was Michael Hayward. One of his own pack. There was a slap of metal on metal and the clinking of the cuff locking in place around a bar beneath the stretcher. Eli's hand was forced in the same direction.

Eli wondered if he was hallucinating the smug smile he saw on Michael's face as he hovered there. Obviously, "call Caelan" wouldn't garner any attention. What the fuck was going on? If he couldn't trust a shifter from his own pack, who could he trust?

"Back off, Detective. You can meet us there."

The stretcher rolled and bumped into the ambulance. Bright white lights washed over Eli as he was pushed inside and he wondered if anything else would come shooting out of his stomach again. He slammed his eyes closed and willed his stomach to settle. Inside, he caught the metallic smell of blood. So that's the wet he felt on his forehead.

Jesus, if only he could remember, he thought, and let the calming blackness surround him.

🐕 🐕 🐕

After complaining for an interminable amount of time about his lack of Mountain Dew, Caelan had finally gotten her to sit and eat some breakfast. If you could call what she was doing to her food eating. The sun hadn't completely risen yet, but was well on its way. Time to start talking about the nightmare that had sent her running to the toilet earlier.

"How's the tummy?" He wasn't so much of a monster he would pass over her obvious discomfort before going on to the necessary evil.

"Fine," she grunted.

He smiled. She crumbled her toast into a pile of toast dust.

"So..."

"He killed her. Except he was a man this time."

Caelan inhaled sharply and snagged her fingers to hold in his hand when she took intense interest in her fingernails. This is what he'd been waiting for. What he could have gotten out of her earlier had they not ended up wrestling naked on the floor.

"Are you sure the man and the wolf you saw before were the same shifter?"

"I don't know," she shouted, making him jump in his seat. "Their eyes were the same, like yours and your wolf's are the same, and his hand…" Her words trailed off so he didn't hear anything past hand, but the way she was squeezing him was all the testimony he needed. She was scared.

"What about his hand?"

"Well, not really his hand, but his wrist. He had on the same watch as you. The same one the driver wore also. And I noticed this morning you have a tattoo beneath yours."

Caelan's gaze drifted to the ancient symbol of a wolf he and Eli had gotten tattooed with when they were twenty-one. It was small enough not to stand out, especially beneath the watch, but still visible because of their position. The top of the wrist was an abnormal placement for someone who wasn't covered in permanent drawings, but surely there were a few. More than just he and Eli, at least. Weren't there?

"Did that person also have a tattoo?" he asked, hoping she said no.

Tieran shook her head. Caelan closed his eyes. *Thank God. It was definitely not Eli she'd seen then.*

"I…can't remember. Something just stood out at me when I saw yours this morning."

Caelan released the breath he hadn't realized he'd been holding. Not the answer he wanted. If she didn't see it, was it because the tattoo wasn't there, or because it was hidden beneath the watch?

211

He cleared his throat and his mind. "Where were they?" he asked, redirecting Tieran to the vision.

She shook her head again. "I don't know. A warehouse somewhere. It was empty, old." Her free hand came up to wipe at the goose bumps breaking out along her arm. "She was tied to a chair in the middle of the room and there was only one light on, right above her." She swallowed and her eyes glistened with unshed tears.

Caelan wanted to pull her into his lap and wrap his arms around her in comfort, but he couldn't. Not now when she was entering that trance-like state again. If he'd learned anything in the last couple of days, it was to let her work through the episodes at her own pace.

"He watched her from one corner where she couldn't see him," she continued, "like he was waiting for something. Then he went to her and grabbed her hair. He yanked her head back, forcing her to look at him. It was dark and he had a hat on. With the light above him, I couldn't see his face." Tieran's monotone drone raked at his nerves.

The pulse in her wrist jumped in tempo and Caelan damned himself for putting her through this. If it weren't vital, he'd give her his shoulder to cry on and listen to her fears.

"Then he said, 'We won't have this problem when I'm Prime.'"

Caelan slammed to his feet, overturning the chair and inadvertently letting go of her hand and flinging it aside. Tieran screamed beside him, jolted out of the spell she was in and grabbed the table, swaying in her seat as if he'd pushed her.

"What are you doing?" she said, breathing heavy.

He almost laughed at the incredulity in her voice. If what she'd said hadn't just thrown him for a total loop, he might have. At least now he knew the motivation of their killer.

"Do you even realize what you just said?" Of course not, she'd been back in her vision, probably couldn't even hear what she said. He thrust his fingers through his hair. Righting the seat, he faced her.

Her face was white, her eyes too wide and tears shimmered along the lower lids.

Her chin trembled and a myriad of emotions crossed her face. "You're a Prime," she whispered as if she'd just come to the conclusion.

She had, he reminded himself. Getting angry with her would solve nothing. What he needed to do was drag every bit of information out of her.

Things were beyond his control because as soon as the elders discovered her ability and the information she had, the choice of whether or not to involve her would be taken out of his hands. It already had been, the moment she murmured something about a Prime.

The sick bastard wasn't playing at murdering mates, he was clearing a path to take out a Prime.

And Tieran was about to stand directly in his path.

"Yes," he answered, even though she'd only made a statement. "I am Prime, and I don't know exactly where you go when you recall these visions, but I need to be able to converse with you about them."

"You're the only one?"

He sighed. "The only one what?"

"Prime. Are you the only Prime?" she asked getting slightly hysterical. "Is he coming after you?" A tear slipped down her cheek and his heart thudded. Despite the very short amount of time they'd known each other, their bond was already very strong. The baby made it more so.

213

"No," he said, wiping the tear off her cheek then cupping the back of her head. "Every pack has its own head alpha and there are about thirty packs in our community. We're just one of many across the country, my own."

"But he's here, in yours, he could be coming after you." Tieran dug her fingernails into his arm and squeezed closer. "You have to leave," she begged.

"I will not leave my pack," he growled, sounding harsher than he meant to. "There's no way of knowing which pack he's targeting." He brought her forehead to his and kissed her nose. "Unless you've seen something that can help us catch him?"

His cell phone rang before he could get any further and he grumbled at the intrusion. It might be Eli though with some new information anyway.

"We'll talk in a minute," he said, scraping a hand over his face and flipping the phone open as he stormed out of the kitchen.

Tieran's heart raced. Someone was out to kill him. She knew it. Could feel it in the pit of her stomach. All the visions were suddenly clear to her and with a heaviness that weighed her down, she remembered Eli's words. "What it really means is that as a Prime's mate, you are the alpha bitch. The only way I'll *ever* get to touch you is for me to fight Caelan to the death and take over the pack." But he'd also said he wasn't too intrigued by that prospect. Words to throw her off, or truth?

God, she didn't know. More confused than ever before about Eli, she buried her head in her hands. She jumped about a foot in the air when Caelan slammed his cell phone down on the table in front of her. Tieran wondered how it didn't shatter into a million pieces.

"Let's go," he snarled.

"Where? What's wrong?" Her stomach rumbled, reminding her she hadn't really eaten anything yet. Yesterday it seemed like she'd done nothing but eat. How could she possibly be hungry again? Tieran laid a hand over her belly and sighed. At this rate she'd be as big as a whale in no time.

"That was the police." A mixture of rage, hurt and confusion clouded his features when he turned to her. "They fucking arrested Eli for the murders."

Tieran's knees threatened to give out. Please, God, no. Not now after all the times Caelan had insisted Eli was innocent. She'd been trying hard to believe it herself ever since the car vision. She didn't want to go back to thinking of him as a cold-blooded killer. Damn.

"Maybe you should go by yourself," she said. He would need the time to deal with Eli's betrayal.

"And leave you here, vulnerable? I don't think so." He grabbed her wrist and tugged her toward the door.

"You don't need me there, Caelan. I'll only be in the way."

"The hell you will. This would be a perfect opportunity for the killer. It wouldn't surprise me if he'd set this up just to get at you."

He was delusional. Her heart ached for him at a time when his world was about to be ripped apart, leaving him without a twin. She loved him. Tieran sucked in a breath with the realization. And she hated Eli for the pain he would cause her mate.

She stopped, ignoring the pain as her shoulder wrenched in its socket. "You need to go alone." Not that she didn't want to support him, but she hated police stations. If she ever saw one again it would be too soon.

"Damn it, Tieran. I don't have time for this. Eli's rotting in a jail cell, he's hurt, and I need to get over there before somebody makes him their prison bitch."

Despite the grave situation, a short laugh escaped her pursed lips. Envisioning Eli as anybody's bitch was too much. The man was testosterone on wheels, the same as Caelan.

"You think this is funny?" Caelan rounded on her, gripping her elbow tight.

"It is, yes, when you've got him rotting in a cell he's probably only been in for a few short hours, and have him tagged as Butch's Bitch." Tieran tilted her head and put her hand on his cheek. "What happened to all that talk about him not being capable of doing this? I think I was beginning to believe it," she whispered.

Her gut twisted in sympathy for both of them. After yesterday, she could see they were both protectors by nature. Otherwise, why would Eli have hidden in those trees just to watch over her? Or had he had other reasons for wanting to watch her? There had to be a reason for the police to arrest him.

Caelan jerked again, throwing her off balance and into his chest. "I know what you're thinking, Tieran, and you're wrong. I don't care if they found his fingerprints, hair, blood and semen tied up in a nice little bow on top of the body. He didn't do it." He pivoted on his heel and dragged her out of the house, pausing only long enough to slam the front door shut. Which it did the first time, without bouncing back open and mocking them like her door would.

"Caelan, please," she cried, digging her feet in all the way to his truck.

He threw open the passenger's side and bodily hauled her into the seat. Before she could even speak in protest, he had her buckled in.

"Stay." He stabbed her nose with his forefinger, his eyes promising retribution if she so much as twitched. He closed her in with a thump and jogged around the hood, jumping into the driver's seat in the blink of an eye. The engine roared to life and the tires squealed with the slamming of his door.

"Not one word, my own, just listen." Caelan took the corner so fast Tieran was thrown against the window.

He would kill them before they got there. "You won't do your brother any good dead."

"You are the most stubborn..." A vein throbbed in his temple and his teeth were clenched tighter than a sprung bear trap.

Fitting considering that's about what his twin had gotten himself into. She sighed.

"Do you remember telling me what the man said in the warehouse?"

"Do you want me to answer, or is that a rhetorical question?"

"Son of a bitch."

She didn't know whether his curse was for her smart-aleck remark or the traffic. He slapped the steering wheel and slammed on his brakes when a slow-moving tractor pulled out in front them. An oncoming semi prevented him from immediately passing the farmer. At least Caelan's brain was still functioning properly.

"You said he wanted to take out a Prime." His fingers drummed with impatience. "Right?"

Tieran jumped in her seat at his shout and nodded. Did he want her to speak, or didn't he?

"Besides a mate, who else would have to be gone in order for him to take over a Prime position?"

How the hell should she know? Her knowledge of werewolves was extremely limited, and it certainly didn't include their hierarchy.

"The second-born son is the next in line."

Well that made everything clearer. Pfft. She was still clueless as to what he was getting at.

Caelan stomped on the gas as soon as the truck passed, sucking Tieran back into her seat. She'd be bruised from his crazy-ass driving.

"With no mate in the way and no second-born son, and in my case, no other sons at all to contend with, if something should happen to me, the Prime is up for grabs. It's the strongest who'll survive."

Tieran grabbed the "oh shit" handle above her head when they came to a screeching halt at a stop sign. She panted in relief. Another foot and Caelan would have creamed the car crossing the intersection. Because she'd been thrown forward with the stop, now her damn seatbelt was locked and pressing into her sternum. For someone who'd once said it was his job to make her happy, he wasn't doing too good a job right now.

"They're framing him to get to me," he ground out, oblivious to the fact he'd almost careened into another vehicle.

She swallowed. As impossible as it seemed, what if he was right?

🐺 🐺 🐺

"Where is he?" Caelan smashed through the double doors leading into the detective's area, sending them crashing into the wall. He ignored the few gazes of the early shift detectives whipping in their direction and stormed in with Tieran in tow. Hayward sat directly opposite him in the far corner, typing on a laptop keyboard. Motherfucker didn't look bothered one iota by his arrest of the Prime's brother.

Hayward stood, his chin rising in a superior gesture. They might be on his turf now, but Caelan didn't stop until he was a foot away from the smug little bastard. Even in the human world, Caelan was still Prime. If Hayward didn't like it, he could shove it up his ass.

"Not where he should be. He should be rotting in a fucking jail cell for what he's done to our kind," Hayward hissed low enough that none of the other detectives could hear.

Caelan cocked his hand back to punch the son of a bitch. Tieran stopped him.

"That won't solve anything, Caelan."

The prick grinned. "Take her advice, Prime," he muttered. "Don't make me arrest you for assaulting an officer."

"Where's my brother, Hayward?"

"At the hospital, Prime. Under lock and key until they release him. He had a poor wittle bump on his head. Then he'll be in a jail cell," Hayward sneered.

"He didn't do it." Caelan ground his teeth until he thought they would crack.

"Let's go, Caelan. We'll go to the hospital and see him." Tieran entwined her fingers with his and led him backward to the door. He glared at the smirking Hayward the whole way. He'd rather put his foot through Hayward's face than walk away right now. How could he do this? Hayward knew Eli. Was one of

219

their pack for Christ's sake. If anyone should be sticking up for Eli, it was Hayward.

Tieran's hand brushed across his back, returning his sanity. She was right. He had to talk to Eli first. Obviously Hayward wasn't going to be any help. Caelan spun around and yanked open the double glass doors again.

"Fuck." He swiped a hand over his face and kicked at the water fountain on the opposite wall. The resulting crash rang throughout the quiet hallway. A door opened further down the hall and a man poked his head out. Caelan grabbed Tieran's hand and hauled her out before the man said anything. A confrontation was the last thing he wanted.

"This is un-fucking-believable."

"Yes."

He couldn't tell if she was truly agreeing with him or simply trying to keep the peace. He didn't care. The only thing that mattered was getting to Eli.

Not three minutes later they were back in the truck and headed to the hospital. "God damn it. What the hell was he doing out there anyway?"

"You said he had a meeting." Tieran's soft voice banged around his head like a sledgehammer.

"That's it," he whispered. "The meeting was just a cover. He's been fucking set up. Why the hell didn't I see it sooner?" Caelan ground his hands around the steering wheel in frustration. While he'd been schmoozing his mate, his brother had been a target, plain and simple.

And Caelan had no idea who in holy hell Dane Christian was.

🐈 🐈 🐈

Eli's head hurt so badly he could hardly lift it off the crappy papery pillow. Wouldn't do him any good anyway since both his fucking arms were handcuffed to the bed. His goddamned nose itched!

He turned his head toward the door, wincing when a lightning bolt of pain sliced through it, turning his stomach at the same time. Ah Jesus. *Please don't puke, please don't puke.* Not again. His abdomen hurt from the number of times he'd done it already.

He wondered if he smelled as bad as he thought he did. Had to, because the tiny little plastic bowl the doc had held to his mouth more than once hadn't contained half of what had come out of him.

And worse than anything else was the fact he couldn't remember a fucking thing before waking up face-down on the pavement with that cocksucker's knee grinding into the middle of his back. Thank God that EMT knew his job, or Eli would probably still be lying there eating gravel while Hayward spat shit at him.

It had taken him awhile to figure things out, but when he had, he'd nearly flipped the bed over in a rage. When he got out of here, Eli was going to smash the fuck out of Hayward's nose for even thinking he could do something like this.

His head exploded in pain and he groaned. He tried to yank his hands up to his face. The metal gouged into his wrists before he made it further than about four inches up from the bedrail.

Eli dug his heels into the mattress and silently cursed everyone around. Where the fuck did they think he was going to go? He couldn't even lift his own goddamned head. No way would he be able to stand, let alone walk.

The door opened and let in a stream of hallway light that pierced every millimeter of his skull with what seemed like a barrage of bullets.

"Hayward catches you here and my ass is grass, Caelan."

"Nobody's gonna *catch* me here, Stark, least of all Hayward," Caelan gritted out. "He's my goddamn brother, did he think I wouldn't come?"

Ah, sanity returns, Eli thought. Caelan would get him out of this bullshit somehow.

"How're you feeling, E?"

"Like I got hit by a Mack Truck." Speaking even hurt. As a shifter, he would heal quicker than the average human, but until then, he hurt just the same.

"You look like it. Who did this to you?" Caelan asked quietly and stood directly over him, blocking out the light from the open door. His eyes widened as he caught sight of Eli's shackles. "Son of a bitch," he hissed.

Eli watched a battle pursue inside his twin. His wolf begged for release despite their high profile visibility. The cop outside the door was a shifter too. Hayward must have thought only another one of their kind could stop him if he somehow got loose. He'd have to turn into the fucking Hulk to do that. Even one of his ankles was cuffed to the rail. If laughing wouldn't hurt so much, he'd be the first one doing it. Hayward must have convinced someone he was a flight risk.

He wasn't going anywhere. Not until he got to the bottom of why he'd been set up and fingered for the murders.

"Like the new jewelry?" he joked, trying to lighten up the air in the room. His lips ached when he tried to smile. "Don't know. Never saw a thing as far as I can recall. Got out of the car and wham. Next thing I know, I'm waking up on the ground chowing on the pavement." Eli inhaled, swallowing back the nausea and fear that flooded his esophagus once again and smelled her. "Tieran's here?"

"Hell, yeah. Someone's bound and determined to get you out of the way to get to me, Bro. I'm not stupid. The next to go will be her, whether she believes it or not."

Eli nodded. "Why wouldn't she believe it?" He twisted slowly to try and see her around Caelan's wide torso. When his twin cleared his throat he jerked his gaze back to him. "What's going on, Cael?"

"How's my patient?" The booming voice of Dr. Taylor broke the tension in the room. Eli didn't like the almost disgusted, yet somehow embarrassed look on his brother's face. "How's the nausea?" The doctor swept past Caelan as if he weren't there and descended on Eli with a penlight. Eli yanked his head to the side and immediately regretted the action. "Not any better, I see."

Eli clenched his hands into fists. It was bad enough some nurse came in to check on him every fifteen minutes to make sure he was still alive. He didn't need any more tests run. What he needed was a way out of here.

"Can you give him something for the pain, Doc?"

Yes, yes, Eli silently begged, his eyes suddenly feeling very droopy. Several times since he'd arrived, he'd felt this way. One minute he was wide-awake, the next, he was ready to fall into an abyss.

"No can do, not with a concussion."

"There's got to be something," he heard Caelan ask again.

"Hmm, I can give him something for the nausea, but that's about it. He'll need to be watched for the next twenty-four hours or so with this head injury, and since waking him up might be hard enough as it is, we don't want to mask it with drugs that will make him sleepy."

The noise faded into the background until a female voice intruded.

"Can he sign these, or should I have his brother?"

Sign what? "I'll do it," Eli mumbled, hoping he made some sort of sense. He lifted an eyelid and looked around, wondering for a minute where he was. How could he forget? Jesus his head must have taken a shot. "What are they?"

"Privacy papers."

"Jesus, does he have to do them now? Why can't I? You can clearly see he's out of it," Caelan ground out.

"Gi' 'em to me." Christ his voice was slurred in his own head, he could only imagine what everyone else heard.

The fingers of his right hand met with plastic and he flicked it away. "Other," he said wanting them to get this over with and go away so he could go to sleep.

"He's left-handed," Caelan said.

Eli thought he heard a gasp from the corner of the room but didn't care. He held his eyes open, a true battle of the wills, and grasped for the pen. It might have been a little easier if he could move his arm at all. The nurse held the paper right where he needed to sign. He hoped to hell Caelan knew what it said because the words were jumping all over the page.

"You're left-handed?" Tieran's high-pitched, hopeful voice grated on his overtaxed brain. She may as well be screeching.

"So what, my own?"

"But you're not," she insisted.

Where the hell was his twin's mate going with this? Wherever it was, perked him up.

"No," Caelan answered. "We're mirror-image twins."

"He didn't do it." Tieran's voice shook with excitement. "Oh my God, Caelan, he didn't do it."

Caelan grunted when his mate leapt into his arms in an obviously overjoyed state.

"I already knew that, my own. I've been trying to tell you all along. What made you decide?" He kissed her before setting her back on her feet.

Ah damn, Eli thought, watching the two of them through his drooping eyelids. He'd give anything to be doing that with Nikki-Raine right now. Wouldn't this be the perfect time for her to find out about who he really was? Right when the police had arrested him for killing all those women.

"What's she talking about, Cael?" Eli asked. Tieran acted like she thought he was the one doing it all along. The doctor and nurse quietly backed out of the room giving them the privacy he'd ironically just signed for.

He squinted in the gloomy interior and got his answer from the pasty white, albeit blurry pallor of her face. She had thought he was the killer. Everything fell into place then. Her reactions to him when they were close, the scar issue, the meeting with the elders. He ground his teeth together.

"The killer was right-handed," she whispered.

Both his and Caelan's gaze flew to her slowly unfocusing one. "What?" they both said together.

"He was right-handed." She swallowed and he could tell she was being drawn back into a nightmare. "When he cut her throat, he used his right hand, like this." She drew her hand threw the air in a cutting motion. "A lefty wouldn't be able to do that, would he?"

"Not a true lefty, no. An ambidextrous one, maybe, but not Eli. He can't even brush his teeth with his right hand. Jesus, that's it, baby, that's the key we need to get E out of this." Caelan picked Tieran up and swung her around.

Tieran pushed away and hugged her arms tight. "And how will we tell Hayward how we know this evidence, Caelan?"

Fuck. Eli closed his eyes. There was no use pretending she didn't have a shitty past with the police believing her claims. He knew from those damn reports.

"Doesn't matter," Eli croaked. "Eventually the medical examiner will discover what you just said. It's all the evidence we need." He nodded slightly. "Everything will be fine." Damn, he sure hoped he believed his own words.

Caelan looked more than a little grim but nodded just the same. He grabbed onto his mate like a lifeline and again, Eli longed to touch Nikki-Raine. *Not here, not when he was handcuffed to a fucking hospital bed and close to going to prison,* he commanded himself.

When Caelan spoke, it was with a voice that wavered. "You're right, E. It'll all come out. Give me some time and I'll get you out of here."

Chapter Twelve

It was time to bring this charade to an end. He threw the cigarette down and ground it into the dried leaves of the forest floor. The lights were still on in Caelan's wing. They were still up, meaning this was the perfect time to make it all work out just like he wanted it to. He grinned and rubbed his hands together. In a few more hours he'd be able to go to the elders and claim his spot. No one would refute his ability to do the job.

Tonight would be fun.

🐈 🐈 🐈

Tieran stared at the vast array of movies in front of her and contemplated which one to choose.

"Oh my God. You've been looking for five minutes. Choose one already."

Irritable bastard. She was doing this to get his mind off his brother. They'd left Eli at the hospital earlier this afternoon, still handcuffed to the bed with a massive headache and an even more incredibly bad mood than Caelan's.

What the hell had she done?

"You didn't do anything, Tulla."

"Well, not exactly, but I insinuated over and over that Eli was the one." And he wasn't. Yet he still sat locked to a hospital bed, charged with several murders. No amount of begging and pleading with Detective Hayward had helped. In fact he'd laughed at her, an almost odd gleam in his eye when they'd sat down to discuss it with him. Something that had taken most of the morning to get the courage to do and it had turned out the same as Florida. She sighed.

Just sitting there in the cold, metal, beaten-to-hell chair had given her the willies. Then when the smirking had started...damn. She'd wanted to punch the egotistical bastard in the eye. Somehow sensing her distress, Caelan had put a hand on her forearm and soothed her by rubbing his thumb slowly over her skin.

Since there'd been no way around it, she'd told Hayward exactly what she was and what she'd seen. His gaze had never faltered as he watched her from beneath his lowered lashes. One by one she relayed the reasons Eli couldn't have done what Hayward had accused him of. She was particularly careful in telling him about the right-handed killer and the fact Eli was left-handed.

Hayward didn't giving a flying fuck. He'd laughed at her. "What am I supposed to do with a dream?" he'd said. His captain would roll on the floor if he went in there with this kind of "witness". Then he'd looked at Caelan, a smile still stretched across his face and told him, "Take your little mate home, Prime, I've got better things to do. Like put your brother in jail."

A split second later Caelan lunged from his chair and threw a punch at Hayward, narrowly clipping the man's jaw as he flung himself out of the way. Two more officers tackled Caelan, belly down, to the floor, yanking his arms behind him and kneeing him in the small of his back.

Thank God he hadn't been arrested. Hayward stood over them as Tieran knelt next to Caelan. When she'd looked up, Hayward was wiping away a trickle of blood from his lip with his tongue. A gleam had sparkled in his eye. Just the thought of it made Tieran shiver even now. Something about his expression had made her uneasy.

"Let him go, boys." He'd chuckled. "Man's just worried about his twin." Then he'd turned and sat at his desk as though nothing had happened.

She'd had to help Caelan up and stop him from going after the detective a second time. The whole scene hadn't surprised her one bit. She was used to ridicule. Caelan wasn't.

Tieran let the tension drop from her shoulders and forced herself to stop thinking about it.

One of the DVDs caught her eye and she pulled it out of its spot on the shelf with a small laugh. Who'd a thunk it? She turned to Caelan and waved the box in the air, grinning.

"It's my mother's," he mumbled.

"The Princess Bride? By the look on your face, I'd say you're lying."

"Fine. It's Eli's."

She snorted. "Wrong again. It's yours and you know it."

"Just put the damn movie in."

Tieran cracked up laughing and inserted the video. Two grown, very macho men living in the same house and their tastes ran to girlie movies. The machine clicked and whirred performing its functions when the otherwise quiet of the house was shattered with a pounding on the door.

"What the hell?"

"Christ, that scared the shit out of me." Tieran followed Caelan to the door despite his bark that she "Stay".

What did he think would happen? The killer would come to the door and knock first?

"Open the door, Prime," came the angry growl from the other side.

Caelan opened it in time to save the wood from another brutal beating from Hayward's fist.

"What the fuck do you want?"

"Where the fuck is he?"

Two grown men circling each other. Great, bring on the sumo diapers. The air vibrated around them making the hair on the back of her neck prickle. She wasn't the only one with problems. Caelan's skin seemed to bubble and move. His fingers elongated then shortened right before her eyes.

Tieran shook her head, fighting off the illusion. Only it wasn't an illusion. It was real, she just hadn't seen it before. They bristled and snarled and snapped at each other, yet neither was in full wolf form. Or human for that matter.

She stepped between them and held up her hands, spreading their bodies apart. Caelan was the first to react. His shift disappeared, his eyes cleared. Hayward's lip curled up in distaste. It would take more than a calming influence to pacify him. The man looked like he was out for blood.

"What is going on, Detective?" she asked. If Caelan couldn't be sensible, she could.

"He's fucking gone, that's what. Your precious little brother is an escape artist," Hayward spat around her, never taking his eyes off Caelan.

Shock kept Tieran frozen in place.

Caelan stepped back. "What?" He was as genuinely shaken up about Eli's disappearance as she.

"Don't play the goddamn innocent card with me, Prime. He's gone and there's another mate missing. Still think he's not the fucking one?" Hayward sprang around Tieran and lashed out at Caelan with fingers ending in claws.

Tieran screamed in warning but Caelan was quicker and easily dodged the swipe.

Caelan stilled, breathing heavy, his face white. "Another one?"

She saw him swallow. It wasn't Eli. She knew that for certain. Something was very wrong.

"Where would he go, Prime, and you'd better think fast, 'cause if I find him first, I'll rip his throat out with my bare hands."

Caelan jerked at the malice emanating off Hayward. He'd never seen the man like this. And where in the hell was Eli? When they'd last left him, Eli hadn't looked like he would have been able to *stand*, let alone finagle his way out of those cuffs and run. So where'd he go? And why hadn't he called and asked for help?

Because he wouldn't want Caelan involved.

"You're running out of time, Prime. And so's the girl."

Caelan waved him off. "Maybe if you had picked up the right man, there wouldn't be a missing girl. Go out and do your job and find her. I'll worry about Eli."

"Sure," he scoffed. "And help him get away with murder." Hayward lunged again, this time his snout forming on his face.

With a quick roundhouse, Caelan threw him off.

Damn it. He had to find Eli. The quickest way to do that would be to shift and hunt him down in wolf form, leaving Tieran here alone. Something he loathed doing. He could call his dad and have him come over. They only lived a few miles away, it wouldn't take him long to get here.

Jesus. What the hell could he do?

"You're wasting time, Prime."

"Fuck you, Hayward."

"Go, Caelan." Tieran dragged a sympathetic hand down his arm and clasped his fingers. "Find your brother."

He hesitated, then nodded. "I'll get the keys." He might waste precious time when he could be out looking, but he couldn't leave her alone here. He'd drop her off at his parents' house then be on his way.

"No."

The emphatic word stopped him.

"I can see in your eyes what needs to be done, so do it. I'll be fine here alone."

Caelan blew a breath out through clinched teeth. "Fuck. I don't want to leave you."

"Ahem." Hayward cleared his throat. "Go, Prime," he sneered. "I'll stay here with your mate."

I'll just bet you will. Probably just to make sure I come back. "Don't you have better things to do? Like finding the missing woman?"

"Caelan," Tieran warned.

"I have a whole task force out there looking for her," Hayward gritted. "Besides, whenever you find that traitorous brother of yours, you'll find the woman. Let's just hope she's still alive when you get there."

"You son of a bitch." Caelan swung his fist, connecting with the soft tissue of Hayward's cheek with an audible thud. The detective stumbled backwards and lifted a hand to his face.

When he'd steadied himself, he grinned and moved his jaw back and forth.

"I'll remember that."

"Caelan, please. Go." Tieran put her hands on his chest and pushed.

He stared at his mate, the woman he loved, and saw the pleading in her eyes. She was right. Getting arrested wouldn't help his brother. Not to mention all the time he was wasting on this asshole.

"I'm calling Dad. He can be here within fifteen minutes."

"I'll call him, you go," she assured him.

Caelan glanced at Hayward. Despite the animosity between them here tonight, the man was a cop. A good one, too. Or had been until he'd decided Eli had murdered mates. The smug bastard loved this. His smirk turned into a grimace and he had to work out the kinks in his jaw again.

Served him right. The satisfaction of smashing his face was worth every ounce of pain still flaring through Caelan's hand.

"Fine," Caelan said, and scratched his number on a piece of paper he found on the foyer table. "Call him now, don't wait. I don't trust Hayward to stay if he hears something is going down."

Tieran nodded and pushed him toward the door. He yanked off his shirt and pants before opening it and shoved his clothes into a bag, which he could carry in his teeth to be put on later.

Uncaring of his nudity in front of another shifter, Caelan locked Tieran's face between his hands and kissed her long and hard. She squirmed beneath the onslaught of his lips and tongue, then melded into him and held on for dear life. With a moan, she caressed the small of his back, tickling him. He'd find his little brother and finish this off. It would never be enough. Not in a million years. She had to put up with him for the rest of her life.

Breaking the kiss, he stepped back and opened the door. Her eyes widened as his body contorted in its shift. Caelan embraced the oh-so-familiar change and stood on four feet before her. His heart thumped.

A tiny tear escaped the corner of one of her eyes and fell to land with a plop on his wet nose, making him sneeze. Instead of more tears, she laughed and laid a hand on top of his head then ruffled the scruff of his neck. Damn. She was the most beautiful creature.

"Be safe," she whispered and knelt in front of him, her head tilted in wonder. "You are the most magnificent—"

"Time's a wastin', Prime."

Caelan growled. *Prime, that's right. I am Prime. When I get back, I'll help you to remember, Hayward.*

Tieran's mouth twisted at the interruption. "Go," she mouthed.

He turned and leapt off the porch, heading for the woods. He knew of two places Eli might run to. With one last look over his shoulder at his mate, he raced into the trees.

🐄 🐄 🐄

"Better lock the door. Wouldn't want the Prime thinking you're not safe."

"You know, you're a real condescending bastard," Tieran hissed and picked up the portable phone from the same table where Caelan had scratched his parents' phone number. She walked into the living room and stood looking out the window toward the trees where Caelan had disappeared. Waiting here seemed as good a spot as any.

Seeing her mate change before her very eyes had been the most amazing and magical and unthinkable thing. She wondered if she'd really just imagined it. Maybe she was sleeping. Having a dream.

"Put the phone down."

Tieran jerked at the low growl behind her. A shiver ran down her spine. Slowly turning around, she faced the detective. He licked his lips, like a wolf licking his chops, ready to devour her. When he grinned, sharp white teeth poked out from beneath his lips.

Keep it together. She swallowed. "Why should I do that?" *Please God don't tell me I've made a mistake in trusting this cop.* "Caelan asked me to call his father, remember?"

He laughed. "Now why would you want to do that when the party's just starting?"

Oh hell. A time like this and you'd think her eye would be twitching like crazy. She had a feeling instead of seeing this vision, she was going to be living it. *Caelan? You forgot something, come back. Crazy psycho killer here. Mate Killer.*

"Put the phone down!" he barked, making her jump.

She carefully laid the phone down as if it were made of the finest crystal. Too bad she couldn't hold onto it. It might have made a pretty decent first strike weapon. Wouldn't hold him off for long, but she could have at least gotten a good crack in.

"All this time, it was you?"

Of course it was. Same build, same height, same hair color. He and the twins might easily be confused, especially in one of her dream-like states. She'd thought the same yesterday when first meeting him.

Think. Think. Nobody's coming to save you.

Distract him.

"Why are you doing this?" That's it, make him talk. *"Gramama? A little advice here."*

"I'm here, Tulla. Hold him off a little while longer."

"That's your advice?"

"Because it should be me here living in this house," Hayward snapped. "Not that pansy-faced boy and his twin."

Boy? The detective didn't look any older than Caelan. Who was he calling a boy?

"I am the strongest of the pack," he continued, stalking toward her. "My grandfather should have been Prime. When his leader died, leaving no heir, there was a scramble for the position. Three men fought as wolves. Two of them died. The Graham cheated. My father told me so."

Oh my God. The man was delusional. Because of a story passed down through the generations, he thought he should be Prime. Tieran edged away from the window, keeping her back to the wall. The door on the other side of the room, behind Hayward, seemed a mile away.

"Every fucking day of my life I am reminded of what should be rightfully mine," he snarled, reaching behind his back.

When his hand came forward, a wicked-looking knife sat cradled in his fingers. The same knife he'd used to kill the woman in the warehouse. The woman he'd killed and pinned on Eli. He twisted his arm in front of her, taunting her with the knife. His watch shifted on his wrist, revealing the tattoo hidden beneath every time the back of his hand faced her. Tieran's breath caught. It was the same as Caelan's.

"Why not just kill Eli?" She crept ever closer to the exit, somehow dragging him further away as he moved around the sofa. In his demented state of mind he wasn't even aware of her direct route to an out. "He stands to take over if something happens to Caelan."

"Not from jail he won't." He took a longer stride around the end of the sofa.

Damn. He was on to her. An evil grin spread across his face.

"You can run, but you can't hide," he said with a glance at the door.

How cliché was that? she thought insanely.

"But I thought you didn't know where Eli was. Aren't you the least bit worried this will backfire on you?"

With an evil grin, Hayward shook his head.

"Oh my God. You let Eli go, didn't you? You set him free so it would look like he escaped and came here to kill me. This whole thing is a setup to lure Caelan away from here."

The smile widened across his face. She was getting sick of that smile.

"You're a smart girl," Hayward said, moving closer. "It was easy to get rid of Eli. Release him from his bonds, tell him he was free to go. He fell for it, like I knew he would. Dumb fuck. Eli made it easy for me to tell my captain my prisoner had somehow escaped. Just think of all the commendations I'll get when I 'find' him."

Tieran swallowed. "So you didn't kill him?" Please God don't let Caelan be searching for his twin's body when this was all over.

"Not yet, no." He never stopped his stalking. "But, I kind of like the idea of him spending the rest of his life in prison while I take over the pack. It'll give him something to think about."

"And what about Caelan?" she taunted. The doorway was only about five feet away. She could make it. To do what, exactly? Grab the lamp? Bash him over the head? Not likely. "Don't you think Caelan will be a little upset about your plans? Were you afraid you couldn't take both of us on at the same time?"

Jesus, shut up, Tieran. His nostrils flared, his eyes lit up with pure hatred.

"Caelan will be lying beside you in the grave," he roared and lunged at her.

She screamed and tried to dodge him but wasn't quick enough. She'd only taken one step when his hand fisted around her ponytail and yanked her backward. His arm bent around her neck, squeezing her air off, the knife edging dangerously close to her face. Tieran clawed at his arm, gagging and choking. Her toes barely reached the floor as she thrashed in his hold.

There was no purchase beneath her feet. No leverage with which to kick off. Red spots danced in her vision. She was going to die and never see Caelan again. Or the baby growing in her belly. A baby created with their passion for each other. A baby who didn't deserve what was happening, who would never even get the chance to follow in his father's footsteps. It was a boy, too. A dark-haired, golden-eyed boy, the spitting image of his daddy. She saw him clearly.

"Yes, think, Tieran. You see him clearly."

Her lungs burned. The boy turned, running in the grass and pushing a toy airplane in the air. His hair was mussed and he was laughing. Alive.

He was alive, which must mean she wasn't going to die.

Renewed strength overwhelmed her. She dug her fingers into the arm strangling her. Time to fight. Tieran lifted her leg and kicked back with all her strength, slamming the heel of her tennis shoe into Hayward's knee.

He buckled and howled in pain, releasing her with a shove forward at the same time. Her forehead hit an end table with a sickening crack, sending her sprawling to the ground. She lay there, stunned, and on her stomach while her head swam.

Tieran gasped, short, pathetic breaths that were all she could handle passed her smashed throat.

"You bitch," he bit out.

As if. She crawled to her knees and swiped at her sweaty forehead. The red evidence that came away on her hand said there was more than sweat up there. A trickle of blood ran down her cheek. Swaying on her knees, she watched several crimson plops fall to the floor and soak into the cream-colored carpet.

"You're gonna pay for that."

No, I think you're going to pay for the gash on my head, wolf-boy.

He limped over and pulled her to her feet by the hair. She winced but stayed silent. Content with the knowledge she would live through this night, she stayed stoic.

Caelan was another matter. She hadn't seen him in her vision, just the boy. Would he die tonight leaving her alone for an eternity?

No. Not if she had anything to say about it.

The point of the knife pricked her battered throat.

"Move."

Not much choice but to move when he kneed her, prodding her forward and toward the door. His unsteady gait got stronger as they walked silently, except for the harsh breathing, into the kitchen and out the back door.

Where were they going?

🐾 🐾 🐾

Caelan turned in the circular clearing in front of his parents' house, his chest heaving from the heavy run. He hadn't found Eli in the first place he thought to look, the ramshackle barn they'd played in for hours on end as kids. It was one of the few places either of them felt totally safe.

The lights glowed brightly in several rooms of the house. Caelan cocked his head. Was Eli here? He wouldn't make his presence that obvious. Had his dad left in that much of a hurry or...

He didn't let himself finish the sentence. Bounding up the front porch steps, he shifted into human form and groped beneath the potted plant by the door. After unlocking it, he threw it open and rushed inside. The TV was on, some comedy by the sound of a crowd erupting in laughter.

"Son? What the hell you doin', boy?" Liam laughed.

Caelan closed his eyes briefly, sweat coating his naked body. Fuck. "Why aren't you at my house, Dad?" he asked cautiously.

"Well now, why would I be?"

Caelan swallowed. "Son of a bitch."

"What's going on, Son?" his father asked, all business now.

"Hayward just showed up at the ranch. He said Eli had escaped and another woman was missing."

"Where's Tieran?" Liam threw his newspaper to the ground and began unbuttoning his plaid shirt.

"There, with him," Caelan choked.

"What are you waiting for, let's go get her."

"What about Eli?"

His father laid a gentle hand on Caelan's bare arm. "He was in the hospital at least up until two hours ago. I know because that's when your mother left him to go play Bridge. Realistically, do you think he was capable of leaving under his own steam? With as bad as his concussion was, even if he could have shifted he still had to get out his cuffs and past the guards. Someone had to have let him out. Think, Son. Who stood to gain by doing that?"

A red haze overtook Caelan's mind. He'd handed his mate over to the real killer. His heart slowed to near stopping, his chest felt like it might explode. He hadn't been able to protect her.

He shifted with no thought to the grinding bones or popping joints. It would take them a good ten minutes at a flat-out sprint to reach Tieran. He hoped his father was up for the pace.

Caelan ran, hell-bent, dodging trees and the normal debris littering the forest floor without seeing anything. His superior hearing picked up a scream as it split the air, stopping him in his tracks. He lifted his muzzle to the sky and let out a series of howls, alerting the pack to the danger and asking for help. He hoped they would make it in time. Caelan found his feet moving even faster. He would feel it in his soul if it were too late, wouldn't he?

The underbrush crunched beneath his paws and he heard his father close behind. How much longer? He passed the huge oak tree that they often used as a reference point. Only about a mile to go. *Hang on, my own. I'm coming.*

🐈 🐈 🐈

"You'll never get away with this, Hayward. It'll never work. You have to see that." Proud of how calm she sounded, Tieran relaxed a fraction. She would get through this. The bastard got off on scaring women. She wasn't going to be one of them.

"Shut up."

He'd brought her out to a barn, which looked more like a garage inside. Caelan's truck was parked here along with a small red car. Several pieces of lawn equipment and a tool bench lined one wall.

Hayward dragged the chair from the tool bench in between the cars and placed it directly in front of the wide double doors. Pulling out a plastic zip tie from his pocket, he spun Tieran around and bound her hands together. She grunted and bit her lip.

Please, Caelan, hurry. He was coming for her. She could feel their connection growing stronger. Something sewing their two separate beings into one whole.

"When I'm Prime, we won't have this problem anymore."

Jesus, he had said the same thing to that woman right before he slit her throat. "You mean you'll stop killing women to get what you want?" she goaded. Sick bastard.

He backhanded her, splitting her lip. Tieran recovered slowly from the shock. He smiled and pushed her into the chair, yanking her arms up at the wrists and fitting them over the chair back. Wrenched as they were, her shoulders screamed in agony. She yelled out in pain.

"I must apologize to the Prime's mate for hurting her."

The sneering was really getting on her nerves.

"Does it make you feel like a big man to be stronger than us females?" She just couldn't keep her mouth shut, could she?

That strange feeling inside her grew stronger. Caelan was very close.

"There's a certain justice in the Prime getting saddled with a bitch like you."

"Eli told me any challenger had to fight the Prime to the death to take over," she said, ignoring his comment.

"But this is so much more fun, don't you think?"

"I think it's the coward's way out."

Hayward growled menacingly and grabbed hold of her feet. He slammed them together, bringing tears to her eyes as the anklebones smashed into one another.

"Afraid you'll lose to him in a hand-to-hand?"

"I will never fucking lose to a Graham," he shouted. His eyes were wild and searched the confines of the enclosed space lit by strong overhead lights.

"Why here?" Tieran asked.

"Why not here?" His top lip curled up. He was definitely not firing on all cylinders. There was a craziness about him, a jerkiness that told her he was close to losing it. Whatever *it* was.

"I meant in this particular spot." She jumped in the chair, emphasizing the space where he'd sat her.

"Because when Graham gets here he's gonna open those doors and see you a second before you die."

Well, that was comforting. "But if you kill me first, you'll enrage Caelan and still have to fight him." She swore his eyes changed color. The skin on his face rippled, his jaw elongated. Then it was gone.

Caelan was home. She could feel him just outside the door. Maybe if she got Hayward rattled, he wouldn't see Caelan come in and this whole mess would be over.

"How did you do it? Make yourself look so much like them, I mean?"

His cruel laugh echoed. "Saw me, did you? I had so much fun after I found you there in Elizabeth's head."

Tieran gasped.

"Made things so much easier for me to try and pin it all on Eli." He shrugged. "Make myself look like him, follow him, lead you to believe I was him."

"But what about the scar?" *You can't fake a scar on a hairy wolf's body, can you?*

"Oh the scar's real. My daddy gave that to me one night after I'd lost a fight with that no good son of bitch Eli. Daddy said I ought to look like the man I'd tucked my tail between my legs and run from."

Hayward sniffed and wiped his sweaty brow on his shirtsleeve. "Should have been done with this the first night Caelan spent in your bed. Eli was supposed to meet me. I'd been watching your house, waiting for Eli to leave first so I could follow him. He did, but a little too early for me, so I stuck around. Then Eli called and said he had car trouble and couldn't make it. So I stayed and you left the house and I followed you instead. The whole night gave me the perfect excuse to jump into your dreams."

"Oh my God," she whispered. "It was you that night in my room. Not Eli."

"Nobody, especially not a Graham, can do what I do with my mind," he gritted out.

The vision of the man stranded by his car swam before her. *He was going to miss his meeting with the Christian guy.*

"Supposed to meet with Eli that night," she whispered, working things out in her head. "You're Dane Christian."

Somewhere she'd overheard Caelan say that name. A false name to throw everyone off.

Christ, she'd done so many things wrong, had believed everything this psycho had led her to believe, which made her visions less than reliable. What if it happened again? What if she really didn't get to see her son? Tieran swallowed back the sudden bitter taste of fear in her mouth.

She glanced at the single door to her left along the far wall. A shadow passed in front of it. Caelan. His face appeared through the glass, a brief look and then he was gone.

Her entire body relaxed in its restraints. The game was almost over.

"I still don't understand how you think you're going to kill Caelan."

"It doesn't fucking matter how, bitch," he shrieked and lunged for her, his hands outstretched, the knife falling to the ground.

The door burst open. Caelan, in his wolf finery, dove through the opening in a growling, snarling, twisting mass of fur and teeth. Hayward fell to his side, shifting even as he hit the ground, but wasn't quick enough. Caelan's teeth bit into Hayward's shoulder and ripped a strip of flesh off.

Hayward howled in furious pain and slashed back at Caelan who was much bigger and faster in wolf form than the detective. In the confined space between the double doors and the truck, the wolves attacked, parrying back and forth. Both their pelts were dark, but Tieran easily picked out Hayward's from the familiar scar bisecting one shoulder.

A hand on her own made her squeal and jump in her seat. She twisted her head to see a buck-naked Liam standing guard. Her cheeks reddened and she quickly averted her gaze. Even in the midst of a disastrous situation, it wasn't right to see your

245

lover's father in the buff. Liam made quick work of her shackles and led her out of harm's way, completely unabashed by his state of undress. The god-awful barking and screaming of the wolves made her want to cover her ears but there was no doubt in her mind who the winner would be.

"God, but you do have a mouth on you, girl. Be prepared for a nice, long disciplining tonight." Liam grinned. "Thought Caelan was gonna bust through that door and jump on you for the things you were saying. Why did you have to taunt him?"

"I was trying to distract him while Caelan took his sweet time coming in to rescue me."

His belly laugh was drowned out by the snarls. One of the wolves yelped and backed off feebly. Hayward. His hind legs collapsed beneath him and he fell to his haunches. Caelan stood over him, his lips curled back, his eyes squinting.

Tieran saw why the detective had yelped. Blood poured from a wound in his neck, draining his life with it. Her heart pounded. A fight to the death and she had stood by silently and watched it happen, unafraid even for her mate. Deep in her heart, she knew he would survive. Somehow she understood that when the day came, she would know when he wouldn't be with her any longer.

"It is the way of our people," Liam whispered in her ear, somehow picking up on the direction of her thoughts.

"It's insane."

Caelan shifted and stood on two feet, gloriously naked, sweating and breathing heavily. He swiped at a patch of blood across his chest. Three angry stripes marked him there.

Hayward whimpered and gurgled one last breath. He hadn't even had the strength to shift back to human form before succumbing to Caelan's attack.

Caelan lifted his head and stared at her. The intensity stunned her. He stalked to her, his chin dropped to his chest, his cock... She swallowed. She watched it grow the closer he got. Liam laughed behind her and she thought she heard him say good night.

Without a word, Caelan tenderly caressed her split lip with his tongue before taking hold of her hands and laving the tender spots on her wrists. When he was satisfied, he led her out the double doors. Tieran sucked in a breath. A huge group of people, his pack, most of them in their birthday suits, stood waiting there, all of them silent and looking at her. How they'd gotten there so quickly, she didn't know. Didn't care.

Heedless of his nudity, Caelan stepped forward.

"It is done. Michael Hayward is our traitor."

A collective gasp flowed through the crowd. Caelan was pulled aside leaving Tieran to be engulfed by the pack. She was hugged, her cheeks squeezed, making her wince, and her limbs checked to make sure she was still in one piece. Satisfied, they all started talking at once.

Caelan came to the rescue before she could even open her mouth to speak. He grabbed her hand and tugged her along in his wake. She didn't protest. The group parted and let them pass. Several people shook hands with Caelan or patted him on the back. Many more simply said, "Thank you."

"Oh my God, Caelan." Tieran stopped. "What about Eli? Hayward said he'd disposed of him somehow. He's out there somewhere. How will we find him if Hayward's dead?"

Caelan turned and put a finger over her lips. "That's what I was doing a second ago. They've already picked up his scent and are going after him."

"Don't you need to go with them?"

"No. I've got more important things to take care of right now." Caelan started dragging her again and although he paused more than once within his pack, he never actually stopped moving until they were in the kitchen. Alone. He closed the door quietly behind them and yanked the blinds closed, shutting out the spectators.

"I promise retribution for the way you tempted Michael Hayward tonight, my own."

She shivered at his softly spoken words. One could only imagine what his form of retribution would be.

He pressed her against the counter. The small of her back dug into the marble and he slanted his mouth over hers, careful not to hurt her lip. Screw careful. She deepened their kiss, tasting his tongue. A little cracked lip wasn't going to keep her from doing this. Every ounce of her anxiety and fear vanished with the simple touch. Tieran wrapped her arms around his neck and held on tight. She needed this. She needed him. Now.

"Bedroom," he said.

Her clothes somehow disappeared along the way and she found herself laid out across the bed. The wounds on his chest already looked better. She wished she had that kind of healing power.

Caelan knelt between her legs and pushed them wide, making more room for himself. When he knelt, his breath tickled across her pussy, enveloping her in warm heat.

"Please, Caelan, make love to me."

"Oh, I will, my own. I will."

His lips caressed her clit and she arched into his mouth, trying to get closer. He backed off until she relaxed, and started again. His tongue snaked out along her slit, licking the moisture from her and adding his own. It wasn't enough.

Caelan seemed to understand. Either that or he couldn't wait himself. He reared up, lifting her knees into the crook of his elbows and sank into her sheath in one long agonizing stroke. Tieran groaned as he filled her and grasped the blanket in her fists.

Clinching her vaginal walls, she fought to keep his cock inside when he began to pull out.

"Fuck," he said, his head dropping back on his shoulders. He pressed in a little quicker this time. Both of them moaned.

"Can't go slow."

"No, don't want you to," she begged.

He leaned over her and set his teeth on the crook of her shoulder, prepared to mark her once more. The headboard shook along the wall with his heated thrusts. Mere seconds went by and she felt the sharp prick in her skin. His fingers played magically with her clit, circling and teasing it until she exploded. A shower of white lights sparkled behind her eyelids. The orgasm took her breath away.

With a final thrust, Caelan held himself still inside her. His come pulsed from his cock, bathing her in warm spurts.

When he collapsed in a panting slump, Tieran hugged him close, accepting and loving his warm weight on top of her. After a few minutes of catching their breath, he rolled them to the side, his cock sliding out of her.

"I think that's what you call a quickie."

Caelan's chest vibrated on a growl. "If you ever do something so stupid again—"

"You'll what? Spank me?" she asked, grinning from ear to ear.

"God, I thought I was going to lose you tonight." He nearly did right then when he squeezed the life out of her.

"I knew you wouldn't," she whispered.

"You saw this?" He pulled back to look in her eyes.

She rubbed the fading scratches on his chest and walked her fingers to cradle his cheek. "No, but I saw something else just after you left."

He searched her face. "What?" he rasped.

Tieran took his hand in hers and laid it on her belly.

"Our son.

About the Author

Annmarie McKenna lives just outside of St. Louis with her husband and four children. She loves to hear from her readers. To learn more about Annmarie, please visit www.annmariemckenna.com or send an email to annmarmck@yahoo.com.

Look for these titles

Now Available:

Blackmailed

Coming Soon:

Checkmate
Two Sighted

What's an alpha shape-shifting wolf to do when the woman pre-destined to be his mate no longer trusts men?

Checkmate
© 2006 Annmarie McKenna

After returning home from an eight-month security job, Eli Graham is ready to claim his best friend's little sister as his mate. Instead of the stubborn, independent, carefree girl he left, Eli finds a shell of the woman he once knew.

Having lived through a near fatal attack, Nikki Taylor has hidden herself away from the world. Now the time has come to face head-on the one man who could devastate her completely, Eli Graham. She's loved him forever, craves him, body, heart and soul, but he's never treated her as anything but a little sister.

When Nikki witnesses a murder, she has no choice but to rely on Eli's expertise. Eli is more than up for the challenge—both to win her heart and to protect her from the man bent on wiping out a witness.

Coming in February 2007, from Samhain Publishing.

fly AWAy

Discover the Talons Series

5 STEAMY NEW PARANORMAL ROMANCES
TO HOOK YOU IN

Kiss Me Deadly, by Shannon Stacey
King of Prey, by Mandy M. Roth
Firebird, by Jaycee Clark
Caged Desire, by Sydney Somers
Seize the Hunter, by Michelle M. Pillow

AVAILABLE IN EBOOK—COMING SOON IN PRINT!

Samhain Publishing Ltd

WWW.SAMHAINPUBLISHING.COM

Printed in the United States
118854LV00005B/115-213/A